Wicked Good

A Novel of Unconditional Love

by

Amy Lewis Faircloth and Joanne Lewis

TELEMACHUS
PRESS

This book is a work of fiction. Names, characters, places and incidents are either the product of the author's imagination or are used fictitiously. Any resemblance to actual persons, living or dead, or to actual events or locales is entirely coincidental.

Wicked Good

The publisher does not have any control over and does not assume any responsibility for author or third-party websites or their content.

Cover designed by Warren Lewis

Cover art Copyright © 2011 Sean Faircloth

Published by Telemachus Press, LLC
http://www.telemachuspress.com

Visit the author website
http://www.amyandjoanne.com

ISBN 978-1-935670-97-1 (eBook)
ISBN 978-1-935670-98-8 (Paperback)

Version 2011.07.21

Printed in the United States of America
10 9 8 7 6 5 4 3 2 1

INTRODUCTION FROM THE AUTHORS

"Asperger's syndrome" is a disorder on the autism spectrum. It was discovered by Dr. Hans Asperger in 1944 but not in the public conscious until after 2000. It is diagnosed from a checklist of symptoms. Individuals with Asperger's syndrome appear eccentric. Rory is no exception.

"Wicked" is a slang term originated in New England. To be used properly it must be followed by an adjective. It is used to add emphasis. For example, Rory is wicked smart when it comes to removing those wicked pesky squirrels. And we are wicked excited that you are reading *Wicked Good*.

PLEASE VISIT OUR WEBSITE

www.amyandjoanne.com

WE WOULD LOVE TO HEAR FROM YOU

amyandjoanne@gmail.com

This book is dedicated to Brendan Faircloth and Ryan Faircloth, our two big guys, without whom this book could not have been written.

Wicked Good

A Novel of Unconditional Love

CHAPTER ONE

"Mom, I don't feel safe." Fifteen year old Rory Falcon said.

Archer Falcon opened her eyes and tried to focus on the illuminated hands on the clock beside her bed. It was either ten minutes after midnight or two in the morning. A cool September breeze blew through the open window. A Bangor, Maine sanitation truck rolled along the street, whirling brushes spraying water and sweeping the road.

Lit by a moonbeam, Rory paced at the foot of her bed, following the path he had previously worn in the carpet. Five steps forward, five steps back. Repeat.

I don't feel safe. Archer knew the meaning of the words. Rory's counselors used it; the high school used it; the psychiatrists used it. He was contemplating suicide.

She pulled the string on the faux Tiffany lamp next to the bed, feeling tears in the back of her eyes and tightness in the hallows of her throat. She looked at him to assess. There were no new cuts on his arms or chest. His face had narrowed over the last year and his chest and shoulders had broadened. His deep blue eyes were watery and sad. His mop of golden hair was mussed. He was wearing black flannel pajama bottoms peppered with white skulls. He wore black, even his pajamas, so people would not approach him.

Archer had prepared a written list years ago for moments like this. She no longer needed to refer to it. She had it memorized.

Speak quietly. Assess the situation. Keep calm. Involve Rory in his own care. Call crisis hotline. Call psychiatrist. Go to Emergency Room.

He stopped moving and faced her. Dark circles lurked under his eyes.

"Have you slept at all?" Archer asked.

"No, and I have a really bad headache." He pointed to the top of his head. A tear escaped down his cheek. He quickly wiped it away.

What were the best options? She didn't want to take him to the emergency room since she didn't want him admitted to the psychiatric hospital. The last time he had been there, four years ago, he had befriended a boy who had stabbed his cousin over a Nintendo game. He didn't need to learn anything else from the teenagers there. Tomorrow was the first day of school. Would this latest crisis end by morning or would he miss the start of tenth grade?

Archer slid out of bed. "I'll get you some Tylenol."

In the bathroom, she shook the red and white bottle until two caplets landed in her palm, giving her just enough time to make a decision.

She returned to her room. "Let's call the crisis hot-line."

No longer necessary. For the moment. Five foot nine inch Rory had taken her place in bed, wrapped from head to toe in her blanket. She touched his cheek, smoothed his hair, loving the feel of him, hoping he would find his way.

CHAPTER TWO

At her office, Archer leaned back in her chair and thought about that morning. Rory had insisted on going to school. He hadn't wanted to miss the first day. She had felt anxious. She wanted to excuse him from school so she could watch him "eyes on", as the experts said. He probably would be fine. He had made his own lunch, searched for the specific black t-shirt he wanted to wear and left on his bicycle for school in a good mood.

Archer looked at the document on her desk. Motion to Decrease Child Support. She shook her head, felt anger boil in the pit of her stomach. This time, it wasn't a client hiring her to defend the motion. It had been filed by Wayne, Rory's father.

"What a loser," Archer said.

"What?" Delores, her secretary, called from another room.

"Nothing." She put the pleading down and picked up the phone, about to dial Wayne's number, then stopped. Talking to him would get her nowhere. As usual. She thought about her response to the motion. Would You're An Asshole be legally sufficient?

Delores walked into her office, dropping several pieces of mail on Archer's desk. "Did you want me to schedule mediation for the Tamina case?"

"Yes, and I put some pleadings on your desk for Goodrich. I'll need those to go out today." Archer turned in her chair and looked at the mementos and photos of Rory hung on her law office wall, crooked no matter how many times she straightened them.

"Oh, I forgot to tell you." Delores said. "Judge Morton called again.

He said to remind you of your plans for lunch and he wouldn't take no for an answer. Do you know what he's talking about? I don't have that on your calendar."

Archer shuffled through her mail. She knew what he was talking about but didn't want to say, yet. The phone rang. As Delores left her office, Archer stuffed the linen envelope from the Governor's Judicial Appointment Committee into her purse.

She turned again to her wall. Rory with Grandma Rose and The Little Mermaid at Disney World. The story Rory had written in second grade that began "onca pana time". The note from his sixth grade Assistant Principal congratulating Rory for not being sent to detention for an entire month, failing to mention that for two weeks, school had been closed for winter break. The photo of three-year-old Rory with his head in the dog's bowl.

Her favorite photo was of four month old Rory wrapped in the little yellow blanket she had brought him home in. Only his perfectly round face was visible. His eyes were wide and alert. His mouth was formed in a happy oval.

At first, it had been cute when Rory would insist he sit under the rotating ceiling fans at Wal-Mart. It had been endearing that he would not go to day care without his toy dump truck, its wheels worn down from the constant pressure of his spinning. It had been funny that his pounding on the floor at day care during nap time disturbed the prickly principal on the floor below. His behaviors became less cute when he was almost kicked out of kindergarten for spinning on his bottom during circle time and refusing to stop. And then there was the one parent-teacher conference Archer would never forget.

"I'm retiring," Rory's first grade teacher had said, "unless you get Rory to behave."

Archer had tried and failed. The teacher retired.

Could she commit to a judgeship *and* parenting Rory?

Delores' voice rang out on the intercom, "Kara's on line one."

Archer snapped out of her trance and froze for a moment. Why would Kara, her best friend and the school principal, be calling her so early?

She picked up the phone. "Is he alright?"

"He's drunk. Get over here. Now."

CHAPTER THREE

Archer slammed on the brakes and parked the Subaru at an angle, not caring what cars or school buses she blocked. She should have followed her gut. She should have made him stay home.

She jumped out of the car and saw Kara rushing toward her. Archer tried to send brain waves. Don't hug me, I'll cry. Don't hug me, I'll cry. Kara reached toward her.

Archer raised her arms like the victim of a hold-up. "Just tell me he's okay."

She raced past Kara, unable to look her in the eyes, and entered the school. She slowed at the trophy case displaying the gold cup bearing hers and Kara's names dated 1982. They had been the dynamic duo, the driving force behind the girls' high school state soccer championship. But that had been twenty-five years ago when they had dreamed of the perfect lives, the perfect families, before law school, before Kara's rise to principal of Bangor High.

With Kara on her heels, Archer headed for the nurse's office to retrieve Rory. Archer knew the nurse too well from Rory's frequent complaints of headaches or stomach aches when he hoped to be sent home in order to avoid school work and the kids who made fun of him.

"Is this his?" Kara matched her steps and held up a silver canteen with a black imprint of a skull on it. Its eyes, nose and the slit of its mouth were sparkling white, derisive, laughing at Archer. "Rory drank vodka from this canteen. Said he brought it from home. He gave a few sips to Evan during first period."

Archer stopped at the nurse's office door. "Is Evan okay?"

"Yes. I had to call his parents and tell them. I thought you were done with this." Kara faced her, held up the canteen.

"Rory didn't get the vodka from me." Archer looked away.

"I'll go to meetings with you again."

Archer shook her head. "Kara, I…It was just one time over the summer. July Fourth weekend. I didn't even drink the whole bottle. It was in the cabinet and…"

"…Rory found it."

Archer nodded.

"I can keep the police out of this. Campbell isn't working at the school today. He could summons him for being a minor in possession of alcohol, and for giving some to Evan. But I have to suspend Rory for five days."

"Why? What will that do?"

Archer wanted to disappear, knowing she wasn't asking the most important questions, the ones which engulfed her and for which she knew there were no answers. How did my life end up like this? How can I be in control of every aspect of my life—including running a successful law practice—but I can't help Rory? And how come no one can help him, not all the psychiatrists, social workers and doctors he's seen from Maine to New York to California?

"Five days suspension is standard policy when students have alcohol on school property," Kara said.

"Rory is different than the other kids." Archer grabbed the doorknob.

Kara reached for her hand. "I know how special Rory is. But I have to follow school policy. And he shouldn't have had access to vodka. You have to watch him better. And," she lowered her voice, "you need help."

Feeling the tears about to escape, Archer opened the door. "I'm going to take him home now."

Inside, Rory was lying on the green vinyl couch, giggling. His grin widened when he saw her. She stopped for a moment, taken aback by that smile, those deep blue eyes. He wore a pair of black baggy shorts and a black cut off t-shirt. From across the tiny room, she smelled alcohol.

He sat up, held his head then lay down again. "I'm really sorry. I'm really drunk." He hiccoughed then laughed. "I can't walk. I didn't know this is what it would feel like to be really drunk. I really love you, mom. Don't cry, mom.

It's okay. I love you. I shouldn't have come to school today. I should have listened to you. Can we go home now?"

With Kara's help, Archer got Rory into the back seat of the Subaru. Rory never sat in the front. It made him too nervous. Driving toward their home on Willow Street, Archer finally let her tears escape. She didn't need to hide them. Rory was asleep.

CHAPTER FOUR

Spark plugs, small motors, tools, wires, computer pieces and fan blades were scattered on Rory's bedroom floor and cluttered the tops of his dresser, desk and end tables. Dirty mountains of clothes and sneakers were toppled over. Red lights glowed from the power buttons of a television, a DVD player, a VCR, a turntable, two boom boxes, an I-pod and three MP3 players. The room smelled of Axe cologne and soil. Several potted plants were lined on a shelf hung below a window. The plants were well-cared for with plump and brightly colored leaves; except for one. Archer dropped it into a wastepaper basket and swiped the back of her neck. Early menopause, just like her mother.

Wrapped tightly in his blanket, only the top of his head visible, Rory groaned. "My head is killing me."

"Why did you drink the vodka? Why did you take it to school?"

"Save the lecture. I'm gonna' puke." He threw the blanket to the floor.

Archer grabbed the garbage pail from under the desk in time for Rory's donut breakfast to hit the sides of the aluminum basket and cover the dead plant. She watched and waited, her stomach turning from the sight and the stench.

Finished, he lay back in bed.

She put the pail in the bathroom and wet two towels. She handed one to Rory and used the other to wipe her face and neck. She fanned herself with a horticulture magazine.

"It's really hot in here," Archer said.

Rory sat up. "I can put an air conditioning unit in the window in your room. I saw one at the dump the other day. I'm sure I can refurbish it and make it new and then..."

"I just want a fan that works."

"That's easy." He got off the bed, fell back down.

"Stay in bed. You're still drunk."

He laughed. "I can do this." He stood again, teetered.

"Where are you going?"

"I have the perfect fan for your hot flashes." He rubbed his head.

"Do you want to take something?"

"I don't wanna' take anymore drugs. I take too many as is."

"You shouldn't mix alcohol with your medications. You shouldn't drink at all. I shouldn't have to watch you all the time."

"Whatever."

He disappeared into the closet. Several Beanie Babies flew out, along with wires and cables. Rory emerged holding a battery-operated pink fan.

"You're right. This is perfect." She held the fan to her face and looked around. "Maybe while you're home for the next few days we can clean your room and the guest room."

"They don't need to be cleaned." His words were slurred.

"There are parts for lawn mowers and snow blowers everywhere."

"I have to keep them somewhere. I'm going to figure out a way to run them without gas or oil. And we need new spark plugs. I had to use one for a lawn mower from the weed whacker. Can we go to the store now and get it?"

"The school grounded you for five days. And so have I. Maybe longer. And you're still intoxicated. You're not going anywhere."

His eyes narrowed. "That's what you think."

Archer felt it coming. His insistence on having things his way, on his schedule, on his terms. She thought about the hole in the guest room wall hidden behind a framed print of Andrew Wyeth's Christina's World.

The professionals had told her to be firm, don't back down, show him who's the parent and who's the child. Others had said to reason with him. And then there were the ones who liked to bundle Rory's problems into neat packages, like a restaurant menu with no substitutions.

His anger is a manifestation of a low frustration level.

He finds comfort in repetitive actions.

He has a poor ability to soothe himself.

He is adverse to crowds, loud noises, flashing lights.

He is inflexible, needs to lead conversations, is sensitive to touch, easily distracted.

None of those professionals really knew Rory. The twin diagnoses of Asperger's syndrome and Bipolar Disorder did not define Rory. He was more than the sum of his symptoms.

She looked at the end table next to his bed. "What's this?" It was small and felt like lead in the palm of her hand.

"A bullet from the Civil War re-creation we went to last month."

"I told you not to bring it home."

"Well, I did. Put it down."

"No, Rory. It's not safe."

He grabbed it and shoved it into his pocket. "It's fine. Okay?"

"Why'd you take the vodka to school? Why'd you drink it? You could have died. People die from drinking too much."

"I didn't drink that much." His phone jingled, indicating he had received a text message. Rory looked at the phone then put it back in the side pocket of his shorts.

"Who is it?"

"No one."

"Rory, please…"

"It's Trish, okay? She wants to know why I'm not in math."

"Was it your idea to bring the vodka to school?" Archer asked.

He lay down, closed his eyes. "Some kid from the Y said it'd be cool."

"So you listened to him?"

"It's no big deal. Forget about it."

"I can't forget about it. Last night, you were so upset. I worry about you. Were you trying to kill yourself?"

"No." He rolled on to his side, his back to her, mumbled something.

"What did you say?" she asked.

"Nothing."

"Rory, turn over. Face me. You need to show respect."

He didn't move.

She went to the other side of the bed, locked eyes with him. "I have to stay home from work for the next five days because they won't let you back in school. For those five days, you can't leave the house."

There, she was firm. Just like the experts had told her to be. She left and closed the door behind her. As she headed down the stairs, she heard the dead bolt slam from inside his room.

CHAPTER FIVE

Seated at the kitchen table, Archer looked at the document on the laptop screen without seeing it, grateful for the cool air blowing from the pink fan. She was preparing a marital settlement agreement for a couple who was divorcing after thirty-seven years. She represented the husband who had made an excellent living as an executive at the paper mill only to discover his wife had been having an affair with her dermatologist.

Archer and Wayne had been married twelve years. Rory had been eleven when their divorce was finalized. Wayne hadn't put up much of a fight after she had caught him with a woman from his acting troupe.

She looked back at the document on the screen. Permanent alimony, property divided, debts paid. She had been lucky Wayne had agreed to waive alimony. She would probably still be paying.

She heard the front door open and jumped up. "Rory, where are you going?"

"It's me," Wayne said.

She faced him, hands on her hips. "What are you doing here and why do you have a key to the house? You should knock or ring the bell. Don't just walk in."

She didn't see him very frequently and was a little surprised by how grey his hair had become. Running her hand through her own hair, she couldn't help but consider the injustice of it all. He looked quite distinguished, handsome even.

He had been funny, positive and engaging when they had first met in college. And when he had played the guitar and sung folk songs, she thought she had found the man of her dreams. But dreams die and his obsession with acting sucked the life out of him. She didn't think he owned a guitar anymore.

"Is he okay?" Wayne asked.

"Yes. He's sleeping." She held out her hand.

He dropped the key into the soft part of her palm.

"How'd you hear?" she asked.

"It's a small town. But I should have heard it from you. How did he get into your vodka? You need to watch him better."

She felt her face get hot. "Maybe you could do some watching instead of trying to reduce your child support."

"Lay off, okay? I've been auditioning for a play in Portsmouth. I think I'm going to get the lead."

"Great."

"Just tell me what happened."

"He was drunk, okay? Our—" she emphasized Our—"son was drunk by nine in the morning. I had to leave work to get him and, as usual, I called and you were nowhere to be found. " Archer's voice raised several octaves as the words spewed out of her mouth. It was her Wayne voice. She didn't know where it came from, only that when she stopped and listened, she heard a stranger.

"I didn't have my first drink until I was seventeen," he said. "Don't tell me you have alcohol in the house. I thought you were done with that. Are you drinking again?"

"Of course not. It was left over from July fourth. Friends brought it."

"Is he really suspended for five days?"

She took a deep breath and calmed herself. For Rory's sake, she had to find a way to communicate with Wayne without screaming, cursing, or wanting to pummel him.

"He's really suspended for five days and there's more. Last night he was up in the middle of the night pacing and complaining of a bad headache. He said he didn't feel safe. I think the alcohol is a cry for help. I don't want to leave him alone while he's suspended. You'll need to watch him. I can do some work from home but I'm going to have to go to the office, probably every day."

"I have to work at the library and I'm pretty sure I'm going to get the lead in this play so I need to rehearse and…"

"Did you hear what I said?" she interrupted. "I'm worried he is going to hurt himself."

"I know. But do you really think he will? It seems like a way to get attention. He's just bored. He should be running cross country or playing football."

"Are you serious?" She screeched, felt herself becoming someone she didn't want to be. "I don't know if he'll really hurt himself but we can't ignore it. And you need to spend more time with him. He thinks you don't like him."

"Of course I like him. I love him. I've been busy. I'm working two jobs and trying to get this play and..."

"If you're working so hard, why do you need to lower your child support?" She felt the heat in her chest, did nothing to stop it from boiling into her throat and shooting out through her words. "You shouldn't have left the library and Maine for two years to pursue your acting career. You wouldn't be in so much debt and you would have been around for him."

"I'm following my dreams."

She heard the defeat in his voice but felt no sympathy. "What about my dreams?"

"You have dreams? I thought you just wanted to make money."

"Fuck you. You need to see him more than once a month. And when he spends time with you, stop giving him your broken crap. My house is like a garbage dump."

"He likes to collect things."

"Let him collect them at your house."

"Fine. Look, I have to tell you something."

She felt the truck barreling toward her.

"Mary Beth is pregnant. We're going to have a baby."

Archer's stomach clenched.

"But the doctors said we couldn't..." The words barely came out.

He shrugged. "I just wanted you to hear it from me. It is a small town, you know." He turned and walked away.

She closed her eyes until she heard the front door shut; then opened them and stared at the space where Wayne used to be. Her cheeks grew hot, her neck clammy. She turned the pink fan on and pointed it toward her face. Her tears scattered.

Rory came down the stairs, his gait unsteady. His eyes were bloodshot. His hair tousled. She was glad he looked nothing like Wayne.

"You okay?" he asked.

"I'm fine."

He put a hand awkwardly on her shoulder. "Don't be sad. I'm sorry I drank the vodka. I was just trying to fit in." His words ran into each other but he appeared to be sobering.

"I know."

"So we can go get those spark plugs now?"

"Good try."

He smiled.

"Why don't you go back to bed? Sleep the rest of it off."

"No. I was just thinking."

"About what?"

"That Grandma Rose died." Rory started to pace. His hands moved rapidly like he was conducting a concerto. His body swayed as he spoke with hardly a breath, danced his frenetic dance. Five steps forward, five steps back. Repeat. "I don't know what I would do if grandma died. Would she be cremated or buried? What is her favorite landscape? Would she want to be by the ocean or in the woods? What is her favorite flower? I would want to plant flowers for her. Maybe Lupines. I don't think I could go to school if grandma died. What would you want to remember her by? I would want some of her cats. We should put a family photo in her casket. She would like that."

"Yes, she would."

"Think I should call her?"

"If you want."

He pulled his cell phone out of his pocket. "She'll ask me why I'm not in school and I'd have to tell her the truth."

"Yes, you would."

"I'll call her later."

CHAPTER SIX

Archer had discovered the benefits of a bath when she and Wayne were separating. They would leave her alone when she was in the tub. Rory would respect her privacy and Wayne ignored her, which was just as good. Fearing she would disappear into the luxury of a bath forever, Archer made a deal with herself. She would only take a bath as a reward for exercising or as relief from paralyzing depression. Having just learned Wayne and Marybeth were pregnant and Rory was again sleeping off the vodka, this moment qualified as paralyzing depression.

When the cast-iron claw foot tub was filled, she submerged until her nose and mouth were above water. Her thoughts took her to Gloucester, Massachusetts, November, 1991.

She and Wayne had spent one week in Gloucester during the worst storm she had ever experienced. The winds were fierce and the rain a downpour. As they waited for permission to take Rory home, they spoke with social workers and met Kitty, Rory's birth mother. Archer and Wayne were pleased Kitty was an older woman. She was unmarried, a hard worker and sure of her decision to give up her baby for adoption. They weren't supposed to know her last name but someone had failed to delete it from the papers. Archer had the documents in her safe deposit box.

What Archer and Wayne hadn't been able to do during the storm was talk to the officials who would give them permission to leave the state with the newborn. Rory had come into the world during the height of one of the worst storms in the history of New England. The whole state had been shut down.

And no one, including Kitty, could stop talking about the Andrea Gail, the sword fishing boat that was lost at sea. Seemed like everyone in Gloucester was trying to help the Coast Guard locate the fishermen. The only places open were The Crow's Nest, the bar where Kitty worked which served as headquarters for the families of the missing fishermen, and one movie theater. Archer and Wayne loved movies so it gave them something to do while they waited to meet their son. Finally, with the storm moved on but the devastation severe, they drove back to Bangor in silence. Without Rory.

The call came a few days later. Rory was ready to be picked up. Archer flew to Boston alone since Wayne was in rehearsals for "Pippin". When she landed at the airport, a woman waited with Rory snuggled in her arms. The social worker hesitated then handed Rory to her along with a small bag. Archer was surprised to see tears in the woman's eyes.

Rory was heavier than Archer had expected. The crisp, clean smell of diaper wipes and baby powder mixed with the scent of formula filled her nostrils. He smelled perfect. She studied the shape of his face, eyes and nose. He was wrapped in a yellow blanket, large oval eyes stared at her. She fell in love, especially with the red angel bites on his eyelids.

When the announcement was made to board the plane to Bangor, she held Rory tight to her chest as she walked up the portable stairs and into the twelve seater prop. On the plane, she held him on her lap, not knowing what to do with the newborn. All she had were several bottles filled with formula and the yellow flowered blanket. She bounced him, cooed, gave him a bottle, sang to him.

He cried the entire trip. Archer cried too.

Back in the tub, Archer added hot water and submerged until only her nostrils were above water. She liked the sound that filled her head like she was afloat in the middle of the ocean. She thought of Rory, Wayne, the vodka. She had been clean three years, except for that small regression on July Fourth. Why hadn't she thrown out the bottle? She knew the answer all too well. Just in case.

She popped up, a pang of guilt in the pit of her stomach. She got out of the tub and put on a robe. She walked down the hall and knocked on Rory's door. There was no answer.

"Ror," she called. "You okay?"

No response. She opened the door, searched the room, looked in the closet. No Rory. She noticed the window was open and ran to it, hoping she would see him. The only movement in the yard came from the willow tree, its branches and leaves swaying gracefully. She and Rory had planted the tree shortly after the divorce was finalized. Archer had told him it was in honor of their street name but the truth was the tree was symbolic of her freedom, of her hopes, of her dreams for the two of them.

"Where is he?" she whispered, knowing the willow could hear.

But she knew it wouldn't answer. It kept its secrets well.

CHAPTER SEVEN

Archer auto-dialed Rory's cell phone. No answer. She called Wayne. No service. She threw on her clothes and headed into the garage. She would look for Rory at the Mobil-To-Go first, then at Trish's trailer.

Was he still impaired by the vodka? Was he feeling safe?

She backed out of the garage then slammed on her brakes when she saw the police car blocking the driveway. She ran to the driver's window.

"Is Rory okay?"

"He and Trish were in an accident," Mike Campbell said.

"Are they hurt?" The familiar lump in her throat and the nausea in the pit of her stomach took root.

"We think they're okay but we can't find them. The whole police department is looking for them. He and Trish stole her neighbor's car. The neighbor chased them down Route 1A. The car flipped a bunch of times. Rory and Trish ran into the woods."

"Rory wouldn't steal a car."

"I know." Campbell took out a pad and pen. "When was the last time you saw him?"

"Recently. I was taking a bath. I thought he was asleep. He must have climbed out the window." Archer's legs became weak. She leaned on the police car. "I need to find him."

"How come he wasn't in school?"

"Um, I, uh, kept him home today. He wasn't feeling well."

He closed the pad. "If you see him, call me." Campbell touched her hand. "Don't worry. We'll find him."

Archer stepped back from the car and watched him drive away. She stood in the driveway, alone, missing Rory, hoping he was safe.

Her cell phone rang. She didn't recognize the number. "Rory?"

"It's Darcy Cyr. You represented me in my divorce a few years ago. Remember?"

"I remember but this isn't a good time. How'd you get my cell number?"

"From Rory. I'm working a double in the ER at Bangor General. He has a slight concussion and burn marks on his hand. He's going to be fine."

"Burn marks?"

"He says they're from a bullet. Do you know what he's talking about?"

"No. I mean, yes. I'm on my way. Don't let him speak to the police."

"Police?"

"I'll explain when I get there."

Archer got into her car and drove that all too familiar route to the hospital.

CHAPTER EIGHT

Archer had made the drive to Bangor General many times. She remembered at least seven. Four to the emergency room—three lawn mower related accidents, one a sledding mishap. Rory was lucky to have all of his fingers. Plus three trips to the psychiatric wing. The first time, he was eight years old. The last, he was twelve.

As she drove, she tried Wayne's cell. No answer. She wondered if he had forgotten to charge his phone again.

She hesitated then punched in Kara's number. She needed to talk to someone right now. Friends since they were seven, Archer had moved into the house behind Kara's in the middle of second grade. A transplant from Boston, Archer had felt out-of-place with the other kids in Bangor. It was Kara, with her long braids and peasant tops, who had made her feel at home when she showed Archer the Magic Eight Ball.

"Ask a question," Kara had waved the black ball like it was a magic wand.

"Will I like my new home?" Archer had asked.

Kara shook the ball and when Definitely floated in the little window, Archer made her best friend for life.

They had attended Middlebury College in Vermont together; earning work-study monies by gathering information about cadavers to be donated to medical schools. When they graduated with degrees in the useless major of American Studies, they applied to the Peace Corps. Archer didn't meet the language requirement but Kara, who spoke French, did. She went to Ghana for two years, where ironically the official language was English. Archer went to law school. Over twenty years later, they lived within one mile of each other.

Kara answered on the first ring. "How's Rory?"

"I'm on my way to the hospital. He got into a car accident and a bullet blew up in his hand and I don't know what's going on."

"A car accident? A bullet? Where'd he get a bullet? I can't believe he's awake after all the vodka he drank. Is he okay?"

"I think so."

"I'd meet you but I can't leave right now. I'm sorry. Are you okay?"

"I don't know. I'll find out soon enough. How's Evan?"

"I spoke to his mother. He's fine. She's willing to forget that Rory gave him vodka. Evan talks about him all the time. Says Rory is his best friend. In sign language, of course."

"Thanks for taking care of that. I'll call her later. I'm just getting to the hospital. I have to go."

Archer parked the Subaru outside the emergency room. Inside, Darcy grabbed her arm. Her hospital top was green with scattered, smiling Barneys. Archer remembered when Rory would have laughed at the shirt and sing the *I love you* song, adding a line about mommy being a dinosaur. Archer matched Darcy's quick, long strides down the corridor and through the waiting room.

"He's going to be fine," Darcy said. "The ER doc wants to observe him for a few hours due to the head injury but he'll go home tonight."

Archer stopped as Darcy was about to lead her through a side door into the triage. She put a hand on her shoulder. "Thanks. I really appreciate this."

"It's the least I can do after all you've done for me. My divorce was really hard. You got me through it. I couldn't have done it without you." Darcy opened the door.

Archer walked through, surprised at the praise. It had been the reason she became a lawyer—to help people. When she actually succeeded, it made all the madness of the legal profession worthwhile. She thought about Chief Judge Morton. Did he really think she would make a good jurist? Could she commit to a judgeship? Would she even make it to lunch with him?

"He's down the hall," Darcy pointed.

Like a MASH unit, gurneys lined the hallway. This is Bangor, Maine, Archer thought, and still there aren't enough beds. She wondered what ERs were like in cities with large populations and high crime rates. She was glad to live in Bangor. Rory needed the small town life. He hated crowds. Refused to go to the movies. Wouldn't go to water parks, carnivals or fairs. He wouldn't stand a chance in a town larger than Bangor.

Archer rushed down the hall. She passed an elderly woman who was snoring, an IV pumping clear fluid into her veins. A man in his twenties held his arm out like a broken wing, groaning as Archer walked by. A boy, about seven years old, watched as she passed, offering no clues to his ailment beyond a watery stare. Nurses, doctors and aides mingled, seeming oblivious to the humanity around them.

Rory was at the end of the hallway, alone and parked on his gurney next to the exit into the hospital lobby. His eyes were closed. His right arm was by his side, his left hand bandaged and placed over his heart. He had a cut on his forehead and a bruise forming under his right eye.

Right before Rory woke was Archer's favorite time to look at him. It was a chore getting him out of bed each morning, but those few seconds before the daily struggle began begged Archer to see the potential in him. Sometimes, when he was at his worst, she tried to visualize him sleeping with his face perfectly aligned, even a slight smile on his lips, just to remind herself of all he could be, of all she hoped one day he would be. She touched his cheek with the back of her hand.

He opened his eyes. "Man, my head feels like it's going to explode"

"Did they give you anything for it?"

"I don't know. I never smelled burning skin before. When the bullet exploded, my hand caught fire. It didn't hurt when it happened. It hurts like twenty-seven mother fuckers now."

"Please don't talk like that."

"Whatever."

"What happened? Did you really steal a car? How did the bullet blow up in your hand?"

Rory shrugged.

"Talk to me. I need to know what happened."

He closed his eyes, his expression almost peaceful as if he hadn't been involved in wrapping a stolen car around a tree, as if he had no connection to the havoc he had caused. As if he didn't even know she was there.

It was then she noticed the blue markings on his right hand. She picked up his hand. He pulled away.

"What's that?" she asked.

He opened his eyes and glared like she was an intruder. "Trish and I wrote it." He turned his face toward the wall but his hand lay across his chest so she could read the magic marker, each letter occupying the top of a knuckle.

FATE.

CHAPTER NINE

Archer had just finished sweeping "her side" of the garage. Rory sat crossed legged on the other side. A lawn mower tipped on its side rested in front of him. Gas cans, funnels, and assorted tools surrounded him.

"Do you know where the trowel is to plant bulbs?" she asked.

Rory gave the mower a swift kick. "Work, dammit. Where's my tool box?" He pushed aside fan and computer guts, gardening tools, snow shovels, and used bicycle tubes from a corner. "I can't do anything with this bandage on my hand. And I told you not to clean up my stuff but you never listen. I can never find anything because of you."

Before Archer could tell him she had no idea where his tool box was, let alone anything *she* needed, Rory jumped back.

"I found it! This is how that squirrel keeps getting in." He pushed aside several oil containers and pointed to the hole in the wood, a perfect circle. "Do we have moth balls?"

"No. Why?" Archer leaned towards the squirrels' entrance and picked up the empty containers to throw away.

"Just leave 'em there."

"I'm going to throw them away."

"I need them where they are so I can find them. Are you sure we don't have mothballs? I saw on the Discovery channel that squirrels stay away from moth balls. If we put some in a box right here," Rory pointed his bandaged hand toward the hole, "we'll get rid of 'em. I don't want to have to replace that rubber strip at the bottom of the garage door again."

They both looked at the garage door. The black rubber strip was half eaten off.

"If I could ever leave this house again, I could ride my bike to the hardware store and ask whether moth balls hurt squirrels. The hardware guys know all about that stuff. I don't want the squirrels hurt, just gone."

Archer thought about the two days left of his grounding and looked at her son, surrounded by the flotsam and jetsam of his life, concerned for the squirrels and the garage.

"Please, mom, I really don't want to hurt the squirrels. Let me ride my bike to the hardware store."

"C'mon," she said, "I'll drive you."

CHAPTER TEN

With only one day of his suspension left, Archer sat in her living room, looking at the letterhead of the heavy linen paper in her hands, running her fingers over the raised seal and reading it again. The Office of Judicial Appointment invites you to interview with the Governor's Judicial Selection Committee on Friday at three o'clock. In one week, she would be interviewed to be a Judge. She smiled, feeling surprisingly pleased. She had worked hard. It was a long time coming.

Rory sat in the oversized cuddle chair messing with a small carburetor and drinking from a can of Vault. Grandma Rose was preparing dinner. Each clunk and clatter from the kitchen tightened the vice in Archer's head.

"Mom, must you make so much noise?"

"Where's the kosher salt?"

Another bang. Another clatter.

"It's there somewhere. You and Rory used it for the popcorn last night." Archer walked into the kitchen. She looked inside the microwave then reached behind the toaster oven and handed her mother the salt.

Nothing ever had a permanent spot in her house.

"What are you cooking?"

"Chicken a la king. Rory asked me to make it. He thought it would give him strength for his return to school."

Archer sat at the counter and watched her mother bustle around the kitchen. Rose Peskin was seventy years old but looked and acted much younger. She kept her hair brown with frequent visits to the home salon of her friend; her nails were manicured by another friend. An eternal optimist, she saw only good in people and situations. Her part time work as a nursing home inspector was perfect for her. It allowed her time to enjoy card games and Mahjong, yet gave her extra money for her hair and nails but mostly to spend on Rory. Archer wondered how The Trust left by her father was faring during the economic downturn. Rose had been living very comfortably from the interest from the trust but 2007 and 2008 likely changed that. Rose never complained.

The sounds of *Phantom of the Opera* came from deep within her mother's purse. Rose scurried to it and began the search for her cell phone; placing on the counter her wallet, a bottle of Tylenol, a box of mints, an eyeglass repair kit, lipstick, and tissues before finding her phone.

Having missed the call, she listened to the message. A deep voice vibrated from the speaker. "Mrs. Peskin, you promised to call me today but I haven't heard from you. Did you talk with The Trust officer? I expect to hear from you tomorrow."

Archer looked at her mother. "Who was that?"

"Who was what?" Rose opened the refrigerator.

"Your phone, mom. You just listened to a message."

"Um, it was my hairdresser." Her voice was muffled as she reached behind cans of black olives which Rory insisted be kept cold

"It was on speaker phone. I heard it. Who was it?"

Rose unfolded from the cold box, holding a package of defrosted chicken. "I don't know who it was."

"He knew you."

Rose put the roaster on the counter. "Where's the cleaver?"

"Is something going on with The Trust?"

Rose dug through another drawer and pulled out the cleaver. She hacked at the chicken. Her back turned to Archer. "They're giving me less money each month."

Archer froze. How could she not know this? How could she be so wrapped up in her own problems, in Rory's situations, and forget about her mother? That nagging thought invaded her brain. *I am unkind to one of the people I love the most.*

"I can help you."

"I don't want to talk about it. Should I save the gizzards?" Rose held up a bloody mass of poultry organs.

"Only if you want to make chopped liver."

"We'll see." She plopped the innards into the sink.

"Mom, please let me help you."

Rose returned to dismembering the chicken, chopping violently at its raw legs and wings.

Archer sighed, walked into the living room. She would figure out later how best to help her mother.

On the cuddle chair, Rory tugged at the bandage on his hand. Generally, she kept Rory off her chair by stating the one rule of the house that actually terrified him—if he sat in the cuddle chair, she would get to cuddle him. She knew he sat in it when she wasn't around. The small mechanical springs, screwdrivers and Allen wrenches lodged under the cushion gave him away; and the crumbs. She could always tell where he was and what he had been doing by the trail of tools and junk food left in his wake.

"Leave it alone," Archer said. "It comes off in a few days."

"I can't work on my lawnmower with this thing on."

"Dad should be here soon. He'll help you."

One day left of his suspension and finally Wayne was helping out.

"Mother fucker," Rory threw the carburetor to the floor, grabbed the Vault and took a long sip. "I can't do anything with this bandage. And why do I have to hang out with dad? He ignored me for like two years. I should ignore him for two years. Let him see what that feels like. He doesn't like me and I don't like him. Why can't he understand that?"

"Your father likes you and loves you. Plus, you need to respect him. He's your father."

"I want Officer Campbell to come over instead. He knows how to fix a carburetor and change spark plugs. All dad knows how to do is read and lecture. And you don't get respect handed to you on a silver platter. You have to earn it."

He walked through the kitchen toward the garage. Archer followed, passing Rose who was draining the blood from the chicken and humming a Liza Minnelli tune from *Cabaret*.

Rory switched the light on and pressed the automatic garage door opener. The small engine strained to lift the heavy door. The squirrel who lived in the garage scampered away.

"I oughta' shoot that thing," Rory said. "Moth balls didn't work."

Archer knew he didn't mean it. He loved animals and plants. Could do without humans.

"Why don't you ask your dad to help fix your lawn mower? He's smart, he can figure it out."

"He doesn't know the first thing about mechanics. He can't even change a light bulb."

"Don't be like that."

"I wish Officer Campbell was my dad. He'd be a cool dad."

From behind his three bicycles—one Grandma Rose had bought him, two purchased for less than five dollars at garage sales—Rory pulled out the red Craftsman lawnmower he had pushed home from the town transfer station several months ago. He kicked aside a package of tulip bulbs and pulled the mower to the end of the black top driveway. He sat on the ground, tipped the machine gently over, grabbed a large wrench and started tinkering with its engine. Archer watched from the top of the driveway. She considered ordering him back into the house. He was still grounded since his five day suspension hadn't officially ended. But after four days in the house, she was relieved he was outside.

They lived on a dead end street with ten houses on the block; five on each side. Even with the thick woods behind their home that lead to the City Forest—a public park with trails for hiking in the summer, snow shoeing and cross country skiing in the winter—it was a safe neighborhood for Rory. Archer knew all the neighbors on Willow Street and the cars they drove. She knew most of the cars of the people who visited them. They were a close neighborhood of professionals, many with children, all protective of each other.

"I'm not talking to dad when he gets here," Rory said.

"Tell him yourself."

Wayne pulled into the driveway, his old red pickup coughing and wheezing after the engine was cut off. The door squeaked as he stepped out.

He looked at Rory. "You think you can help me fix this truck? She's hesitating like crazy."

Rory concentrated on the lawn mower. "I don't know anything about cars."

Wayne squatted. "Why don't we take an auto mechanics class? We can learn together."

"No, thanks."

Wayne looked up at Archer, his eyes signaling that he needed help. She didn't blame Rory for being mad at Wayne. She was furious with him too. But she did wish he'd give his father a break. Wayne was trying.

"Why don't we see a movie?" Wayne asked.

"I'm good."

"How about we go to the skateboard park?"

"I'm working on my lawn mower. And I'm grounded, in case mom didn't tell you."

"I can help with the mower."

Rory looked at him. "You don't know anything about lawn mowers and you don't know anything about me. So stop pretending."

"I'm your father. I know everything about you. "

"You're not my real dad."

"I am your real dad. And you cannot talk to me like this. "

Archer tried not to feel bad for Wayne. It was like he and Rory didn't even speak the same language.

An old Ford Mustang stopped in front of the house.

Rory jumped up. "What a sweet car. Sick."

The passenger window rolled down.

Archer bent over to see who was driving. "Trish, what are you doing here?"

"Nothing, Mrs. Falcon."

"I'm gonna' have to take this fuckin' thing off to fix this mower," Rory tugged at the bandage on his hand.

Archer stepped toward him. "Don't."

Rory loosened an end of the bandage then began to unwrap it.

"Rory. Stop," Archer said.

He mangled the bandage into a ball and threw it to the ground.

"Can you take me to get gas for the mower?" Rory asked Trish.

"Sure. Get in."

"I'll take you," Wayne said.

"Trish, whose car is that?" Archer asked. "You don't have a driver's license. And you just flipped that jeep . . . . "

Rory got in the Mustang. "I'll be right back."

"Let me take you," Wayne said.

"Wait…," Archer called.

Too late. They were gone.

Archer watched them drive up the block, then around the corner. She looked at Wayne, then at the lawn mower, wishing she knew how to fix it. All of it.

"Where did they go?" Wayne asked.

"Probably the Mobil-to-go."

Archer slowly picked up the mangled bandage and turned at the sound of a car, hoping to see the Mustang. Instead, it was a Bangor police cruiser. Campbell stepped out, holding a folded piece of paper. He handed it to Archer. Wayne stepped next to her.

"Thanks for doing a summons and not an arrest warrant," she said. "I'll bring him to court for the hearing."

"No problem. I know he'll show up. I'm not so sure about Trish. I still need to serve her folks."

"I'll make sure he gets to court, Mike," Wayne said.

Campbell looked at Wayne, then back at Archer. "You okay? You look tired."

"It's been a long week."

"Where's Rory?"

"Took off with Trish."

"How long have they been gone?"

"Not long."

"I was just going to look for them." Wayne hitched up his jeans.

Campbell turned to Archer. "Trish has no one watching her, you know. They don't care what she does. "

They locked eyes.

Archer pulled her gaze away. "I have to get Rory."

CHAPTER ELEVEN

Archer pulled into the parking lot of the Mobil To Go, knowing Rory would be there. His home away from home. She didn't know where Wayne had gone and certainly did not care.

Rory liked that the convenience store/gas station was rarely crowded and the corn dogs were crisp and hot. He liked to sit on Mr. Jenkins' red riding mower kept out back. Rory had dubbed it the Monster Mowchine since Mr. Jenkins had spruced it up with new spark plugs and over-sized tires. Once, Mr. Jenkins even let Rory drive it. Rory had talked about it for weeks, not caring that the Mowchine barely topped five miles per hour.

Through the large glass windows, Archer saw Rory at the counter speaking to Connie, the petite, elderly woman who usually worked double shifts. A gas can, a container of oil, a bag of Funyons, a tin of Pringles and a can of Red Bull were on the counter. Archer didn't see Trish. She pushed the glass door open and walked in.

Rory leaned on the counter. "Do you ever wonder what color a zebra's balls are?"

"Black?" Connie asked.

"Don't you think they're striped?"

Archer touched Rory on the back. "Let's go."

"In a minute. I'm getting oil for the lawn mower. I think that's what it needs. And look at this gas can. I think there should be a uniform color for gas cans. I never knew there could be so many shades of red. Why can't they pick one color red and stick to it? What do you think?"

"Yes, Rory. I agree. Now, can we go?"

"In the old days, they used to make gas cans out of metal. They were wicked good. I've never seen one in-person, only on-line. Now, they're plastic. I think they should make them out of paper or orange peels because those are biodegradable, only takes a few months before they're gone. Metal and plastic take like a million years, if ever."

Archer heard rustling, looked down an aisle where she saw Trish slip something into her pocket.

Trish was beautiful the way fifteen year old girls were beautiful. Unlike Rory, she appeared to have escaped the roll-over accident unscathed. Her skin was unmarred and her belly flat. Her hair was blond, dark at the roots, and pulled back into a high ponytail with a thin pink ribbon. She wore little makeup except around her eyes which were lined with black pencil and brushed with green shadow. She was thin-hipped and wore flannel pajama bottoms with kittens on them and a tank top that rested above a silver belly button ring. Thin purple bra straps peaked out. She had a butterfly tattoo on her left shoulder blade.

"We should go," Archer said, loud enough for Trish to hear.

"If we could turn dirt into oil we would solve the world's energy crisis and not have to rely on other countries," Rory said. "Don't you think that's a great idea? Connie does."

The clerk nodded.

"Yes, Rory, it's really smart. I'm tired. Can we go home now?"

"Yeah. I need money."

She looked at Rory's bounty on the counter as Trish walked up next to them. Archer held out her hand. Trish took the Milky Way out of her pocket and dropped it into Archer's palm.

CHAPTER TWELVE

Archer pulled into the garage on Willow Street. The garage door closed behind them. The car engine rattled.

"I don't want you to hang around Trish anymore," she said.

"You can't tell me who to hang out with." Rory opened the car door.

"Yes, I can."

"You don't want me to have friends. You don't know shit about me. Get that through your head." He jumped out of the car.

She sighed. "Why don't you relax, take a shower?"

He leaned in through the open door. "I'm not taking any more showers."

"Then take a bath."

"I don't like drains."

"That's ridiculous."

"What's ridiculous is you sitting here in a closed garage with the car running." He ran into the house.

Archer shut off the car and listened for sounds of breaking light bulbs or objects being thrown against walls. She heard nothing, took a deep breath and walked into the house. It was quiet. Her mother had left, accustomed to the chaos that was Archer's life. The pot of chicken a la king sat on the stove. She heard Rory's bedroom door shut, the deadbolt latched. Archer hoped he would stay there all night.

Two hours later, Archer put her ear against Rory's bedroom door and heard her own voice from inside the room.

"I don't want you to hang around Trish anymore," she said.

"You can't tell me who to hang out with."

"I'm your mother. Yes, I can."

"You don't want me to have friends."

She stopped listening, padded to her room. Rory often used his cell phone as a recorder. He liked to review what was said because sometimes he forgot. She wondered how many conversations he had of her on his cell, how incriminating they might be, how long before she was going to reach her breaking point.

In her room, Archer read the Talmudic saying hung above her dresser next to the bedroom door. Wayne had framed it and presented it to her on Rory's second birthday.

Every blade of grass has its angel that bends over it and whispers, grow, grow.

As an angel, she sucked.

She thought about taking a bath but got into bed instead. It was late and she had a hearing in the morning. She closed her eyes, too weary to shut the light off, too tired to get up and throw the deadbolts to her own bedroom door. She let the exhaustion cradle her, seeking calmness in its haze. She heard Rory's door open, his stomps down the hallway. Hopefully, he was going to relax in a hot shower. Instead, he barged into her room.

"Why are you such a bitch? Trish is my friend." He paced in front of her bed. Five steps forward, five steps back. Repeat.

"Rory, you need to calm down."

"I was calm. I was just buying a gas can and stuff. You never trust me. You're an asshole and you ruin my whole life."

"I ruin your life? How about my life? I can't work. I'm always being called away because of your bad behavior. You're rude. You got drunk at school, stole a car, ended up in the hospital..."

Archer stopped. Her throat hurt and Rory wasn't listening anyway. He was still pacing, but his head was down. His hands covered his ears. The angel who whispered had turned into the devil who shouted.

"You are a dumb fuck." He slammed the door behind him.

The Talmudic frame fell to the floor. Archer picked it up and threw it in the bathroom garbage pail. She went back to the bedroom door and slid the three deadbolts into place. The angel had been demoted and probably was a dumb fuck.

CHAPTER THIRTEEN

Archer's bedroom door rattled. The deadbolts were secure, three gold titanium locks slid into place. Rory had installed the deadbolts on both their bedroom doors as a mother's day gift to protect them from intruders. It had become unclear who they were shutting out.

When her door wouldn't open, Rory quietly called: "Mom?"

No rage in his voice. No blame. She slid the deadbolts open. Rory shuffled in, wearing red and white flannel pajama bottoms, no shirt. Rudolf's face was repeated on the PJ's thirty two times. It had taken Rory five tries to get the right count since each time he'd come up with one extra or one less; but he was sure of the number now. Thirty-two. He had told Archer he liked how each face was an exact replica of the face next to it. He liked that Rudolf with his nose so bright looked sad.

Rory looked sad as he paced at the foot of Archer's bed. "You know, a window AC unit will cool all year round. Even if it's cold out, you might still need it with your hot flashes. When Mrs. K gets hot flashes at school her face gets so red she looks like Rudolf's nose." He wrapped his arms tightly around his chest.

"Are you shaking?" Archer asked.

"Naw. I was just wondering..."

"What?"

"Why can't I have a friend?"

"I don't know if Trish is really your friend. What about Evan? You could hang out with him."

"You need to have faith in me. Remember, you thought the willow tree was going to die?" He looked out the bedroom window, into the dark night, toward the willow tree, the back of the house and the City Forest. "I mean, you're always telling me to make better choices but if you don't trust me, what's the point?"

"Making better choices comes before the trust."

He leaned on the window sill. "Maybe we could go for a hike in the City Forest tomorrow. Or you can go for a run and I'll ride my bike. I know you like to do that."

"You're still grounded, Rory. After taking off with Trish today, you're grounded for even longer. But good try."

He smiled. "That's not fair. I try to do the right thing. I'll try and do better. I promise. I love you, Mom. I really love you."

"I love you, too."

"You don't know what's in my head. Nobody knows. You wouldn't like it if you were inside my head."

"I'm tired, Rory."

"Remember you said you'd tell me about my birth parents?"

"Yeah?"

"I kinda' want to know."

"Now?"

"I can't sleep."

"I have court in the morning."

"Please, Mom, I won't ask for anything again."

They both laughed, knowing that was impossible.

"All right. Guess I can't sleep either." She patted the empty side of her bed.

Like a player who finally gets to take the field, Rory leaped onto the mattress. He shoved his feet under the comforter.

"Where do we start?" Rory asked.

"We start," Archer said, "with The Perfect Storm."

CHAPTER FOURTEEN

"The Andrea Gail was a seventy two foot fishing boat. It had a crew of six men," Archer said.

"What were they fishing for?" Rory's head was propped up on his hand. She lay on her back. "Swordfish."

"People think swordfish have a spear that comes out of their nose but it's really their jaw. It's wicked long and they use it to pierce prey."

"How do you know that?"

"There was this book I loved that Dad used to read to me called Tales of Swordfish and Tuna. I can't remember the last time Dad read to me."

Archer ran her finger over the bump on his forehead. "You okay?"

"Yeah. It doesn't hurt."

"It's healing great. Let me see your hand."

He held it out for her.

"It's like you weren't burned."

"I'm a quick healer."

"That's for sure. Why don't you ask Dad to read to you again?"

"'Cause he'll look at me like I'm an idiot like he always does. And I'm too old for that stuff."

"Your father is a librarian. That could be something you do together. He loves to read. He loves books."

"More than he loves me."

"That's not true. He loves you very much." The words came out stilted.

Rory rolled his eyes. "Tell me about the swordfish boat."

"The Andrea Gail left port from Gloucester, Massachusetts on September 20, 1991. The last anyone heard from the ship was October 28th."

"That's the day I was born. What happened?"

"The Perfect Storm."

"How can a storm be perfect?"

"It was perfect to those who studied storms. Two enormous air masses called Nor'easters collided. The results were severe. At one point, it was a cyclone. Then, it turned into a hurricane. People died and homes were lost. There was flooding and major erosion."

"What happened to the crew members?"

"They were never found."

"The ship too?"

"The Coast Guard searched for about a week. They found a few parts but that's all."

"Seems like something as big as a fishing boat would be easy to find. Think I can learn to scuba dive?"

"Sure. Why?"

"'Cause then I can look for the...what's it called?"

"The Andrea Gail."

"Maybe I could find clues as to what happened. I bet the crew was scared. I bet the waves were big."

"Over one hundred feet at times."

"That's three times bigger than the Paul Bunyan statue at Bass Park. How do you know so much about the Andrea Gail?"

"I studied it. I wanted to know everything about the Andrea Gail and The Perfect Storm."

She hesitated to say anything more. She had always promised herself she would be honest with him about his birth parents. Even if it filled her with jealousy, even if it reminded her: he's not my blood. She never thought he would be interested in finding out about them until he was older, eighteen at least. She should have known. Rory never did anything as expected. He was the other perfect storm.

CHAPTER FIFTEEN

Archer watched Rory study the ceiling fan slowly turning over the bed.
"It's spinning backwards," he said. "Sucking the cool air up not down. No wonder you need a fan. I can switch the direction for you."

"That'd be great," Archer said.

He didn't get up. "Mrs. K taught us about long line fishing in school, before she was the principal. They use hundreds or thousands of baited hooks hanging from a single line to catch swordfish but they trap sea birds and loggerhead turtles. You think they did that on the Andrea Gail? You think they killed birds and turtles?"

"I don't know."

"There must be some way to fish without trapping birds and turtles. If they wanted to, they could pick the birds and turtles out of the nets and put them back in the ocean. That's what I would do. When I have a boat, I'm going to name it the Archer Rose after you and Grandma. You know, The Perfect Storm is an oxymoron like jumbo shrimp or wicked good." He hesitated. "You think I'm an oxymoron?"

"I don't think a person can be an oxymoron."

"Yeah. I guess not. Do you know my real mom's name?"

She hesitated, wanted to say I am your real mom, but didn't. "Your birth mother's name was Kitty Warren."

"Warren? Like the moving truck company?"

"Yeah. But not related. She lived in Gloucester, not in Bangor."

"Did she have blonde hair? How tall was she? What about my real dad?"

She squirmed. She couldn't defend Wayne as his real father. Definitely not enough evidence to support that.

"I'm sorry. I don't know his name."

He watched the fan for a moment. "So what's the big deal about the Andrea Gail and that storm?"

She hesitated then spit it out. "Your birth father was one of the crew members."

Rory sat up. "My real dad was a crew member on a swordfish boat? Is that why he didn't want to keep me?" Rory's eyes teared. "How long have you known?"

"Since you came home with us."

Rory jumped off the bed and paced. "So, my real dad might have killed birds and turtles? I wish I could have stopped him from fishing forever. Maybe we could have opened a lawn mower shop together. And when the lawns were dead and there was snow, we'd turn the signs around and we'd have a snow blower shop." He ran out of her room.

Archer sighed, turned on her side and curled her knees to her chest. She considered going to Rory's room, but how could she relieve his pain when he was hurt by everything she said? She didn't really know what to say. How many times could she tell him that she loved him?

She heard clanks and clatters from his room. With each jolt, her heart jumped. Blood rushed to her head. Afraid of the noise, but more afraid of silence, she snuck into the hallway. Her moose slippers swished gently on the wood floor, and she listened at his door for some sign that he was okay. She pushed the door slightly ajar and saw him wrestling with a black wooden fan. He tugged at the wires in the back. Rage hot on his fingertips, seeming to rattle down his arms and legs. He pulled the wires out, tossed them aside, then broke the blades off one-by-one; throwing each one against the wall, leaving black scuff marks and indents behind.

Even in the calmest of moments, he was unable to control his emotions. His happiness was uncontrollable euphoria, his sadness was the deepest of depressions, his anger was chest- pounding fury. She knew he scared even himself at times. Her heart pounded. He was scaring her.

"Fuck you," he yanked at a fan blade, "for not telling me about my real father sooner. Fuck you for adopting me." He looked at the door and appeared startled to see her standing there. "You know what," he screamed, " I wish he would have lived. He would know what it's like to be me. And then me and my real dad would have opened our shop together and I wouldn't be living here. With you."

Pain gripped her chest. Her entire body went weak and shaky. She leaned on the door. Her face burned with anger and hurt.

He threw the last blade against the wall, grabbed the record player—the one Grandma Rose had purchased on E-Bay—and raised it high over his head. Before letting go, before smashing it to the ground, he looked out the bedroom window at the front of the house. He threw the record player on to his bed, went to the window and peered out.

"What is it?" She clung to the doorknob for support.

"Someone who really cares about me."

He put on his hoody sweatshirt—black and dotted with tiny white skulls—over his Rudolf pajama bottoms and stuffed the sweatshirt pocket with his cell phone, wallet, a small flashlight, a screwdriver, a pocket knife and a couple of AAA batteries. Then, he ran toward the door.

Archer didn't move out of his way. "Where are you going?"

He pushed past her. "Why didn't they want me?" His voice was a hoarse whisper.

"Rory. Stop. Where are you going?"

He turned back, hesitated, then balled his hand into a fist. She saw the swing of his arm, his knuckles aimed for her face. Then felt the smack. Her knees buckled. She fell to the floor.

As he ran down the stairs and out the front door, he yelled: "Change the direction of the fan above your bed yourself, you dumb bitch."

With her head spinning and her eye throbbing, she crawled to a front window in time to see the taillights of the old Mustang speed away.

She sobbed and climbed into Rory's bed. She pushed the record player off the bed with her feet and wrapped herself in his blanket. Her head hurt. Her eye ached. The blanket smelled like Rory.

CHAPTER SIXTEEN

The morning sun streamed through the window. Archer tried to bring the events of the last few hours into focus. They had been in her bed and she had told Rory about his birth parents and The Perfect Storm. She recalled his outrage, her fear, his fist against her eye. And then the slam of the front door.

She tried to open her eyes. The right one was crusted closed and ached like — yes - like she had been punched. The air smelled like sweat and fried onion rings. She groaned and unwrapped herself from Rory's blanket, trying to recall if there was anything she was supposed to do, anyplace she had to be.

She closed her eyes then opened them again. Rory's room was cluttered with broken fan and stereo components, marred with indents in the walls, littered with candy wrappers, chip bags, uprooted plants and broken flower pots. Beanie babies lay like fallen soldiers along the wood floor.

She heard ticking, reached for the nightstand, pushed aside spark plugs, funnels and batteries, and unplugged the Barney clock Grandma Rose had given Rory when he was three years old. He never got rid of anything given to him by Grandma Rose. Archer squinted. Barney's long arm pointed at the twelve, his shorter arm at the nine.

She jumped up as the fog in her head lifted, stepped on the record player and hopped to her room. She had to be in court at ten. Should she try and find someone to cover the hearing? No time. Besides, what else was she going to do? Lie in bed and lament her son hitting her for the first time? Burrow into the cuddle chair and grieve for her lack of parenting skills? Clean the dryer vent and question for the umpteenth time how her life had ended up like this? No, she would get out and keep busy with work. She would do something she was good at. She would feel needed, important.

In the shower, she forced herself to think about her cases. All she had scheduled for the day was an informal conference with Judge Murphy then she would concentrate on Rory. She knew she should call Wayne and try to find him now, but she didn't pick up the phone, didn't do anything about it.

She felt guilty for not feeling more guilty.

CHAPTER SEVENTEEN

Archer's client was a woman from Hampden, Maine. After months of stalling, her soon-to-be-ex and his lawyer had finally provided Archer with a box of financial documents. Every document was cut in half. Archer had filed a motion seeking to hold the husband in contempt for his failure to abide by the court rules. The hearing was set in front of Alan Murphy, the Judge who had presided over her divorce.

Judge Murphy was short tempered and lacked patience for wordy lawyers and weepy litigants. He made up his mind quickly, too quickly according to some. Archer was one of the few who trusted his judgment. In fact, she frequently agreed with his decisions and his belief that any decision was better than indecision. They also shared a common bond. They both had children with special needs. But two parents raised Judge Murphy's son while only one was raising Rory.

The courthouse was a three minute walk from her office. Archer carried the box of mutilated documents. Opposing counsel, Steve Finelli, caught up with her as she walked into the courthouse. She shoved the box into Steve's pudgy hands.

"Here. It's your box. You carry it."

"Everything was provided by my client, right?" Steve was out of breath.

"You're joking."

"I didn't have time to go through it. What with my Dad being in the hospital and all. My paralegal was home with a sick kid and I knew the discovery was late so I had it delivered to your office. What's missing? I tried to call you to work this out but you didn't return my call." Steve panted. He was ten years younger than her but fifty pounds overweight. "We don't need to have the hearing. Tell me what's missing and I'll get my guy to supply it."

Archer stopped. "You can't get your client to do anything and I'm not playing games anymore. He's not giving her any money. The house is about to go into foreclosure. She's going to have to get food stamps to feed their son. The only way he's going to cooperate is from a jail cell."

"Not every husband is a dead beat."

She tried not to think about Wayne. She knew she shouldn't project her contempt for him on all the men in the world.

"I know, Steve. I represent plenty of men who do the right thing and many women who don't. But in this situation, your guy is wrong."

"Give me a chance. I'll speak to him. He'll fire me if he goes to jail."

"Are you going to buy food for my client and their son?"

"No."

"Then I'm going forward with the hearing." She walked toward the Judge's chambers.

Silver-haired Joe, Judge Murphy's bailiff, sat behind a desk in the waiting area. "Uh, oh." He smiled at Archer. "Here comes trouble." He looked at the box. "What'cha got?"

"A discovery dispute." Steve said. "Archer wants to put my client in jail."

"If the judge would do it, I'd suggest you go to jail instead," Archer glared at Steve.

"Save it for the Judge," Joe said. "Go on in. He's ready."

Archer held the door for Steve who carried the box inside. Judge Murphy sat at the head of a large conference room table.

"Looks like a discovery dispute." Judge Murphy eyed the box.

Steve put it down on the table. "Your honor, my client and I worked hard to get all the documents requested. They're all here."

"He's right." Archer said. "The documents are there. Twice."

"See," Steve said, "this is a waste of the Court's time. My client wants fees and…Twice?"

"Mr. England cut all of the documents in half," Archer said. "Every bank statement, every corporate invoice, every check provided from the last three years."

"Let me see." Judge Murphy shuffled through the papers and looked to Steve.

"Did you know about this?"

"No, Your Honor. My father has Alzheimer's and…"

Judge Murphy pushed the box toward him. "Take it back and organize it. Get new documents for Ms. Falcon or tape those back together if you have to. And have your client pay for her time." He looked at Archer. "Three hours worth. Is that good?"

"Yes," Archer said. More like five hours, but she didn't want to appear ungrateful for the positive ruling. She decided not to ask for jail. This time. Compliance would be better.

"Get the documents to Ms. Falcon by Monday at two. If anything is missing or indecipherable, let me know and I'll re-consider your Motion for Contempt. Have a nice day and, Mr. Finelli, tell your client he almost went to jail today. Next time, he might not be so lucky."

Steve grabbed the box and left. Archer followed, a few steps behind. She waved to Joe and promised she'd bring him a hot cup of tea Monday morning when she was next scheduled to appear in front of Judge Murphy. She walked toward the exit, watching Steve huff his way out of the courthouse. As her heels clanked on the tile floor, Rory popped into Archer's head. She touched her eye and winced. She hoped the make-up she had applied that morning still covered it.

Judge Murphy stepped along side of her. "How are you?"

"Good. Busy at work. I've always wondered how such a small town can have so many divorces. It seems like we would have gone through everyone by now."

"How'd you get that black eye?"

She flinched, saw Rory's fist and felt surprisingly relieved to be free of him, even for a little while. Shouldn't she be more concerned? Shouldn't she have called the police by now? Or at least his father? And what was she going to tell her mother?

"I slipped on an ice cube and hit my face on the kitchen counter."

"I see. How's Rory? I've been pleased to see his absence on Tuesday juvenile days. Although I heard about him and the Dooley girl stealing a car."

Archer had no response. She could defend Rory but it would serve no purpose. If it wasn't stealing a car, it was something else like bringing alcohol to school. Tears welled in her eyes. She looked away, embarrassed, feeling ineffective.

"My son is nineteen now." Judge Murphy shuffled down the hall with his hands behind his back. "He's non-verbal and in a wheel chair. He graduated high school going through what they call the MR room. He's not mentally retarded but that's where they put the non-verbal kids. He's living in a group home outside Boston."

Judge Murphy opened the door to the outside. Archer stepped into the cool air and wiped the tears from her eyes, grateful to be a step ahead.

"You always had hope for Rory even if you didn't realize it," he continued. "I knew you would never give up on him." He lightly touched her arm. "Truth is, I was impressed by the Skittles."

She smiled at the memory. When Rory was young and feeling bad and Archer didn't know how to help him, she put Skittles in a medicine bottle and told him they were feel good vitamins. Every time he took one, he felt better.

"You'd make a wonderful judge, Archer." Murphy pointed to a coffee shop. "This is where I get off. Have a good day."

She watched him go inside and sit at the counter. Stunned, she stood on the sidewalk. It was time to find Rory.

CHAPTER EIGHTEEN

He wasn't at the Mobil-To-Go telling jokes to Connie. Not at the mall in his favorite electronics repair shop trying to scam left-over wires or cables from a new employee. Not at the hardware store talking up the guys behind the counter about powering lawn mowers with the fat Grandma Rose skims off the top of her chicken stock.

As Archer drove, heading home, hoping he was there, her eyes darted side-to-side, her neck turned sharply as she looked up and down every street. No Rory.

She pulled into the driveway on Willow Street and released a long sigh. Rory was seated on the front porch, hunched over, his shoulders curled and heaving. She jumped out of the car, sat next to him, her knees sticking tall above the step because of the high heels she wore. She took them off and threw them into the grass, grateful to let her toes wiggle free.

"Hi." She injected false energy into the greeting.

He wiped his face with his sleeve. His pajama bottoms were torn. His hoody scuffed with mud. The right sleeve was ripped. There was a road rash on his right hand and forearm. She wanted to take him into her arms, pull him into her lap, and cuddle him like the little boy she had first brought home. But she knew if she touched him, if she even reached out to him, he would rebuff her. Hard.

"What happened? Are you okay?"

He didn't respond.

Archer touched her eye and winced. She stood. "C'mon inside. I'll get you some water." He followed her into the house. She poured two glasses of water and sat at the kitchen table. Rory paced, five steps forward, five steps back, repeat.

"Why don't you take a shower?"

"I told you. I'm not taking a shower or a bath ever again."

"How'd you get so dirty?"

"At the City Forest."

"How did you end up there? Is that where you spent the night?"

Although trails in their backyard connected to the City Forest, it was a long and meandering journey to get there. They had tried to hike it a few times but had turned back, usually because Rory became anxious as the brush grew thicker and the trail turned dark. Besides, the tall grass, thick trees and the swamp by the old railroad bed made the twenty minute drive much more appealing.

"I shouldn't have come back here," he said.

Archer touched her eye again. "This is your home."

"You never give me a break. Do this. Do that. Clean this. Clean that. Wear your helmet when I ride my bike. Take off your shoes. Get in the shower. You don't let me have any friends. Maybe I'll go find my real mom."

She flinched like he was hitting her again, like she was cornered in a boxing ring.

"I am your real mom."

"You're fake. Just like those feel good pills you used to give me. My real mom would never lie to me."

Archer's face grew hot. Her head pounded. Her arm went numb again. She wanted to smash Rory, pulverize him, knock some sense into him. She raised the water glass over her head and threw it against the wall. Glass shattered. Water splashed. She ran to the bathroom and locked herself inside, relieved when she heard the front door slam.

CHAPTER NINETEEN

Archer sat on the floor in the bathroom regretting her outburst. Throwing the glass of water was exactly what Rory would have done. She was a terrible role model.

She remembered the first time she had lost her temper over Rory. She had taken one-year-old Rory to Florida for her parents' thirty-fifth wedding anniversary. Wayne had refused to go since he was rehearsing for a play. She vividly recalled the fight they had which ended with Wayne storming out the door, yelling, "The Show Must Go On!"

Normally, her family didn't have parties and celebrations but her father had been dying. This was going to be their last anniversary together. Lung cancer and emphysema had robbed him of the ability to walk. He was in a wheelchair. Rory spent the whole week sitting on his lap. His first word wasn't mama or dada, but "spin" for the wheels on the chair.

The flight home had been horrendous. Rory had stood on her lap in his feety pajamas and bounced while looking out the window. When she tried to settle him with a toy, his screams reverberated through the cabin until she bounced him again. Feeling fatigued, lonely and sad, her grip on Rory had tightened and she had bounced him harder. He only giggled louder and repeated, "spin, spin, spin." Archer couldn't hold back her tears any longer. When the flight attendant asked if she could help, Archer gratefully handed him over.

In the downstairs bathroom on Willow Street, Archer slowly stood, tugging on the skirt she still wore. Her court uniform. She was happier in loose jeans, a baggy shirt and Birkenstocks, carrying a knapsack or hip sack and not a briefcase or pocketbook.

She had felt so happy and relieved to see Rory sitting on the front steps when she had returned from Court. But this wasn't working. She was not a good mother for Rory and he was not a good son for her. What would she advise a client? Go to counseling? Talk with his father? Adjust Rory's medications? But she didn't have the patience to explore her own feelings. It was easy to tell other people what to do. She wanted answers without feelings. Feelings only hurt.

Walking into the living room, she saw Rory's muddy footprints on the hardwood floor. When would her life be her own? Of all the parenting classes she had taken, all the books she had read, and all the psychologists and social workers she had spoken to, none had ever warned her it would be like this. The tension with Wayne over disciplining Rory, her inability to date because she couldn't leave Rory alone for any length of time, the time lost from work, the missed opportunities to make friends with other parents at pre-school, boy scouts, soccer and other events — all made her an outsider. Although she would nod sympathetically, she couldn't relate to the parents' complaints about their kids staying up late to do homework or not taking the garbage out. She would never talk over coffee with other mothers about the exorbitant cost of clothes for the prom. She and Rory were outsiders and it wasn't their fault.

She went into the dining room, opened the credenza, gently pushed aside her grandmother's wine glasses and felt for the bottle. She took her hand out and sat on the floor. Thick, stinging drops fell from her eyes. The vodka was gone. And she remembered. Rory had taken it to school.

CHAPTER TWENTY

Archer put the tall vodka bottle on the counter of the Mobil To Go.

"Isn't it a little early? It's not even two yet." Connie scanned the bottle and put it in a bag. "You just missed Rory and Trish."

"They were here?"

"Rory bought chips, drinks, another gas can. I don't know what he does with all of them. Maybe he's starting his own business selling gas cans."

"Did they say where they were going?"

"That Trish girl is bad. She must have taken almost ten dollars worth of candy. I never call the police because her life is hard enough. I hear her mama beats her. She was all covered up this afternoon with a hoody, like what Rory wears all the time. I think something happened last night."

"Did Rory pay for his things?"

"With a brand new ten dollar bill. Said he made it mowing lawns. Your son is a hard worker." Connie hit buttons on the cash register. "That'll be seventeen dollars and thirty two cents."

Archer handed Connie a twenty dollar bill. "You sure you have no idea where Rory and Trish were going?"

"I know they were driving far since Rory said he needed energy drinks to stay awake and keep Trish company while she drove. Those kids should be in school. My boys never missed a day of school."

"I wish you would have called me."

"Not my responsibility." She pushed the bottle toward Archer. "I'm thirty seven years clean. I still go to AA meetings."

Archer grabbed the neck of the bottle through the bag and headed for the exit. She pushed open the door, chimes echoing, mocking her like the skull on Rory's canteen. She stumbled to the Subaru, got in and shoved the bottle under the driver's seat. Rory didn't need his mother, but Archer surely needed her own. Her hands shook as she fumbled with her cell phone.

"Hi, baby." Her mother's voice was always upbeat. "Everything okay?"

"Yeah. Fine." The words barely squeezed out of Archer's throat.

"How's Rory? Did he like the chicken a la king?"

"Yes. He's fine," she said.

"I'm playing Canasta with the ladies at The Elm. Can we talk later?"

Archer fought the tears, tried to swallow the lump in her throat. She shouldn't have called. She shouldn't burden her mother with Rory's problems, with her own inadequacies. What was the point of them both being miserable, worried, ashamed? Her mother had enough problems of her own.

"Sure. We can talk later." Archer hung up.

She leaned back, closed her eyes. The hard raps on the window startled her. She opened it, watching the glass disappear into the door.

"They told me where they were going," Connie leaned in, "but they made me promise not to say anything."

Archer wanted to explode but instead tried a technique that often worked in court. Say nothing. Wait. In court it was fun. Now, though, she picked at her cuticles and waited. It wasn't fun.

"I didn't know Rory was adopted," Connie said. "He told me about his dad being this famous fisherman, like Jacques Cousteau. How does Rory know about Jacques Cousteau? I didn't think kids his age knew things like that. He said his real dad died trying to save his friends' lives during The Perfect Storm. I remember that storm like it was yesterday. I was living in New Hampshire at the time and..."

Archer pulled a piece of skin off her middle finger. She could wait no longer. "Where are they, Connie?"

"I said I wouldn't tell."

"You raised three boys, right?"

"Sure did. One's a mechanic in Bath, the other's in the Coast Guard and one's still lost but I know he'll find his way."

"Where's Rory? If he were your son, you'd want to know."

Connie looked away, then back at Archer. "He trusts me."

"He's a fifteen year old boy. Trish is a bad influence and Rory will do whatever she wants. Did Trish make him go somewhere?"

"It wasn't Trish's idea."

"Where are they?"

"Gloucester," Connie said. "They're on their way to Gloucester, Massachusetts."

CHAPTER TWENTY-ONE

The Subaru's tires screeched as she pulled into the library parking lot. Wayne was perched at the Help Desk.

"Rory is on his way to Gloucester with Trish," Archer said.

"Who's Trish?"

"Don't you know anything about your son? That girl he drove off with to get gas."

"Keep your voice down. This is a library." He pulled her by the arm behind a stack of medical books. "I didn't know her name. He never talks to me and you never tell me anything. What do you mean he's going to Gloucester?"

"He's looking for his birth mother."

"You told him about Kitty? How could you? We're supposed to talk about that together."

Archer was surprised that he remembered Kitty's name. "That's a joke, right?"

"No fucking joke, Archer. I know we're divorced and you have custody but I'm still his father. We're supposed to discuss important issues as a family."

"Are you kidding? When have you ever been there for him?"

"Always. Why do you think he knows so much? It's because I read to him when he was little."

"Big deal. You were so busy reading you forgot to listen. And you can't just put kids on hold for two years while you go around New England auditioning."

"It's better for him that he have a dad who is successful. I tried, Archer, and if I'm successful I'll be able to give him anything he wants."

"He wants you to know him. Name two of his friends. Who are his teachers? Do you know his favorite color? What he likes to eat? All he's ever wanted from you is your time."

"If I don't know something about him, it's because you've kept it from me. You alienate him and you know it."

Archer sighed. It wasn't worth the fight. "You need to go get him."

"I can't go to Gloucester. I have to go with Mary Beth to an ultrasound in a few minutes. I also got the lead in that play in Portsmouth I told you about and the rehearsals start tonight. It's your fault he's going to Gloucester. You never should have told him about Kitty. He can't handle it. If you had let me raise him..."

"Don't even fucking say it," she got close to his face. "You didn't want him. And you couldn't handle him. And what would you have done with him over the last two years?"

"You never gave me the chance."

"I have to give you the chance? That's insane. You're his father. Take it. Spend time with him. Do something that interests him and not you."

"Fine. I will."

"So you're going to Gloucester?"

"I can't. I have the ultrasound and rehearsals..."

Archer turned away, headed for her car.

CHAPTER TWENTY-TWO

A rcher loved to drive, listen to the radio, sing and wiggle in her seat. To her ears, she was in tune. But as Wayne liked to remind her, she was off-key. So when she was alone, she sang. Loud and proud. And to herself, she was perfectly in tune.

She loved all music except for the head-banger stuff that Rory favored. They did have some of the same musical tastes—they liked some of the same rap artists and R&B singers. But when Rory put on that awful music that sounded like a truck grinding its gears in reverse, she couldn't relate. Likewise, he didn't get her penchant for big-haired eighties rock ballads.

The highway was empty as she sped along, the speedometer teetering around eighty. She wondered what Rory and Trish were doing, wishing he would have answered her numerous calls to his cell phone just once so she would know he was okay. Was he hurt? He was usually cautious, she reasoned. The ride in the jeep had been an aberration. Atypical Rory behavior. But then again, he was almost sixteen with hormones raging. Wouldn't he do things out of character just to please Trish? Wasn't that typical behavior for a teenage boy?

She shut off the radio and tried his cell phone one more time. Right to voice mail. She sent another text. Waited. No response.

Archer tried to be positive. That's what Kara would tell her to do. Imagine good things. Visualize Rory in a safe, comfortable place. Archer saw him in her cuddle chair, his long legs curled around the arm, in his lap a carburetor he had been tinkering with right before he fell asleep. But Rory wasn't home. And neither was she. Life certainly was a highway. One she didn't want to drive all night long.

She wanted to blame it all on Trish and her butterfly tattoo. Archer didn't know much about Trish. Just that she lived in the trailer park off the ironically named Country Club Road. Archer couldn't recall meeting Trish's parents at any school events, around town, in the supermarket or at the transfer station. She only knew one thing about Trish—she had been suspended from school more times than Rory. That, and Rory was enamored by her. But what boy wouldn't be?

Her cell rang. Finally. She didn't recognize the number but knew the area code. Massachusetts.

"Hi Mom," Rory sounded happy.

"Where are you?"

"What was the name of the lady who gave birth to me again?"

"Kitty. Rory, where are you?"

"It's a good thing we don't remember being born. That would be freaky—coming out of someone's body, that's totally weird, isn't it? Remember when we saw that calf being born on The Discovery Channel? How come calves can walk right after their born but it takes humans like a year to learn how to walk? How come animals don't crawl before they walk like we do? When did I learn to walk?"

"Rory, listen to me. Where are you?"

"With Trish and some lady police officer."

"What?"

"Trish drove into a ditch. We bottomed out. It was wicked cool. It's gonna' take a crane to get that car out of there. I bet the transmission is shot. I think I wanna' learn how to fix cars. Can I do that?"

"Are you hurt?"

"Naw, we were wearing our seatbelts."

"Where are you?" she asked again.

"In the back of a police car. The lady cop is taking us to the Gloucester police department."

"Are you under arrest?"

"I don't think so. We're not in handcuffs or anything like that. She didn't read Miranda to us. Remember when I was twelve and that old bag down the street accused me of stealing her lawn mower and the cop read Miranda to me from a card. I said it right with him. I knew it by heart but he had to read it from a card," Rory laughed. "I didn't steal that lawn mower, by the way."

"I know. I've tried your cell phone a bunch of times. How come you didn't answer?"

"I don't know."

"Whose phone is this?"

"The lady police officer's. Wanna' speak to her?"

"Yes. But Rory, wait. Are you okay?"

"Yeah, mom, I'm fine. We're fine. Don't worry. This is just something I have to do, know what I mean? I love you, mom. I really love you."

"I love you too."

"I'm making better choices."

"I don't know, Ror."

"You have to trust me."

"Running off with Trish is not making better choices."

"According to you."

Archer sighed. "Let me speak to the police officer."

Archer heard muffled sounds, then a woman's voice with a distinctive New England accent.

"Detective Ellen O'Neill," she said.

"I'm Archer Falcon, Rory's mother. Are they under arrest?"

"Not yet. I'm taking them to the PD to check out their story."

"What have they told you?"

"The car belongs to the girl's uncle and she's borrowing it. She doesn't have any ID but she says she's sixteen and has her driver's license. Can you confirm any of this?"

"I should be in Gloucester in about a half an hour. Can we talk when I get there?"

"Yes, ma'am. Do you know how I can reach any of the girl's relatives? She said her parents died in a fire that also killed her little brother and her cat. She said she's been living with you and Rory. Do you have legal custody of her?"

"Officer, can we please discuss this when I get there?"

"Thirty minutes, you say?"

"Yes."

"See you then, ma'am."

Archer hung up, threw her cell phone on to the seat next to her. Life certainly was a highway, leading her off a cliff, head-banger music blaring off-key.

CHAPTER TWENTY-THREE

The exit into Gloucester off Route 128 twirled like a breeching tarpon. When Archer was growing up her only awareness of Gloucester was the image of a fisherman in a yellow rain coat selling fish sticks. She never ate frozen fish sticks. She blamed it on her mother who never served them. Archer came from a long line of fish haters. Her line preferred cow.

But they loved lobster. Archer ate her first lobster at the Yankee Clipper in Worcester when she was six years old. It was one of her earliest memory. She was so proud when she sat at the wood table covered with the day's newspaper with empty bowls eagerly awaiting the discarded pieces of shell, metal crackers ready to crush and crack, and her father ordering a two pound lobster for himself, a one and a half pounder for her mother and a one pounder for Archer. Archer beamed, keenly aware she was in the midst of a rite of passage. No more sitting at her mother's side on the hard wooden bench, waiting to be fed pieces of white lobster meat drenched in butter barely hanging on a tiny red pitchfork, butter dripping off her mother's fingers. Archer was finally getting her own lobster. She adored the smell of the hot butter, always asked for an extra monkey dish. She loved when the waitress wrapped the bib around her neck, covering her new dress like a graduation gown.

Little Archer had treasured that first moment when she dipped the luscious meat into the hot butter, then licked her fingers like her mother always did. But the best part, the absolutely most awesome amazing part of the whole thing, she only had to ask her daddy to help her crack the claw one time.

Rory refused to eat lobster. He said he couldn't eat anything that watched him while he ate. Archer offered to take the meat out of the lobster or to have the restaurant serve the lobster without the shell, but the damage had been done. Once a lobster had looked at him with its deep black eyes, Rory could never eat one. He wouldn't go with her to have lobster either. He said it made him too sad.

In Gloucester, the congested street wound past restaurants and gas stations, souvenir stands and whale watching booths. Archer slowed as the road snaked around a lawn mower shop, lawnmowers evenly lined up on the sidewalk. She regretted Rory wasn't with her. He would love that store. Would probably talk the ear off the guy behind the counter as he announced his grand plans to solve the world's problems by building the perfect energy-efficient lawn mower. Her heart swelled for her son. He was simple in the most complicated way. Or maybe he was complicated in the most simple way.

Archer parked in front of the police department located just a few doors from the lawn mower shop, unsure what to think about Rory, unsure what to think about anything. She stared ahead, prepared herself for the interrogation by the police officer. Would she tell the truth or perpetuate Trish's lies? What would be best for Rory? Archer shook her head, knowing she was probably the last person on the planet who knew what was best for Rory.

She sat for awhile, then pushed open the car door and made her way into the police station, having made a decision. Rory wasn't getting in trouble because of Trish. It was enough he was being blamed for the stolen car. It was time for Trish to take responsibility for her actions. And Archer wasn't bailing her out. She had parents. It was their job. Not hers. Besides, she could only parent one difficult teenager at a time. She definitely wasn't equipped to handle two.

CHAPTER TWENTY-FOUR

A rcher hadn't expected the Gloucester Police Department to be so modern. It's brick and glass structure stood conspicuously among the neglected storefronts and homes she had passed since exiting Route 128. Its design was likely intended to instill confidence in Gloucester's law enforcement personnel and assurance to the community. Archer felt little of that confidence as she passed The Policeman's Prayer and entered the building. She approached the officer encased behind thick, smoky glass; wishing there was a prayer for Rory.

"May I help you?"

Archer saw the officer's outline through the glass but could not see his eyes. She needed eyes to talk to. Instead, she looked at the sign on the window. We will provide service with understanding, response with compassion, performance with integrity and law enforcement with vision. She hoped so. She and Rory would need all of it, extra too.

"My son is here. Rory Falcon."

"Have a seat, ma'am."

Archer remained standing. The last thing she wanted to do was have a seat. Have a drink. Have a vacation. Have a new life. But have a seat, no. Her legs whirred like one of Rory's lawn mower engines. She was anxious, antsy. She paced, counting her steps, one, two, three, four, five steps forward, one, two, three, four, five steps back. Repeat. She wanted to get Rory and go home.

The woman who entered the waiting area was dressed in civilian clothes.

Pleated pants, a silk shirt and Ugg boots. Not an acceptable combination in a city like New York, but expected in New England. Her hair was cropped short, her face round and girlish. As she got closer, Archer saw the lines around her eyes. They were probably the same age, both in their early forties.

"Detective Ellen O'Neill," she held out her hand.

"Archer Falcon, Rory's mother."

"Come this way."

Archer followed her through a door and past a maze of cubicles to a conference room. The smell of new carpet and fresh paint made Archer want to sneeze.

Trish sat at a long table, staring at a uniformed officer whose scowl suggested he was frustrated by her lack of cooperation. Trish had the hood of her sweatshirt pulled deep over her face. Rory paced around them, adjusting the buds in his ears and playing with his I-pod. He ran to Archer when she entered the room.

"Did you see the fisherman patch on their uniforms? That's the same fisherman on the box of fish sticks," he laughed. "I don't like fish but maybe I'd like fish sticks. Think you can buy some for me?"

"Sure," Archer looked at Detective O'Neill, hoping she was getting a picture of what Rory was like.

"We haven't charged them with anything yet." Ellen was brusque. "We need to confirm their story. She doesn't have a driver's license or any other identification. The car is registered to Gus White in Corinna, Maine. We haven't been able to reach him. Can you confirm this for us?"

"Gus is Trish's uncle," Rory said. "He lets her use the car."

"Wait," Archer held up her hand to get Rory to stop talking. She turned to Ellen. "May I speak to Rory alone, please?"

Ellen nodded, pointed to a small room. Archer walked in. Rory followed.

"What were you doing?" Archer whispered through gritted teeth.

"I want to meet my birth mother and find out why I'm messed up. Trish said she'd take me. Trish told me that she and her mother both like to dip French fries in their milkshake. I want to see if Kitty likes noodles with olives and ketchup like I do. And," he paused, "I want to find my birth dad."

A lead ball fell from Archer's throat to her stomach. Her heart ached for him. She wanted to set him on her lap and rock him until their hearts were mended. "Trish doesn't have a license and whose car is that?" Archer tripped over words like she stumbled over parts and components on Rory's bedroom floor. She didn't know how to confront their broken hearts.

"I wasn't driving," Rory said.

"I don't care. It was stupid to get into the car with her and . . . "

"You weren't going to take me."

"How do you know?"

"Cause you keep avoiding it, like I'm not going to love you anymore." His eyes filled with water. "It's not about you, Mom. It's about me. I need to find out..." He stopped.

"What?"

"...why I am the way I am?"

"Rory," she sighed, "you have Asperger's syndrome. You know this."

"I'm not some retard."

"I know you're not."

He paced, made one tight loop around the small table then looked at her. "I know all about Asperger's. I'm socially awkward, abnormally hyper-focused and have poor communication skills. I get frustrated easily and sometimes over-react."

She stared at him, stunned. He had actually been listening when they met with the psychiatrist who had explained the syndrome four years ago. Archer remembered the bald, congenial man seated behind a desk, Archer and Wayne in the over-sized Queen Anne chairs and Rory intent on a Rubik's Cube Grandma Rose had sent him. But Rory had actually been listening. That was more then she could say about Wayne.

"I'm the one taking medicine twice a day," Rory said. "I'm the one in special classes. I'm the one who the other kids laugh at. What about them? Who diagnosed them when they lit my locker on fire? Who's going to tell them to go on meds when they make fun of Trish in gym class because of the bruises on her back? And where do I belong?"

Rory looked at his hands. Together, they watched them shake; a side effect of one of his medications. Archer took his hands in hers and felt their vibration. They were puppy hands, thick, meaty and warm. She wanted to take his pain away, if only she knew how. Like that day on the plane when she first took Rory home, she became overwhelmed by a feeling she would do anything for him. He pulled away, paced around the table like it was the school track.

"Rory," Archer said, "I have to tell the Detective the truth. Trish doesn't have a driver's license. She could have killed you both, again."

He looked at her, his face contorted with anger. "If you do that, you will never see me again."

"I know what's best. Trust me."

"You don't know shit," he shot back. "You don't know anything about what it's like to be me and Trish, to be all fucked up like I am or to be beaten the crap out of like she is."

"What do you mean?"

"What do you think I fucking mean? Her mother beats her. That was what Trish was doing before she came by the house last night. She was getting beaten up. Look at the bruises on her back. I oughta' kill that bitch. Ask Trish. God, you're so stupid. I'm fucking outta here."

"Wait. I need to think. Please."

As an attorney, she could make a decision in an instant. As a mother, she never knew the right thing to do or say. Rory waited impatiently by the door.

"How do you know it's her uncle's car?" Archer asked.

"She told me."

"And you believe her?"

He shrugged.

"Let me call her mother," Archer said.

"No, you can't do that."

"I either do it or I tell the police she doesn't have a license."

He tossed her his cell phone.

"What's this for?" she asked.

"You're so stupid. For her phone number, of course."

She tossed the phone back to him. "Find me the number and then wait outside."

He scrolled through his address book, pressed a couple of buttons and tossed the phone back to Archer. As he left the room, Archer heard the phone ringing.

"What?" The woman's voice on the other end was agitated.

"My name is Archer Falcon. My son Rory is friends with Trish. Are you her mother?"

"Yeah but Trish ain't home right now. I don't know where she's at."

"She's with me. Trish is safe and..."

"Tell her to get her ass home. Her Uncle Gus is fit to be tied. He called the police. Serves her right. He told her that'd happen if she took his car again. And who are you?"

"Archer Falcon, Rory's mother."

"That retarded kid she hangs out with? What a loser."

Archer took a deep breath. "My son is not mentally retarded. He has a form of Autism."

"Whatever."

"Don't you want to know if Trish is okay?"

"Oh, she's okay. But she won't be once she gets home. Tell her that." The woman hung up.

Archer steadied herself on a chair. The detective opened the door.

"The car belongs to her Uncle Gus," Archer said.

"She doesn't have a license, right?"

Archer sighed. "Has Rory done anything wrong?"

"Other than lie to us about his girlfriend, I don't think so. He's seems like a good kid. Doesn't stop talking but it's a lot better than the girl who won't say a word."

"You know I'm a lawyer."

Detective O'Neill looked as if she had been slapped in the face. "No, I didn't."

"Why are you holding them?"

"They were in a stolen car. I have a call into the Bangor Police Department but no one's gotten back to me yet. I can't release them but there are no juvenile holding facilities here. We send our juvies a few miles away to ..." Her phone rang. "Detective O'Neill," she said then turned away.

Archer thought about the outstanding charges in Bangor against Trish and Rory. Campbell must not have entered them on the national computer bank. Otherwise, the detective would have picked up on it. The kids would already be on their way to juvenile detention.

"Did you say Margaret Warren?" Ellen asked into the phone.

Warren? Like Kitty Warren, Rory's birth mother? Archer tried not to seem interested in the detective's conversation.

"Who found her?" Ellen asked. "Where?" She paused, then "All right, I'll be right there." She turned to Archer. "I have to go. Don't leave town. I need to talk to those kids."

CHAPTER TWENTY-FIVE

Inside the lobby of the Bass Rocks Ocean Inn, Archer looked at the clerk standing behind the counter which was shaped like the transom of a boat. His name tag read Duffy, Salem, Massachusetts. He stepped out from behind the counter and shook their hands. A twenty-something with long stringy hair tucked tightly behind his ears, Archer wouldn't have picked him to have such good manners. Especially based on his clothes—camouflage pants, military style boots, a black t-shirt with the word POLICE emblazoned on the back. He had a port wine stain on the left side of his face that ran from his jaw to the bottom of his neck.

Archer had chosen the Bass Rocks Ocean Inn because it was the closest hotel to the Gloucester P.D. Located on the rocky coastline of Cape Ann and the Atlantic Ocean, it was perfect for tourists with its view of the Atlantic Ocean, Thacher's Island and lobster boats in season. Not a typical spot for three misfits, but a nice stopping place, Archer hoped. The lobby was decorated like the stateroom of an old ship and smelled like the salty spray of the ocean.

"Cool," Rory eyed the thick soles and high laces of Duffy's combat boots.

"Yeah," Trish said.

Duffy blushed. "I don't normally dress like this at work. They just called me in 'cause Celia had to leave. Some kind of an emergency. I didn't have time to change. I was in the finals of a paint ball competition. There's always next year, I guess."

"Do you have a room with two beds?" Archer asked.

She was physically and mentally exhausted and wasn't interested in small talk. Besides, she didn't care if the kid was naked as long as there was a clean, comfortable bed in her near future.

She and Trish would share a bed or they would each take one and Rory would sleep on a palette on the floor. He had slept on the floor of her bedroom until he was eleven years old. Archer still left a blanket and pillow on the floor for him, just in case.

"Hey, check this out," Rory said.

He and Trish migrated to a four foot fish tank in the hotel lobby. Rory reached into the water. Trish playfully smacked his hand away.

"Hey," Rory looked at Duffy. "You ever see that show Sniper School. It's wicked good. See that sniper on the hill. He's gonna' get that one shot kill," Rory sung. "Do you have a ghille suit? Man, I'd kill for one. That'd be totally chill."

"How do you know about a ghille suit?" Duffy asked.

"I dunno'. They're like over a hundred dollars for a really good one that camouflages you from head to toe. I bet I can make one for less but I'd still have to mow a lot of lawns. You know how to make a ghille suit?"

"You into laser tag or paint ball or something?"

"Naw. I just think everyone should have one, even my Grandma Rose. I think I'll make one for me and one for Grandma Rose. I'm trying to invent an alternative to fuel but if I can't, the world's probably gonna' blow up."

"I know what you mean. What about you?" Duffy looked at Trish. "You want a ghille suit too?"

Trish rolled her eyes. "No way."

"About that room," Archer said.

Duffy went behind the counter, stood at a computer and typed noisily. He reached under the counter and handed the key to Archer. "Room 207. Take the elevator to the second floor. You need help with your bags?" Duffy leaned forward, looking for their luggage.

"No, thanks," Archer walked toward the elevator with only a backpack slung over her shoulder. She would have to get them clothes tomorrow, maybe wash their underwear in the sink tonight.

As she waited at the elevator, she heard Duffy, the wise teacher, imparting knowledge on his eager students: "To make a ghille suit, you need a boonies hat, gloves, a caulking gun, silicone, burlap, a flight suit..."

Archer stopped listening. Fatigue enveloped her. She stepped into the elevator and watched Duffy animatedly addressing Rory and Trish who stared at him in awe.

CHAPTER TWENTY-SIX

Archer was thankful when the day began to lighten outside. She didn't like sleeping in motels. She didn't like the smell of stale cigarettes and disinfectant, reminding her of her great aunt's apartment in the Bronx in the 1960s. Not that she didn't like her aunt, just the smell of her apartment.

It was almost seven in the morning and Trish had slept the whole night beside her, silent and curled in a ball, her hand resting on Archer's arm. Rory had been in and out of the other double bed, into the bathroom, gathering things, stomping through the room, periodically talking about Duffy and someone named Clark who, as far as Archer could tell, was the hotel janitor. She had been too tired to complain and Rory wasn't really looking for dialogue. He seemed satisfied with his frenetic monologue. He was finally asleep, sprawled across the top of the covers, buds still attached to his ears.

A sliver of light through an opening in the thick curtains revealed twine, leaves, grass and tools scattered throughout most of the room. For Rory, it had been a busy night.

Archer gently removed Trish's hand from her arm and went into the bathroom. The floor was covered with white bath towels, mosquito netting and empty shampoo bottles. She shook her head, not surprised that in less than twelve hours the hotel room looked like Rory's room at home. She put on her clothes from the day before and headed to the front desk to get clean towels and shampoo. She didn't want to call and wake the kids.

A pretty woman who looked to be barely twenty years old was behind the front desk, leaning over a newspaper.

"Can you please have towels and shampoo sent to Room 207?" Archer asked.

"You must be Rory's mom," the woman said.

"You know Rory?"

"He's been down here several times since I got on duty at two. He's a talker, that one. Borrowed tape and scissors. Said he's making some kind of a suit. I'm Celia." She held out here hand.

"Archer Falcon. Nice to meet you." Archer looked at the headline of the Gloucester Times. "What's this?"

"My neighbor died yesterday. She was a good lady." Celia tapped the local paper.

"Can I read it? The kids are sleeping and I don't want to go back to the room right now and wake them."

"Sure," she pushed the paper toward her.

Archer sat in a chair near a fireplace. A stuffed swordfish above the mantel eyed her while she read.

Gloucester Daily Times, Morning Edition, September 6, 2007.

Margaret Warren, mother to many, friend to all, dies at 84.

After a lifetime of giving and caring, Margaret Warren died Monday afternoon at her Haskell Street home. Warren, who opened The Crow's Nest in 1963, passed away unexpectedly in her sleep. Warren worked the day before she died.

Warren will best be remembered for her kind spirit and for keeping The Crow's Nest open during the 1991 Halloween Nor'easter to comfort the family and friends of the crew members of the Andrea Gail and to help in the rescue attempt.

Funeral Services will be held on Friday, September 7, 2007, at 5:00 p.m. at the Gloucester United Methodist Church. Warren will be buried on Saturday, September 8, 2007, in Salem where her family originated. The burial will be private.

She is survived by her daughter, Kitty Warren.

In lieu of flowers, the family requests donations be made to the Andrea Gail Fund in support of the relatives of the fishermen who perished during the Halloween Nor'easter.

Archer read the article several times then looked up. Celia was standing over her.

"My mom has been friends with her daughter Kitty since fifth grade. Rory was asking a lot of questions about her."

Archer stood. "Can you have the towels and shampoo sent to my room, please?"

Archer walked away, took the elevator to the second floor and went to the room. Rory was awake. Trish was still asleep, stretched across the bed on her stomach, the blanket thrown to the floor. Archer picked up the blanket, went to throw it over Trish. She leaned in closer, noticed yellow, black and blue discolorations peaking out behind her tank top.

"I never knew peaches had a smell," Rory said.

Archer stared at Trish's bruises, wondering why she had never seen them before. Perhaps it was because she had never looked.

"The shampoo in the bathroom says it's peach smelling," Rory said.

Archer covered Trish.

"Mom, are you listening?"

"Shh. Come here." Archer motioned Rory into the bathroom. She closed the door behind them.

"What's going on with Trish?" Archer asked.

"Her mom doesn't like her, I guess. She says her mom hits her and her Uncle laughs. She wants to hire someone to kill her mother. She said she'd do it herself but she doesn't like blood."

"She doesn't mean that."

"She really doesn't like blood. One time in school this kid cracked his head on the sidewalk and Trish fainted."

"I mean about wanting to have her mother killed."

"I don't know. She's said it a few times."

Archer paused, fearful of the answer to her next question. "Has she asked you to do it?"

"I should do it. No one should beat up on their family."

Archer unconsciously reached up to her bruised eye. Recognition flashed across Rory's face. Neither of them acknowledged it.

He continued, "She knows that's not my thing. She says I'm a lover, not a fighter."

Archer certainly didn't want to ask the follow up question to that comment. Another time.

"Why did she take her Uncle's car?" Archer asked.

"Her mom had just beat the hell out of her. She had to get out of there. And then she said she'd take me to meet my real mom."

"Don't you think I am your real mom?"

"I mean my other mother. The one who gave birth to me. She lives here. She works at this bar named after a nest, near a lawnmower store. The lady downstairs told me. I'm going to find her." He hesitated. "Are you going to help me?"

Archer sighed, knowing she had no choice. Once Rory got an idea in his head, he wouldn't let it go. She would introduce Rory to Kitty. Hopefully, it would end there.

CHAPTER TWENTY-SEVEN

The Crow's Nest was across the street from the pier where the Andrea Gail had departed on its final voyage. A dingy place with low ceilings, a bar in the middle and a pool table to the side, the dozen or so tables seemed to be an afterthought. It looked the same to Archer as when she had last seen it just a few weeks before Rory's birth.

Archer stood inside the entrance to the restaurant and watched a thick-waisted woman with blond straw-like hair and a hitch in her walk clear dishes and wipe a wobbly wood table. Archer did some quick math. Kitty had been forty years old when she had Rory. She would now be in her mid-fifties. The woman putting a tip into her apron could very well be Kitty, fifteen years and thirty pounds later.

Rory hadn't gotten his good looks from Kitty. Archer remembered Kitty looking worn and tired when they had met in 1991 but had attributed it to the stress of her pregnancy and the storm. It didn't look as if life had gotten any easier for Kitty after Rory's birth.

Archer was glad she was going to meet Kitty alone, without Rory and his insatiable curiosity and endless commentary on life; and without Trish and her belligerent silence. Rory had asked questions about where she was going and why couldn't he and Trish go with her? Archer had lied, said she was going to buy a present for Grandma Rose, knowing Rory hated shopping. The kids had stayed behind in the car, Trish kidding Rory about having a crush on Celia, and Rory extremely pleased with the attention.

"May I help you?"

Archer jumped, startled by the presence of anyone but Kitty.

"Will you be eating alone?" The short, stout woman with long, black braided hair asked.

"Yes. I would like to sit at Kitty's table."

"You know Kitty?" The woman's Boston accent was thick. "I'm not surprised. Everyone knows Kitty. Are you going to her mother's funeral? Whole town will be closed at two o'clock tomorrow when they bury poor Margaret. Want me to tell Kitty you're here?"

"No, thank you."

"What are you? A distant relative she hasn't seen in like forever? Or an old high school friend?"

"Something like that."

"Just take that table over there." She pointed at the four-top Kitty had just cleaned.

Archer took a step, then turned and eyed the small woman. "Why is Kitty working when her mother just passed?"

"Kitty hasn't missed a day of work in eighteen years. Except for that one time...," the woman stopped, caught herself like she was about to reveal top secret information.

"What?" Archer asked.

"Nothing. Your table's over there."

The chair scratched the wood floor as Archer sat. A white paper napkin was folded on a plastic place mat which identified classes of fish. Silverware was laid out. Ketchup, mustard and hot sauce formed a triangle in the middle of the table. A porcelain coffee cup with a chipped handle faced down in its saucer.

Kitty scooted by and dropped a plastic coated menu on the table. "Be back in a jiffy with some coffee."

Archer looked at the menu, not hungry, just curious. It was a typical breakfast menu. Eggs, pancakes, French toast. Her stomach growled. Maybe she would eat.

"Coffee?" Kitty stood stiffly, holding a metal coffee pot.

Archer turned the mug upright. The black coffee steamed as it rose to the brim. It smelled rich, delicious.

"Do you know what you want?" Kitty asked.

"No. Yes."

Kitty looked at her, maybe for the first time since she got there. Archer bore into her eyes, hoping Kitty would recognize her. Nothing, just a dull, blank stare.

"I'm sorry about your mother," Archer said.

Kitty relaxed her posture, rubbed her hip. "Thank you."

"How did she die?" Archer asked.

"Are you a reporter or something? I'm tired of answering questions."

"I'm Archer Falcon."

Kitty's gaze was vapid. "Do I know you?" She still held the coffee pot.

"Yes. I mean, kind of. I'm Rory's mother."

"Rory?"

"You had a child in 1991. I'm his adoptive mother. He wants to meet you."

"He wants to…what? Who are you?"

"We met fifteen years ago before you gave birth. I'm Archer Falcon. I adopted your baby."

Kitty's face drooped. Her hands shook. The coffee pot crashed to the floor. Archer jumped up, out of the way of the hot liquid, her chair flying out from behind her.

"Are you okay?" Archer asked.

Coffee dripped down Kitty's legs. She quickly walked away, hands flying through the air, mumbling, repeating: "Black and gold leaves of autumn, gift from above, sent from below, new to old, old to new, keep all evil far away. Oh mighty willow tree, save a place for me under thee."

CHAPTER TWENTY-EIGHT

The small, stout woman with long braided hair rushed Archer out of The Crow's Nest, an unlikely bouncer. As she squeezed Archer's arm and pulled her toward the parking lot, her voice fell hard and fast like rain on a tin roof.

"I've never seen Kitty look like that, like she saw a ghost. Who did you say you were? It's best you leave. Poor Margaret just died and whatever you said to her back there, well, that's not good for Kitty when she's mourning her mother. Who did you say you were?"

"Archer Falcon."

"Kitty's never mentioned you. How do you know her?"

"We're old friends."

"Kitty doesn't have old friends. She only talks to her mother and the customers at the restaurant. Guess you brought up some bad memories."

"I didn't mean to."

"It's weird Kitty reacted to you like that. And she was mumbling that spell. She hasn't done that for a long time."

"A spell?"

"She wants to keep bad spirits away from some willow tree she wants to be buried under. I don't believe it but Kitty does. The last time she said that spell was after she spoke to some man on the phone. It was like ten years ago. I asked who it was and all she said was she just talked to a ghost. Her family dates back to the Salem Witch trials. You hear about them? They were back in the 1600's. Kitty thinks she's a witch. I never disagree with her. You know, just in case she's correct."

Archer saw her car a couple of rows away. She strained to see Rory and Trish in the back seat. "You can let go of my arm now."

"Sorry. I think I'm a little freaked out – what with Margaret's death and Kitty, well, she doesn't seem to be taking it very well."

Archer rubbed her arm, wondering if the bruise was going to be the outline of three or four fat fingers. She craned her neck. Where were those kids?

"Do us all a favor," the woman said, "stay away for awhile. I'm sure Kitty will be back to normal before long."

The woman rushed back to The Crow's Nest. Archer approached her car, wondering what to do next. Should she go back and talk to Kitty? Where were Rory and Trish? Hadn't she told them to wait for her at the car? Had she really thought they were going to listen? She sat in the driver's seat, exhaled forcefully. Just beyond the dock, three men with scraggly beards tossed fish off a boat. A small boy played with a ball by a gift shop. A couple walked hand in hand.

Archer leaned forward. Was that them? She definitely needed glasses, and not solely for reading anymore. Life was softer and dimmer in the distance as forty became a memory. She suddenly felt agitated, took a deep breath and braced herself. Sweat puddled on the back of her neck. Her stomach knotted. She spoke calmly to herself like a coach encouraging a star athlete as she waited for the hot flash to pass.

She leaned forward again, squinted. Yes, Rory and Trish were eating ice cream cones on a bench overlooking a schooner with a torn sail. Archer looked at her watch. It wasn't even ten in the morning. Despite all the trouble they caused, she smiled. She wanted ice cream for breakfast too.

CHAPTER TWENTY-NINE

Archer walked up quietly behind the kids. She stood silently behind them, listening; always hoping for the one clue that would decipher the mystery of Rory. Rory held a small, potted plant on his lap.

"She's too old for you," Trish said.

"No, she's not."

"Celia has to be like twenty years old."

"She's still hot even if she is that old." Rory picked at the plant.

"Why'd you choose that plant anyway?"

"It's a baby willow tree, like the one in my front yard," Rory said. "It has special powers. It can heal wounds and burns. The Greeks used it to relieve pain, like aspirin. Some people even think the willow has the power to heal a broken heart."

Trish punched him on the arm. "How do you know that?"

"I know a lot of things. That doctor who has the oath, he used it."

"The oath?" Trish asked.

"Yeah, some hippo guy."

"You mean Hippocrates." Archer walked to the front of the bench.

"Yeah, that," Rory said.

"That plant can't have special powers," Trish used her ice cream cone to point at the tiny leaves rising from the stem in the clay pot.

"How come?" Rory asked.

"'Cause there's no such thing as special powers. There are no super heroes or super plants or super anything. Just a bunch of super dumb people."

"Maybe, but we can try it anyway." He looked up at Archer and took a bite of his cone. "Sorry, Mom."

"About what?"

"Eating ice cream so early. I know you don't like when I eat sugar in the morning."

"That's okay."

"See," Trish nudged Rory, "I told you she wouldn't mind."

Rory slipped the last part of the cone into his mouth and chewed noisily.

"Ask her," Trish nudged him again.

Rory's mouth was filled with cone. "That lady at the hotel said she knew where my real mom worked."

Archer looked away, stung.

"I mean, my birth mother." Rory pointed at the Crow's Nest. "She works there. I want to meet her. Can I?"

Archer rubbed her bicep. "While you and Trish were getting ice cream, I went into The Crow's Nest. She wasn't there. How about we check out that lawnmower store you were talking about?"

"Maybe she's working later. Can we go back then?" Rory asked.

"We'll see," Archer said.

"That means no."

"It just means we'll see."

"We'll see always means no," Rory yelled. "And besides, you can't stop me."

"Rory, please," Archer looked around to see who was within hearing distance.

"We'll see just means we'll see," Trish said.

"Fine, then I'm going to check out the lawnmowers."

Rory trotted toward Gloucester Lawnmower, Fish & Tackle. Trish and Archer walked silently next to each other, past ships and The Crow's Nest. Archer saw Rory slip into the store, sure to enliven the sales clerk's day with his barrage of knowledge.

Trish bit a hole in the bottom of her cone and sucked the ice cream out. "Could you ever give up a baby for adoption?"

Archer's heart skipped several beats. "That's a very personal question."

"Yeah, I know. It's just that my mom says..."

"What?"

"Never mind."

"I'm sure there are people you can talk to about things."

"What people?"

"I don't know. Like a friend, or maybe your guidance counselor."

Trish laughed. "Everyone thinks I'm a loser freak. No one but Rory believes anything I say."

Trish tossed the remainder of her cone into a garbage can. Archer saw faded half inch slash marks on her left forearm.

"Oh, Trish, why did you do that?" she asked.

Trish folded her arms across her chest. "That's a very personal question, isn't it?"

Archer grabbed her arm. "Did you cut yourself?"

"Leave me alone." Trish yanked her arm free and headed toward the pier.

"Wait," Archer yelled.

Trish kept walking, increasing her steps.

"I could never give up a baby for adoption," Archer said.

Trish stopped, slowly turned. "Why don't you want Rory to meet his birth mother?"

"I don't know if she'll want to meet him."

"Rory thinks you're worried he'll like Kitty better than you."

Archer walked toward her. "I worry about his reaction if she rejects him."

"He can handle it, you know."

"I answered your question, now you answer mine. Why'd you do it?"

Tears filled her eyes. "It hurts a lot less than my mother calling me a loser. And I'm sick of her saying she wished she'd given me up for adoption."

"I'm sorry."

"Don't be. I don't give a shit. I don't need her anymore."

"What does that mean?"

"I can take care of myself. I'm not going back to Bangor."

"What are you going to do? You're only fifteen."

"I dunno," Trish said.

"Why did you ask me about adoption?"

Before Trish could answer, Rory shouted from in front of the storefront window. "Hey, guys, check this out." He waved a white piece of paper. "It was on a bulletin board in the back of the store. There's a funeral for Margaret Warren. That's my real, uh, I mean my birth grandmother. That woman in the hotel told me. I wanna go. I bet Kitty will be there. Tomorrow's Friday, right? It's tomorrow." He shoved the flyer into the pocket of his cargo pants. "This store is wicked good."

Archer and Trish headed toward Rory. Near the store, Archer's phone rang. She looked at the caller ID.

"Go back inside and look around some more. I'll get the car and meet you right here."

Trish and Rory disappeared into the store. Archer took a deep breath then answered the call.

CHAPTER THIRTY

Campbell didn't announce himself. "If you don't come home today, I'm coming to get you. Gloucester P.D. is holding them, right? I can't believe they stole another car and totaled it? What the hell is going on? Why did you lie to me?"

"You wanted to arrest Rory."

"Interfering with a police investigation is a crime."

"Give me a break."

"I have actually." His voice softened. "Trish's Uncle doesn't want to press charges even though she did some major damage to his car. Anyway, there are no warrants from Maine anymore. And for some reason, Gloucester isn't going to charge 'em. Seems like something big is going on there and they don't have time to deal with this."

"Thanks."

"Don't thank me. I'm pissed. Now will you come home?"

"I can't."

"How come?"

"Rory wants to meet his birth mother."

"His birth mother?"

"You know Rory's adopted. I told you."

"Yeah, I know. Why would he want to meet her? I mean, what's wrong with you?"

Archer sighed. She wanted to say: *that's what I want to know* but knew that response was childish. "It's not like that. He's just curious. I think it's natural."

"How are you taking it?"

"Okay, I guess."

"So, where is she?"

"Here, in Gloucester."

"What's her name?"

"Why does it matter to you? You don't know her. You're from Canada."

"I thought I'd run her record. Are you going to let Rory meet her?"

"I already spoke with her. Let's just say a reunion wasn't high on her list of priorities. I guess I shouldn't be hard on her. Her mother just died."

"Her mother? What's her mother's name?"

"Are you going to run her record too?"

"Sorry. I'm just being overprotective. Are you going to tell Rory she doesn't want to meet him? That's going to break his heart."

"I know. I don't know what I'm going to do."

"Maybe you should just come home."

"Good try. I don't know when I'll be home. Maybe tomorrow if I can get Rory out of here. Hopefully after he goes to the funeral…"

"You're going to her funeral?"

"Yes. And it's a big deal too. They're closing the stores and letting the kids out of school early. Seems her mother was a big wig in this town."

"Alright, I guess. Just be careful."

"Why do you want me home anyway? The warrants been lifted. What's the big deal?"

"I guess I miss you"

Archer sighed. "I miss you too."

"Maybe when you get back…"

"Maybe." Her phone beeped, call waiting. She looked at the caller ID, hesitated. "I have to go." She answered the other call with a terse "Rory's fine."

Wayne spoke quickly. "You better tell me exactly where you are. I'm coming to get him. You can't care for him anymore. First, he's drunk at school, then he runs away and now Campbell tells me he stole a car."

"Wait. Don't come here. He wants to meet Kitty. I talked to her. But she doesn't want to meet him. She was saying some kind of witch's spell."

"See, this is stupid. He can't handle it. You never should have told him about his birth mother. Bring him home. Now. I want Rory to live with me."

Had she heard him correctly? Wayne wanted custody of Rory?

"Over my dead body," she said.

"I thought you'd be happy."

"I'm not."

"I can do a better job. He's older now. He needs a man in his life. I've hired a lawyer. I'm petitioning the court for custody."

"With what money did you hire a lawyer?" she screamed. "You owe me a shit load of money. Remember, poor pitiful Wayne? Living his dream? Not supporting his son?"

"It's Mary Beth's money."

"She works at the Children's museum. How the hell does she have money? And what the fuck does she want with Rory?" And then, the bulb lit in Archer's head. "It's about child support, right? If you have custody of Rory, I pay you child support. I support your newborn. Fuck that, Wayne."

She slammed her phone shut and looked up. With her hands shaking, the phone rang again.

"Listen you goddamn, mother fucker, piece of shit for a father…"

"Whoa," Delores said.

"Oh, sorry. I thought you were Wayne."

"Obviously. Want me to call back?'

She took a deep breath, slowly exhaled. "No, I was going to call you soon anyway. How's it going at the office?"

"It's a mess here without you. I tried to put all of the fires out but it's getting to be an inferno. Bill Clark called. Joan won't let him have the kids this weekend and the principal won't let him talk to them at school. Mrs. England sent you an e-mail. Her deadbeat husband hasn't paid the health insurance. She needs supplies for her diabetes and their son needs a refill on his asthma inhaler. Jim Strong wants to know if you'll agree to an extension of time for him to respond to the modification on Kennedy. He's driving his son to New York to start freshman year at Columbia and won't get it done by tomorrow."

"He's had two weeks to file an answer," Archer said.

"The Sheriff was here to serve papers on you," Delores continued. "He wouldn't let me see them so I don't know who they're from. Is someone suing you? I told him you were out of town and I didn't know when you would be back. Did I do the right thing?"

Archer's heart sank. "Yes, you did great."

"Where are you anyway?"

"Gloucester. It's a long story."

"Is something wrong? Is Rory with you?

"Something's always wrong. And yes, Rory's with me. Anything else?"

"There's one more message. Steve Finelli called."

"Does he have the discovery? Hopefully it's in one piece this time."

"He wasn't calling about England. He's representing Wayne."

"Steve Finelli?"

"Yes. What's going on?"

"Wayne is trying to get custody of Rory."

"No way."

"Believe it or not. That's probably what the Sheriff wanted to serve on me."

"Wayne's such a jerk. No wonder he hired Finelli. They deserve each other."

"What time is it?" Archer asked.

"A little past eleven."

"And it's Thursday, right?"

"All day."

"Good. Call Bill Clark. Tell him to be at the school tomorrow when it lets out. I'll call the principal. He'll have his children for the weekend. E-mail Mrs. England and tell her to buy the medicine she and her son need and put it on her husband's credit card. Also tell her I'll file a Motion for Contempt next week."

"What should I tell Jim Strong?"

"Tell him if he wasn't so busy researching the Salem Witch trials, he'd have more time to file an Answer."

"Is that what he does?"

"He's considered an expert in the field. He's written two books on it."

"Should I really tell him that?" Delores asked.

"No. Give him another week to file the answer, but no more. Anything else?"

"You have yourself marked out of the office tomorrow afternoon. Did I miss something?"

Shit, Archer thought. She had forgotten about the interview. How was she going to get from Margaret Warren's funeral in Massachusetts to Augusta in Maine by 4:30 tomorrow afternoon? And what was she going to do with Rory and Trish?

"Archer, are you still there?"

"Looks like I'll be out all day tomorrow."

"What do I tell Finelli?"

She thought for a moment. "Tell him to kiss my ass."

CHAPTER THIRTY-ONE

Archer waited in her car outside the lawn mower store. What was she going to say at that interview tomorrow—if she could even get there in time? They'll want to know why she wants to be a judge. Why indeed? She knew why, just didn't know if she could speak the words. She was tired of the emotion of it. She was tired of her tears for the single mother of two sons, convicted of selling drugs to support her children in rural Maine. She was tired of her concern for that mother's two boys, excellent students, fine young men, about to lose their mother for a year. She was tired of her anger at the husband who exhibited no empathy toward his wife of 22 years and the mother of his children, and, in the midst of a divorce, cancelled credit cards and turned off phone service. She was tired of her sadness for the children of alcoholics and drug addicts, who wanted nothing more than the company of a sober parent during supper and homework time. Didn't judges make decisions without emotion? That's what she wanted. It was too hard to feel.

She looked up at the bar across the street. God, she wanted a drink. A quick swig to remove the edge. She remembered the bottle in her car, under the seat. She was calculating her next move when Rory leaned out of the store and motioned for her to come in. She rolled down the window.

"You have to come see this," he said.

"We have to get back to the hotel."

She didn't know why she said that. They really didn't have to be anywhere at any time, unless Detective O'Neill told them otherwise. After speaking with Campbell, Archer figured they could go home. She had left a message for Ellen at the police department. She wanted to make sure before they left.

"It's wicked cool. You have to see this." Rory darted back into the store.

Archer looked at the bar, longing for it like a lover she'd never see again. She got out of the car, wanted to turn left. Went right instead.

Inside the store, lawnmowers were everywhere. Some intact, many disassembled. The smells of gas and oil permeated the air. A greasy sheen covered everything. If Rory owned a store, it would look and smell and feel like this one.

Archer walked to the counter where Rory and Trish were speaking with a middle-aged man whose barrel-chest burst from his flannel shirt. He looked strong, like he made a living with his brawn, not his brains.

"And this one," the man held up a metal gas can, "is an original Phillips 66. I found it at a garage sale and got it for three dollars. Couldn't believe the guy was selling it. And this one," he put another canister on the counter, "is vintage red. Look at the spout. It differs from the steel safety cans we use today." The man looked at Archer, extended a dirty hand. "Clyde Morgan. And you are?"

"Archer Falcon, Rory's mother."

"You have a lovely son," he said.

Archer was taken aback. This man with dirty fingernails and a layer of grime on his skin had used the word lovely, and had used it in reference to Rory.

"What's that?" Rory pointed behind Clyde.

Clyde picked up a globe and put it on the counter. Rory and Trish leaned in; as did Archer, surprised she was interested.

"This," he spoke proudly, "is an original gas pump globe."

Red, yellow and green stripes arched over the top of the globe. Large white lettering below announced Rainbow Gasoline Motor Oil.

"I have about a dozen more in the back," Clyde said. "Socony, Pan-Am, Texaco, Sinclair. They're collector's items."

"I bet they're worth a lot of money," Rory said.

"I'll never sell them. I'm going to pass them on. Not sure yet to whom. I don't have any kids." The bell on the door jingled. A man walked in. "Be with you in a moment," Clyde said.

"I collect gas cans," Rory said. "Not on purpose. I just keep needing gas for my mowers and I forget to carry the cans with me so I have to buy new ones. Maybe when I die, I can give my collection to someone."

"We should go," Archer looked at Clyde. "Thank you, Mr. Morgan."

"Please call me Clyde. And come back anytime. Your children are delightful."

CHAPTER THIRTY-TWO

Entering the lobby of the motel, laden with pizza and bread sticks from Pizza Hut and bags from Wal-Mart, Celia greeted them with a big smile. Rory ran to the counter.

"I'm going to that funeral tomorrow. We bought new clothes."

"Awesome," Celia said. "There are cookies in the lounge."

"C'mon, let's go," Rory grabbed Trish's arm and pulled her toward the smell of freshly baked chocolate chip cookies.

"Think a lot of people will be at Margaret's funeral?" Archer already knew the answer. The whole town was probably going to be there. Archer was just trying to get some information from Celia. What information, she wasn't sure.

"Should be quite a crowd," Celia said. "Ever since that storm, Margaret's been a folk hero. She was like a mother hen to everyone waiting to see if the crew of the Andrea Gail was going to make it back and then to all the people making that movie. Margaret and Kitty even had dinner with George Clooney and Mark Walberg. Kitty was always with Margaret. She was shy and didn't go out much, worked at the restaurant since she was young. She had a baby, you know. She never said who the father was. But I'm talkin' way too much. I have work to do. We're booked tonight and there are still a couple of rooms to be cleaned. Duffy never does any cleaning. They need to fire him."

Archer thanked Celia and went to the elevator where Trish and Rory were waiting. They rode the elevator in silence; Rory eating the cookies they had collected.

"What do you think my real mom is like?" he asked as they exited the elevator. "Have you met her?"

Archer sighed, wanted to scream. I am your real mom.

Instead, she feigned a calm façade. "Daddy and I met her just after you were born. I don't know what she's like now."

"What do I call her? Kitty or mom?"

"I don't know, Rory. I guess that's up to you."

"I think you should call her Kitty," Trish said.

"I still don't get why she didn't want me."

"She didn't know you," Archer said. "She just knew she couldn't take care of a baby."

"She sounds smart knowing that," Trish said. "Some people don't know when they shouldn't be parents."

"I'm not going to have a baby until I'm thirty," Rory said. "There's too much to think about and then when the baby cries I wouldn't know what to do. I guess I'll wait 'til I have a wife anyway."

"Good thought," Archer said.

Trish set the pizza out on the desk by the window. Rory headed to the corner of the room where the maid had piled his collection of twine, netting, small tools and leaves. Archer went into the bathroom and put the shower on. She stood under the hot water, wishing the bathtub was big enough for her to stretch out in. The white plastic shower curtain wasn't long enough and kept grazing her legs. The drain was half closed, causing the tub to fill with water several inches, covering her feet. She washed then stepped out of the tub, chiding herself for not buying towels. The tiny white ones were rough like sandpaper and non-absorbent. Arguing with Rory at the store over his desire for a pocketknife had certainly not helped her focus on what they actually needed to buy. She opened the bathroom door a crack to let out some of the steam. The hotel room was unusually quiet.

She peered around the corner at the bed she and Trish had slept in the night before. Sitting next to each other, their backs toward Archer, she saw Rory rubbing the salve from the willow plant on Trish's forearm.

"Does it hurt?" he asked.

She shook her head.

"Hopefully, this will make the scars go away. You don't want scars because people will think you're crazy like me."

Archer stepped back into the bathroom. With a scratchy white towel, she wiped the tears from her face. If tears caused scars, she'd be covered with them.

CHAPTER THIRTY-THREE

Archer was too tired to sleep, couldn't get her mind to stop racing about everything from Rory to Trish to Kitty. Work issues also stumbled into her consciousness. And Wayne. Wayne the pain from Maine, as Rory would say. Wayne the drain was how Archer saw him.

She flipped the pillow for the third time, scrunched it, hoping to get the right height for her head. Trish was asleep, curled and covering barely a quarter of the bed. Her hand once again rested on Archer's arm. Rory was busy on the other side of the room; the television a backup singer to his front-stage shenanigans.

Why not agree to let Wayne have custody of Rory? It might be worth the child support she would have to pay. She would have a clean and quiet house, could spend an undisturbed day at work, could take piano lessons and train to run a marathon. Her options would be endless and none would include phone calls from the school, the police, the neighbors. Could she and Campbell try again? It would be nice to burrow into him once more, surrounded by his large furry arms and gentle hands.

She rolled over and adjusted Trish's hand to rest on her other arm. Archer recalled the conversation with Trish's mother. Is that why Trish agreed to drive Rory to Gloucester? To get back at her mother? To run away? Or did it have something to do with her uncle? Archer couldn't really blame Trish for running away. Archer thought about running away frequently.

"Mom."

Rory's voice broke through her thoughts. Archer shook her head to fully wake up. He frequently talked to her in the middle of the night. He would walk into her room, release whatever thought had awoken him and then return to his restless slumber. She could always talk to him even from the deepest of sleep.

Archer opened one eye. She was close enough to see the digital clock. 2:38 in the morning. The room was dark, only the blue of the television screen providing light. Rory paced next to her bed. He wore the camo flannel pajama pants they had purchased earlier. He had his I-pod in one hand, leaves in the other. Archer opened the other eye.

"What if I'm too nervous at the funeral?" Rory asked.

"You'll do the best you can."

"Being around all those people is scary stuff."

"We don't have to go. It's probably a good idea to skip it anyway. We can check out early and be home by lunch."

"No, I want to go. Maybe I'll wear my ghille suit so no one will see me. It's almost done."

"You think no one will notice a five foot nine walking bush?"

Rory laughed. "Remember when you told me about my birth mother when I was little? We called her my tummy mummy."

"Of course I remember. I'm surprised you do."

"I remember a lot of stuff. I really love you, mom."

"I know, Sweetie. I love you too."

"I just need to know about my tummy mummy."

"I know." Archer sighed.

"So can I meet her?"

"We can try."

"Thanks."

Archer closed her eyes, hoping she could get some sleep, wondering what spell Kitty might put upon them tomorrow.

"Mom?"

She opened one eye again. "Yes?"

"You're my bonus mom."

Archer tried to smile but was overcome by sadness. She didn't want to be his bonus mom, she wanted to be his real mom. Didn't she qualify after all they've been through? What had Kitty done that earned her the title of real mom, besides the obvious?

Trish yawned and rolled over as Archer drifted back to sleep. Her slumber grew deep, filled with thoughts of Kitty riding a broom, chanting spells. She heard laughter and realized it was Rory. She opened her eyes. The sun had risen. Rory and Trish were seated on Rory's bed. Trish shook her head, a big smirk across her face.

She turned to Archer. "Rory wants to freeze his farts so they can be smelled later."

Bonus mom, indeed.

CHAPTER THIRTY-FOUR

"It's wicked easy to find Beechbrook Cemetery. Beechbrook dates back to 1870 something. New people aren't allowed to be buried in a lot of cemeteries around here but Beechbrook is an exception."

"How do you know?" Rory leaned on the lobby counter.

"My mom's on the Historical Burial Ground Commission so I know a lot about the cemeteries around here."

"This Historical what?" Rory asked. "What do they do?"

"They're a bunch of ladies who don't let us have any fun. Don't tell my mom I said that. When I was in high school, we used to tear through the cemeteries like we owned them. You should have been there on Halloween. It was awesome. But now they have all these rules. Some of the cemeteries around here date back to the 1700's. I guess they're right. But we sure had a good time."

"I don't like cemeteries." Rory's hands shook. He shoved them into his pants pockets.

"I do," Trish said. "I like the one near my house. No one can ever find me there. It's peaceful."

Archer looked at her watch. "We're going to be late. You sure you want to go, Ror?"

"I guess."

"My boss won't let me go to Margaret's funeral," Duffy said. "Someone's gotta' watch this place. The whole town's gonna' be there. Make sure you check out the Fisherman Rest section. It's neat."

"401 Essex Street?" Archer asked.

"Yeah. Just up Washington. You won't miss it. Hey, Rory, you almost done with your ghille suit?"

"Yeah. I just need a couple more things."

"Too bad you guys are checking out. I sure would like to see it when it's done."

"I'll text you a photo."

"Awesome." Duffy came out from behind the counter, grasped Rory's hand and patted him once on the back. "Later, Dude."

"Later," Rory said.

In the car, Archer tried to remember Duffy's directions. Don't worry, he had said, you can't get lost. Just follow the car in front of you, it's guaranteed to be going to the same place.

"Hey, mom," Rory said from the back seat. "You think a lot of people will go to my funeral?"

"I don't want to talk about that," Archer said.

Rory leaned back, shoulder to shoulder with Trish. "I'm not afraid of dying."

"Me neither," Trish said. "I'm afraid of living."

"Sometimes I think it'd be cool to be dead. Then I wouldn't have to see those kids in Africa with the fat bellies and big eyes. You know, the ones they show on TV when they ask people to send money."

"Yeah. And in National Geographic magazine too," Trish added.

"It makes me sad to see them. Maybe if I make a lot of money I can go over there and feed them. I'd bring a million pizzas. Think Pizza Hut delivers to Africa?"

"If they don't, we can charter a plane."

"Or maybe I can build a giant lawn mower that flies and runs on dirt so we don't have to buy oil from the Arabs."

Archer sighed. "It will be nice to get home tonight, won't it?" She tried to change the subject.

"I'm going to have my funeral before I die," Trish said. "It seems like a waste to have all those people saying nice things about you when you don't get to hear it."

"I don't want a lot of people at my funeral," Rory said. "If it's too crowded, it'll make me nervous."

"How will you know?" Trish asked. "You'll be dead."

"I'll know. And I don't want to be buried in a box either. I'll get claustrophobic."

"How about if we bury you in your ghille suit?"

"That'll be okay," Rory said. "Then if I come back as a ghost, I can really scare people, maybe cast spells on some of the kids at school."

They both laughed.

Rory leaned forward. "You know where you're going, Mom?"

Archer steered the Subaru around a bend and up a hill. As the road twisted, gravestones came into view along the horizon, followed by the roofs of black sedans, then the tops of people's heads. Archer stopped the car, joining the long line of cars that snaked toward the cemetery.

"Wow," Rory said, "I don't think I'll ever know this many people in my whole life."

"There must be hundreds of cars." Trish said. "Your grandmother was popular."

Archer coughed.

"Sorry, Mrs. Falcon."

"I wish Grandma Rose was here. It's so pretty. She might get an idea for one of her quilts. I think I want to get her a present."

Archer pressed gently on the gas, slowly moving forward. The cemetery was in full view now. Headstones arched row after row like single-colored dominos; monuments and crypts occasionally interrupting the symmetry. The Atlantic Ocean sparkled in the distance under the bright sun.

Directed by a police officer in dress blues, Archer pulled onto the swale within walking distance of the Moose Lot where the outdoor service was going to be held. Archer, Rory and Trish joined the line of people dressed in black and gray, walking, their heads bowed, whispering like they were in a library. Archer had found black dresses for herself and Trish at Wal-Mart, black cargo pants and a black shirt for Rory. She was pleased Rory was wearing a shirt that didn't have a skull on it.

At Moose Lot, Rory hopped from one foot to another. He glanced over his shoulder. Mourners stood behind them, craning their necks to get a view of the portable pulpit arranged under an enormous oak tree. They were no longer on the periphery of the crowd but were immersed in its bowels, swallowed whole.

"C'mon," Archer grabbed Rory's hand. He pulled away. "Follow me," she said.

Like the front car of a little train, Archer led Rory and Trish to the outskirts of the throng, hoping to find a place with a little room where they could silently observe. She looked at her watch. It was almost noon. She was anxious to get on the road, maybe make it to the interview. She wanted to get home and put this week in the history books. Rory would be back in school on Monday and maybe, just maybe, she and Campbell could work things out.

"Archer Falcon," a voice softly called.

Archer scrunched her eyebrows when she saw it was Officer O'Neill. Had she done something wrong? Campbell had told her all of the charges in Maine and Massachusetts had been dropped. O'Neill had never called her to give her the final okay to leave. Was Archer supposed to have called her? Was she supposed to have confirmed this with her?

"Officer Campbell told me everything was okay," Archer slipped into a spot just large enough for her and O'Neill. She directed Rory and Trish to stand near-by, next to a headstone with a cherub carved on it. Archer strained to read the faded inscription. Baby Jude, Born: June 13, 1888, Died: August 15, 1888.

"I thought you had already left town," O'Neill said.

"We're leaving right after the funeral." Archer looked at Rory who was still jumping from foot to foot then pacing in tiny circles. Trish grabbed his shaking hands, tried to calm him.

"Think that's a good idea?" O'Neill asked Archer.

"What?"

"Waiting to leave until after the funeral to go home?"

"What are you saying?"

"Maybe you should go now."

"Now? What about the funeral?"

"Kitty told me you went to see her yesterday. Seems to me everybody would be a lot better if you went home."

"Are you telling me I can't stay here?"

"I'm just suggesting..."

"Mom," Rory said.

"Just a minute," Archer waved him away.

"No, Mom. I need to leave."

She looked at Rory His face was pale. His eyes wide.

Archer grabbed his hand. "This way."

She led him and Trish through the crowd. Rory held her hand tightly. He didn't let go until they were back at the car.

CHAPTER THIRTY-FIVE

They got in the Subaru, the slam of three doors booming through the silence.

In the backseat, Rory placed his hand on his chest. "My heart is beating really fast. I think I'm having a heart attack. Wanna' feel?"

Trish placed her hand over his heart. "Wow. Maybe you should take some deep breaths, like you're meditating."

"I should have gone into that restaurant where she works." Rory leaned forward. Trish's hand fell off his chest. "I bet you never went in there to find out if she was working. I bet you made it up."

"Why would I do that?" Archer started the car and pressed on the gas. The engine revved.

"Because you don't want me to talk to her."

"That's not true. Let's go home. Won't it be nice to sleep in our own beds tonight?"

"What about meeting my birth mom?" Rory leaned back and folded his arms across his chest. "I really want to know why I'm so messed up. Did you see her at the funeral? Do you think she's afraid of crowds too? Do you think she wants to meet me?"

"If she doesn't, it's only because she doesn't know you. She only knows that little infant, not Rory. But Sweetie, we need to get Trish home."

"Let's go to the restaurant where she works. Trish doesn't mind. She doesn't want to go home anyway. I'll wait for her. I just want to say hi. If I meet her once, even for a second, then we can probably start e-mailing or texting. I can learn why she didn't want me. And mom?"

"What?"

"Nothing."

"What, Rory?"

"Do you think once she gets to know me she'll be sorry she gave me up? I mean, I was just a baby. What did I do to her?"

"Maybe you farted too much," Trish said. "You fart a lot now. You probably farted a lot as a baby."

"We're going home." Archer steered off the swale, on to the road, and in a direction she hoped would lead them to the highway.

Rory stuck buds into his ear and fiddled with his I-pod. "I really want to meet her. Can we go to the witch place where they're having the ceremony tomorrow? It's on the way home, isn't it? Didn't the newspaper say that ceremony was private? So that'll be a lot smaller. It'll be better."

"I don't think so. We'll just go home. You and Trish have school Monday." She looked at her watch. Could she still make the interview?

Rory kicked the back of Archer's seat. "You never do what I want. Now it's fucking too late. I'm never going to meet my real mom and it's your fault."

Archer focused on the road ahead. Her heart pounded quickly. The lump which sat in her belly was climbing and would soon be strangling her throat. She didn't look in the rear view window, knowing too well what she would see. A red-faced, venom-spewing Rory.

"You knew I would freak out with all those people at the funeral," Rory yelled. "You know who *your* mother is. You know where *you* come from. If you knew what it was like to be me, you would want to find out where the fuck you come from too and why your mind was so fucked up."

The road narrowed as they approached a rotary. Rory kicked her seat again. And again. And again. Trish made attempts to stop him. Archer couldn't drive; couldn't think. Rage built deep like a hot flash, but worse. So much worse, from depths she didn't know she had. She swung the steering wheel to the right and shifted into the breakdown lane, recalling the first time Rory had been admitted to a mental hospital when he was eight years old. On a rainy afternoon, he had spent soccer practice smearing mud on himself and anyone within his reach. She had removed him early when the coach threatened to kick him off the team if he couldn't behave. During the car ride home, he had laughed at the mud he had brought into the car like each handful was a wrapped Christmas gift. He covered the rear window with mud. He threw mud at Archer. He had put a palmful in his mouth and grinned wildly, his teeth brown. She couldn't drive then either, couldn't think. They had passed the Bangor Hospital and without hesitation, she had made a U-turn and drove to the emergency room. That first time, he had been admitted for nine days.

She gripped the steering wheel, her knuckles white. "Relax" she said more for her own benefit than anyone else's.

"You fucking relax." He kicked the chair in six machine gun rapid successions.

"Stop it," she yelled, turning in her seat and glaring at him. "I can't think."

"You don't need to fucking think. Just do what I tell you for once."

"You need to show me respect."

"Respect this." He gave her the finger.

Archer leaned into the back seat and went to smack him with an open hand. Rory laughed and dodged the blow. She tried again. He leaned to the left, laughing harder. Unable to help, Trish cowered to the side, hugging the car door.

Archer stopped, sat back in the driver's seat. Like with the glass of water, she had lost control. Anger is a manifestation of a low frustration level, indeed.

"I'm sorry." She turned and looked at them.

Rory stared back, his eyes dark and blank. Trish was pale, had her arms wrapped around her stomach.

Archer had read in the newspaper that Margaret's private service was to be held at the First Church in Salem, not far from the Witch Museum. Archer opened the glove compartment and pulled out a poorly folded map. She handed it to Trish, who shakily took it.

"Find out where I go to get to Salem once I'm on Route 128."

"I'm gonna be sick," Trish opened the door and leaned out.

"I can't look," Rory said, "If I look, I'll barf too. Are you okay? Was it because we had ice cream for breakfast?"

Trish sat back and wiped her mouth with her sleeve. "I'm sorry. I haven't been feeling well lately. I must have a virus." She closed the car door.

"See, Trish needs to go home." Archer looked at Rory.

"No, it's okay, really. I've never been to Salem before. I hear it's really cool."

"If you're not taking me to Salem, I'm gonna walk there," Rory opened his door.

"Get back in here," Archer shouted.

Rory remained seated; his door open. Her cell phone rang. Wayne. Unable to decide what to do, what not to do, she answered it.

"Where are you?" he asked.

"On our way home."

Rory kicked her seat again then pulled the hood of his sweatshirt over his head.

"Good," Wayne said. "Finelli says your taking off with Rory is really going to help my case. You know, kidnapping is a felony."

"Why the hell do you want him?"

She looked back and saw Rory adjusting his I-pod, eyes down, hood up, avoiding her eyes, ignoring Trish. The knot in her stomach drew tighter.

"Did he hear you say that, Archer? Aren't you the one who said you weren't qualified to have children? Or maybe you should be able to pick your children from a catalogue that way you can make sure you get one you like. What kind of mother are you anyway?"

She slowly closed her phone. Definitely not a bonus mom. Was it fate that she should be Rory's mother or fate that he be her son? She inhaled until her ribs expanded as far as they could, until she was finally able to make one decision. She wasn't leaving Massachusetts today. Breathing deeply, she called the governor's office.

CHAPTER THIRTY-SIX

Archer, Rory and Trish stood in front of The Salem Witch Museum, a rose colored stone Romanesque building that looked like a haunted castle. The statue of a witch with a full, flowing cape cast a shadow and blocked the sunlight. The old Salem clock chimed ten times.

"I don't believe in witches," Trish said.

"They weren't really witches," Rory said.

"How do you know?"

"Mrs. K taught us about the Salem Witch Trials last year. She said the people who were hanged weren't really witches but people that didn't fit in."

"Like us," Trish said.

"Yeah."

"I like being different. I think being like everyone else is super boring."

"I wouldn't mind being a little less different," Rory said.

Trish kissed him on the cheek. "I think you're perfect."

Rory blushed. His eyes smiled as broadly as his mouth. Archer's heart danced and she stifled a laugh.

"Hey, look at that." He pointed at a police car as it slowly canvassed the street. "There's a witch on the side of the car. This town really loves witches."

"Do you want to go in to the museum?" Archer asked. "We have about an hour until Margaret's service begins."

"Think they'll let us in to the funeral?" Rory asked. "It's supposed to be private."

"I don't know," Archer said. "We'll try."

"When I tell them who I am, they'll definitely let me in."

"You sure you want to do this?" Archer asked.

"Yeah."

Archer sighed. "If that's what you want. How about the museum?"

"Not for me," Rory said. "Too scary."

"It's just a big tourist trap," Trish said.

"Well, then let's walk around and kill some time."

"Could you not use the word kill?" Rory laughed.

"*Witch* word would you like her to use?" Trish asked.

Archer laughed this time. Despite the abnormality of it all, at that moment, it all seemed kind of normal. They walked through the streets. Archer was surprised the small town famous for events that happened over three hundred years ago was progressive and charming. Coffee shops and boutiques dotted the tree-lined avenues. They watched a woman feed an ice cream cone to her miniature poodle outside an ice cream shop. A large park with thick grass was an obvious gathering spot, a wedding party organizing for a ceremony as Archer and the kids walked by.

They stopped in front of a small deli. "Anybody want a drink?" Archer asked.

"Yeah," Rory said. "I could use a Vault."

"How about some juice?"

"No fucking way."

"Rory."

"I want a Vault and that's what I'm getting."

"Not if I won't pay for it," Archer said.

"I don't need your money."

Archer sighed, took a deep breath. When would she learn to react differently to his demands? "How about if you drink juice now and after the funeral you can have whatever you want?"

"No, I need it now. I'm nervous. Ricky from school says that smoking cigarettes helps calm you down. When I'm eighteen, I'm going to try that. It's illegal for me to smoke now." Rory walked into the store.

Archer took a breath; that would be a battle for later. Trish and Archer followed Rory into the store. Rory walked to the cooler, grabbed a Vault, opened it and chugged the entire can. Archer watched, helpless. When he was done, he wiped the back of his mouth, burped, then laughed. Rory left the store, leaving the empty can on the counter.

"Do you want anything?" Archer asked Trish.

"No, thank you, Mrs. Falcon. And I'm sorry."

"What are you sorry for?"

"I don't know. I guess I feel bad."

"There is nothing for you to feel bad about."

Trish put her hand on her stomach. Her face turned pale.

"Are you okay?" Archer asked.

Trish ran out the door, vomited in the street. Archer went up behind her, patted her hair then took her into her arms. Trish's body heaved as tears drenched Archer's shoulder. Archer saw the poodle finish his ice cream cone and sprawl out along the sidewalk while its mistress sipped her coffee.

"How far along are you?" Archer asked, her mouth inches from Trish's ear.

"I don't know," Trish sobbed.

Archer pulled Trish an arm's length away and looked her in the eyes. "Is Rory the father?"

"No," Trish said.

"Then who?"

The tears came again, violent drops that fell like bombs. Trish buried her head in Archer's chest and sobbed. They stayed like that for several minutes.

CHAPTER THIRTY-SEVEN

On Essex Street, Archer stepped into the First Church, a grey brick building buttressed by a watch tower. According to the plaque out front, it was one of the oldest churches gathered by the English Puritan settlers of Massachusetts Bay Colony in 1629. She turned to pass on this information to Rory and Trish but the kids weren't on her heels as she had thought. How'd she let them out of her sight? She turned and scanned the street.

A few people, mostly older and conservatively dressed, scurried toward the church. Dressed in black with their heads bowed, they looked like the funeral attendees from the day before. Archer walked to the street, looked both ways then headed toward her car which was parked around a corner and a couple of blocks away. A cool breeze lifted the bottom of Archer's dress.

A block away, Rory and Trish weren't at the car. She looked in all directions, taking in the tree-lined streets, the manicured lawns, the sidewalks. Sweat beaded on the back of her neck. Nerves? Fear? No, a fucking hot flash! Even with the dip in the temperature, her body was still fighting her. And where were Rory and Trish? Not now. Dear God, please, not now. Where are they? She saw a police car, the witch on the side door laughing at her. Steam rose from her body. She turned in a circle like a wobbly top, unsure what to do, where to go. Were they in trouble? Had she failed again as a mother by letting them out of her sight? Did she have to watch them every single moment? She ran back toward the church, her new shoes cutting into her pinky toes. What kind of trouble had Trish gotten Rory into now? Did she steal another car? Rob a bank? What? What? What?

Archer turned the corner, sprinting now, the hot flash thankfully over. If they weren't waiting for her back at the church, she'd call the police. She'd have to. Her kids were missing.

Six, seven people gathered by a tree near the church and looked up. Archer slowed to a walk, out of breath, her pinky toes raw with pain. She followed their collective gaze and saw --- a tree in the tree. She ran again, stopped, grabbed Trish who also looked up, her hands folded in front of her chest like in prayer.

The tree in the tree…was Rory.

"What is he doing?" Archer asked.

"There's a cat stuck up there. See?" Trish pointed.

A black cat cowered on a thin branch, its fur standing on end. Rory, dressed in his ghille suit, hung on to the trunk, one leg balancing on a limb, the other leg teetering in space like a tightrope walker. He reached for the feline who shied away, hissed. Rory looked down.

"I think he's hurt, Mom."

Archer strained and looked more closely at the cat. Its left ear was bloodied.

"He must have gotten into a fight." Rory lunged and swiftly grabbed the cat.

He tucked it into his chest then shimmied, one handed, down the tree. Just like when he was nine years old with a toothy grin and clutching a stunned Rhode Island Red Rooster to his chest at the Common Ground Fair in Unity, Maine. Rory put the cat down. It darted behind the church. The spectators, speechless at his get-up, clapped politely then walked away, murmuring words Archer was glad she couldn't hear.

Archer grabbed Rory and pulled him into her. His suit jabbed her in the side. Rory pulled away.

"I was worried about you." Archer turned toward Trish. "About both of you."

"I ran back to the car to put my suit on and then we saw the cat in the tree and…"

"Next time, tell me where you're going. You're not wearing that in church, are you?"

Rory shrugged.

"C'mon, Ror."

He kicked at the dirt.

"How about you take it off and put it on later?" Archer asked, always the negotiator.

Rory looked at Trish, who nodded. He slipped out of the suit and let it fall to the ground. Pieces of leaves and netting stuck to him like fuzz. Trish brushed his shirt with her fingers.

"C'mon," Archer said. "Let's get this over with."

She turned toward the church, the kids right behind her. She took a step then stopped. Kitty and Officer O'Neill stood a few feet away.

"What are you doing here?" Kitty asked.

Archer stepped to the side and put her hand on Rory's shoulder. "This is Rory,"

"I told you…" Kitty began.

"Hi," Rory stepped forward. "This is my best friend, Trish."

"Hello, ma'am," Trish said.

Kitty looked at them, terror on her face like she was staring at ghosts. She pointed a fat finger at them. "Go away and never come back."

Kitty ran into the church. Officer O'Neill folded her arms across her chest. Archer, Rory and Trish stood silent, speechless.

CHAPTER THIRTY-EIGHT

*T*hursday, October 24, 1991

Early morning rain pelted the windows of The Crow's Nest. Archer cupped her hands around a porcelain mug of hot chocolate, whipped cream piled high and flowing over the sides. She looked at the round-faced, red-cheeked woman sipping coffee and seated across from her. They were the only ones in the restaurant.

"You're due in a week?" Archer asked.

"Unless he decides to come earlier." Kitty rubbed her stomach.

"Thank you," Archer said.

"No, thank you." Kitty shifted in her seat.

"Can I have some. . .forget it."

"What?"

"A shot of something. Like vodka maybe."

Kitty waddled behind the bar, returned with a bottle. She poured a shot into Archer's mug then put the bottle on the table. Kitty sat again, awkwardly falling into the chair.

"Why are you here?" Kitty asked. "I don't mean to be rude but I didn't think I'd meet you. I thought you just show up to get the baby after he's born."

Kitty's stale cigarette breath wafted across the table.

"I wanted to meet you first," Archer said. "To make sure. . ."

". . .you wanted the baby?"

"Something like that."

"And your husband?"

"He thinks I'm attending a deposition in Saco. And your husband?" Archer fished.

Kitty shook her head.

"Boyfriend?"

"Something like that."

A gust of wind rattled the windows.

"Gonna' be a bad storm," Kitty poured another shot into Archer's cup, then added some to her own. "The father is a sword fisherman. He's at sea most of the time. They're supposed to be back any day now."

"You must miss him when he's gone. Should you be drinking vodka? And smoking?"

Kitty shrugged. "It's not like that, about the father I mean."

"What's it like?"

"It's complicated." She looked in her coffee cup.

"Why the secret?"

"If you came here to batter me, I ain't interested."

"I just wanted to meet you."

"Here I am. So you've met me. Now what?"

Archer signed. "A few years ago, Wayne and I had the chance to adopt a beautiful baby boy from Texas."

"What does that have to do with me?"

"Nothing. We picked him up and we were in the hotel room and...I couldn't do it. We brought him back."

"You can do that?"

Archer shrugged. "We did."

"You want to be a mother now, right?"

"Desperately. Wayne and I had been trying for the last two years and nothing. We did fertility testing, injections, everything." Archer sipped the hot chocolate, reached for the bottle then withdrew her hand. If she didn't drink, maybe Kitty wouldn't either. "The doctors said there were no medical reason we couldn't get pregnant but I know it's my fault."

"How do you know that?"

"I just know."

"Are you saying you want a money back guarantee or something?"

"No, of course not."

"If you think I'm Dear Abby, you can forget it. Tell your problems to someone else."

Archer pushed her mug away. "I'm sorry. I shouldn't have bothered you. I just...the baby from Texas had Down syndrome."

"So?"

"I didn't think I could be a good mother." Archer wiped her eyes with a coarse paper napkin.

"It takes a special person to raise a disabled child," Kitty said. "I know all about being different. If you don't want this kid…"

"No, I want him. I definitely want him."

Kitty jumped.

"What?" Archer asked.

"My stomach. I felt pain."

"A contraction?"

"I don't think so. He's not due for another week. Probably gas. I've always had a lot of gas. Owww." Kitty clutched her stomach.

"Should you go to the hospital? I can take you." Archer looked at the rain striking the front window. It was coming at the window sideways. Archer wondered if rain drops could break a window. She hoped the roads were still passable. She wanted to make it home today.

"Can't go to the hospital," Kitty said. "I'm the only one working today. My mother's in Salem visiting relatives. I feel better now anyway."

Archer looked around. "Is the bar always this quiet?"

"Must be the weather."

"Maybe you should close the restaurant."

"My mother bought this place over thirty years ago. We've never missed a day. I'm not going to start now on account of this baby or some storm."

"How come…?" Archer swallowed the rest of the sentence.

"How come I don't want the baby?" Kitty asked. "Maybe the same reason you didn't want the baby in Texas. How come you didn't want the baby in Texas?"

She looked away. "I don't know."

"You need to leave."

"I'm sorry. I shouldn't have…"

"No," Kitty said, "you shouldn't have." She adjusted the elastic band on her pants, went behind the bar and lit a cigarette.

Archer stepped into the driving rain.

CHAPTER THIRTY-NINE

Rory walked away from the church, ear phones plugged in tight, head down, the hood of his sweatshirt covering his face. He dragged the ghille suit behind him like a deflated gorilla. The old Salem clock chimed eleven times. Archer recalled the only poem Rory had ever written.

The horn, the horn, sounds so forlorn

She had to give Wayne credit for Rory's vocabulary, even if she couldn't be generous with anything else he did as a father.

Rory was refusing to talk.

"Ready for Dunkin' Donuts?" Archer asked as they got to the car.

Rory put the ghille suit on and sat in the back seat. He adjusted the volume on his I-pod.

"You're going to hurt your ears."

Rory shrugged. Archer sighed. Trish bit her nails.

"All right," Archer said. "Let's go home."

Downtown Salem was maze-like. Archer navigated the streets, passing the same church at least three times. When Archer finally thought she was heading in the right direction, Trish gagged.

"Again?"

Trish nodded. Archer pulled the car over near the Old Burying Point. A sign marked its establishment in 1637 as the second oldest cemetery in Salem. Trish jumped out. Rory followed.

"Where are you going?" Archer asked.

Rory didn't answer. He stomped into the Old Burying Point, ran past chipped and faded tombstones and toward a large willow tree. With Trish gagging behind the car, Archer watched Rory climb the willow. At rest on a large limb twenty feet off the ground, he called to her.

"What?" Archer yelled back.

"Come here."

She walked through the cemetery and stopped at a tombstone marked Archer. She hesitated then stepped over raised roots of willow trees, around monuments, through thorny bushes. She looked up at Rory.

"I'm not coming down," he said, "until you let me find out about my real family."

"Rory, please."

"I'm not kidding."

"I don't have the energy for this."

"You don't have to do anything."

"How will you find out about them?"

"I'll get Kitty to talk to me. And I'll talk to people who know my dad from the fishing boat. And I'll figure it out. I know I will."

"You're going to be disappointed."

"I'll be disappointed if I don't try."

"You're only fifteen years old. You have a lifetime to find out about your birth family."

"I'm almost sixteen and I want to know now."

"Why now, Rory? What's so important about knowing now?"

"It's something I have to do."

"The only thing you have to do is be a kid. Why isn't that enough?"

"Because I'm different and I want to know why."

Trish walked up next to Archer and took her hand. Archer looked at Trish, then back at Rory.

"Trish needs to go to the doctor," Archer said.

"She has an appointment on Tuesday," Rory said. "Give me until tomorrow. Let me see what I can find out about my real family. Then we'll go home."

Archer sighed. Trish squeezed her hand.

"I'm glad you're going to the doctor," Archer looked at her. "You and the baby have to be healthy and…"

"I'm not going to *that* kind of doctor, Mrs. Falcon."

"What kind of doctor are you going to?"

Trish looked away.

"She's getting an abortion," Rory said.

Trish let go of Archer's hand and walked away. Rory climbed down the tree and jumped to the ground, landing in front of Archer. Leaves and twigs brushed across his face. He looked like a swamp creature.

"Her Uncle is the father." Rory ran after Trish.

Weak, Archer sat on the ground, next to another tombstone bearing her name.

CHAPTER FORTY

Archer sat on the grass next to Nathaniel Archer's tombstone, did the math and calculated he had died when he was sixty-three. His wife Hannah's tombstone was next to his. Dead at fifty-three years old, she and Nathaniel had seven children. Their tombstones were lined in a row. That Nathaniel and Hannah had lived so long during the seventeenth century was amazing - their lives fraught with danger and without the benefits of antibiotics, public water and sewer systems. In those days, children died of diseases now eradicated. Mothers routinely died giving birth. Nobody was diagnosed with Asperger's, Bi-polar or Down Syndrome—they were just outcasts; or witches.

Archer saw Rory, who wore his ghillie suit, and Trish attempting to climb another willow tree. It was all relative—the dangers of 2007 were no less frightening than the dangers of the 1600's.

"How did you do it?" she whispered to Nathaniel.

Her cell phone rang. She jumped, startled for a moment, lost in Nathaniel's 1600s. It was Kara.

"Where are you? We're worried about you."

"We?"

"Well, me mostly."

"We're in Salem. We found Rory's birth mother but she wants nothing to do with him."

"Is Rory okay with that?"

"Of course not. I'm sitting in a cemetery trying to figure out what to do."

"Come home. You found him, now come home."

"I'm trying. There's another thing. Do you know Trish Dooley?"

"Of course. Why?"

"She's here too."

"How did that happen?"

"I'm not exactly sure. She seems kind to him. Have you met her parents?"

"I've met her mom and her uncle. I think her dad's been out of the picture for a long time. They're not nice people and the uncle is creepy."

Rory jumped and grabbed a branch. His legs swung out, barely missing Trish as he swung backwards. Trish pushed his legs forward as if he were a swing. They laughed. Rory in the ghille suit looked like hanging moss.

"You there?" Kara asked.

"I'm here. What's happening in Bangor?"

"Same old stuff. Wayne called a couple of times asking where you were."

"He knows where I am. He said he filed a motion to get custody of Rory."

"That asshole. Can he do that?"

"Maybe. I guess they're going to say I kidnapped him and Trish; and blame his bad behavior on me. Maybe it would be good if Wayne had custody."

"You don't mean that. Wayne ignores Rory; he always has. And what about all of Rory's stuff? Wayne would never let him keep his stuff."

"Maybe that's a good thing. I had a guardianship case a long time ago. This guy lived in a little tiny house, really dark and musty. His sister wanted guardianship over him because he wasn't able to take care of himself. His house was filthy but even worse was the collection of newspapers in his bedroom—under the bed, all over the floor, on top of his bed, piled in his closet. Over thirty years of newspapers. Not like the sister could do anything about it. Sometimes I worry Rory will be like that. Instead of newspapers - oil cans, lawnmower parts, tools."

Archer's phone beeped. She saw Wayne's number.

"Shit, its Wayne."

"You going to answer it?"

"I don't know." She sighed. "I guess I'd better. I'll call you later."

"Let me know if there is anything I can do."

"Sure." Archer switched to Wayne. "What?"

"Are you home yet?"

"No. We saw Kitty. She wants nothing to do with Rory."

"That was a stupid idea. What were you thinking?"

"You don't know how hard it is to say no to him. He doesn't respond to any discipline. To him, the word no is a reason to try harder to get what he wants. Remember, how he loved The Three Musketeers? Never give up, never give in."

"He's my son. I know all about him. I was the one who read that book to him."

"Why do you want him? You've never wanted him before."

"Are you going to make this easy and agree to give me custody or do we have to do this the hard way?"

Rory ran around the trunk of the willow. The ghille suit flapping behind him, Trish chasing him and laughing. Trish tripped. Rory ran to her, helped her up, brushed twigs and dirt from her jeans. He looked at Archer, grinned and waved.

"Easy or hard? Which do you prefer?" Wayne asked.

Her bones creaking, Archer stood. This was her chance to have a normal life, to make friends, to have a boyfriend, to work a full day without interruption, to be a judge. Nathaniel Archer, she wondered, what would you do?

"Hey, mom."

Archer looked at Rory.

"Bonus," he flashed a thumbs up sign.

"Fuck off, Wayne," Archer snapped her phone shut.

She walked to the front of the cemetery, reading headstones as she went, wondering what the lives of these people over three hundred years ago were like. Would Rory have been better off being born back then? She had always imagined him a caveman; self sufficient, creating tools and weapons out of sticks, figuring out ways to shelter himself. In the 1600s, would he have been a survivalist—feeding and clothing his family without help? Or would his pacing and repetitive movements render him ripe to be accused of being a witch? She smiled as she caught herself protecting her son from non-existent non-accusers who had been dead for three hundred years.

A bus pulled up and a tour group stepped off, filing in through the gate. A few seconds later, two cars parked at right angles in front of the bus. Officer O'Neill stepped out of the first car, a late model Camaro. Behind her was a

Salem patrol car, the witch on the side still laughing at Archer. Two officers exited.

Wayne hadn't been joking. He was going to make it hard.

CHAPTER FORTY-ONE

Forty, maybe fifty, tourists stepped off the Scary Salem Witch Tour bus as, in the distance, the Salem clock chimed three times.

The last person off the bus was dressed in ragged knickers and a blousy white shirt and carried a portable microphone and a clipboard. He held the microphone to his mouth. "Welcome to The Burying Point, Salem's oldest burying ground. Justice John Hathorne is buried here. John Hathorne was a judge in the Witchcraft Court who ordered many of the "witches" to die. Nathaniel Hawthorne was his great-great-grandson who changed the spelling of his last name to avoid any connection with the judge." He swooped his arm grandly through the air. "We even have a Mayflower pilgrim buried on these hallow grounds and members of the esteemed Archer family. Move along, folks. We don't have a lot of time. The Wax Museum closes soon and we want to make sure you have plenty of time there. Come alive. Let's go, people."

Archer stepped back, the crowd heading toward her. Adults trampled graves, children ran around tombstones.

"Rory," Archer swung around. "Too many people…"

She darted for the willow in the back of the cemetery where she had last seen them; zigzagging around tourists, passing Nathaniel Archer's grave and the two women who stood on it, debating the best angle for a photograph. When she got to the tree, Rory and Trish were gone.

"Archer," Officer O'Neill was behind her. "Where's Rory?"

She faced her. "I thought all the charges were dropped."

"I'm not here about the stolen car."

The uniformed officers ran up behind O'Neill. The one with the moustache folded his arms across his chest. The skinny one rested a hand on his gun. Tourists gathered around them, more interested in the police officers than the historical gravesite.

"These officers have an Order to serve on you. It's for the return of Rory." Ellen handed Archer a copy of the two page document.

Archer started to read, the words blurry, jumping on the pages. She didn't recognize the name of the judge. Wasn't out of the Bangor court but from Portland, a city she had little contact with. She did, however, recognize two names on the paperwork. In re: The Former Marriage Of Wayne Falcon, Petitioner/Father versus Archer Falcon, Respondent/Mother. And the heading she knew too well, having petitioned for this very Order many times on behalf of clients. Ex-Parte Protection Order. An Order granted without allowing the accused the opportunity to answer. She scanned the allegations.

The Mother refuses to disclose the whereabouts of the minor child.

The Mother is placing the child in emotional and physical danger.

The Mother refuses to control and discipline the child.

The Mother is under extreme stress and requires a psychological evaluation to determine her ability to parent.

The Mother has a history of alcohol abuse and the Father fears she is unfit to parent.

The Mother is a poor role model.

Archer shook her head then laughed, an involuntary, poorly timed cackle. She looked at O'Neill, the police officers, and the crowd that gathered behind them. The irony of receiving Wayne's self serving accusations in the presence of Justice Hathorne was lost on them; but not on Archer.

She turned to the second page of the document, knowing before she had done so that she had been decreed a witch, destined to be hanged.

The Mother is hereby ordered to return the minor child, Rory Falcon, to the residence of the Father within eight (8) hours after service of this Order upon her. If the Mother does not comply, law enforcement shall escort the child to the Father's residence.

"Okay, people," the tour guide's voice boomed, "show's over. Time to get back on the bus. Don't want to miss the wax figures and your chance to get locked into a jail cell just like one used during the witch hysteria."

Another involuntary chuckle escaped Archer's lips.

"What's so funny?" O'Neill asked.

"Nothing," Archer said.

"Where's Rory?"

"Give me a second," Archer put on her lawyer hat and read the Order again, digesting it more thoroughly, giving herself time to think.

"Let's go," the tour guide called to his flock. "Back on the bus. We're on a tight schedule. Be the first to do grave stone rubbing and tie nautical knots at the Wax Museum. You'll be the hit of your friends at home."

A few people headed for the bus, most stayed, more interested in the present than the past.

"If you're not on the bus soon, we're going to have to leave without you. This is your five minute warning,"

"Where is he?" O'Neill scanned the tombstones, looked up into the willow trees.

More people headed to the bus. A few stayed behind, still rubber-necking.

"Time to move on, Folks," the skinny officer said.

The stragglers headed to the bus. O'Neill ambled among the gravesites. The police officers flanked her on either side. Archer stood under the giant willow, hoping Rory would pop out laughing, saying hi, mom, I really really love you. But still, no sight of him, no sight of Trish.

O'Neill rounded back to Archer. "Where is he?"

Archer reread the last words of the Order. If the Mother fails to comply, law enforcement shall escort the child to the Father's residence.

It was time for her to make a decision. "Take him," Archer said. "If you can find him, take him to his father's. I'm not going to violate an order, even one based on lies. And Rory will think it's fun to ride all the way to Bangor in a police car."

"Where is he?"

"Probably in a tree somewhere."

O'Neill nodded and the patrolmen disbursed to look for Rory.

"I thought you were in Salem for Margaret's funeral," Archer said. "I didn't know you were also here on business."

"I wouldn't have come here to serve the Order but ..."

"But what?"

"This is different."

"What's different? Is it because Rory's father is suddenly showing interest in him because he wants money?"

"It has nothing to do with that."

"Then what? Is it about Kitty? Don't worry, we left town just like you told us. I promise, it'll be a long time before I go back to Gloucester."

"Kitty doesn't want to see Rory, but that's not what it's about."

"Do you have children, Detective?"

"Only a cat."

"Rory wants to meet his biological mother. I'm trying to understand why. He's a complicated boy. He knows he's different but he can't help the way he acts. He's searching for answers and he thinks Kitty has them. Why wouldn't she at least say hello to him?"

"You'd have to ask Kitty."

"Ask her? How? Getting near her is harder than getting to Fort Knox."

"I've known Kitty for a long time."

"Obviously."

"I want you to know this isn't personal."

"It seems personal, Detective. Every time I turn around you show up."

"I know. I'm sorry. I wasn't going to tell you this but...I was with Kitty when Rory was born."

"You were? During the storm?"

"He came a few days early. She was working at The Crow's Nest and wouldn't leave despite the bad weather. I couldn't get her to the hospital in time. The roads were closed. It was too dangerous." She caught sight of the officers still searching for Rory then looked back at Archer. "I caught him."

"You caught Rory?"

"He had a full head of black hair. I had never seen a baby being born before. It was a miracle."

"Kitty didn't tell me."

"There's a lot you don't know. A lot you don't need to know. I don't mean to sound harsh. I know you're doing what you think is right for your son. But you're going to have to trust me. This is really hard. It's better off he doesn't know, you both don't know."

"Know what?"

"Nothing. Forget I said anything." She looked at the officers who were headed their way.

Archer spoke quickly. "What was he like when he was born? Did he cry? Was the birth difficult?"

"Detective," the mustachioed cop yelled. He held the ghille suit.

O'Neill joined them near a tree, took the suit from the officer. She ran back to Archer. "Is this his?"

Archer nodded. The bus engine revved. The eight-wheeler backed up and drove away.

O'Neill draped the suit over her arm and pointed at Archer. "Get him to his Father's house within eight hours or else you're in violation of the court's Order. And I will take you to jail if I have to."

Archer watched O'Neill and the officers walk away, the hood of the ghille suit dragging on the ground behind them. They got in their cars and left, the tires kicking up dirt. Archer walked through the cemetery alone, dusk setting in, a cold breeze sending a chill through her body. She checked behind tombstones, around memorial plaques, high into trees, along the brick wall that bordered the cemetery. No Rory. No Trish. She dropped to the ground next to Nathaniel Archer's stomped-on grave and threw the court Order down, then stepped on it, the white pages brown with dirt.

"Where are they?" she whispered.

She would rather be hanged for something she didn't do than lose them again.

CHAPTER FORTY-TWO

The tires of the Subaru locked as Archer jammed on the brakes. She jumped out of the car and ran to the tour guide standing in front of the bus parked outside the wax museum.

"Where are they?" she asked.

"Everyone's inside, ma'am." He pointed at the museum with the megaphone.

"Rory and Trish too?"

"Rory and Trish?" He looked at the clipboard. "No Rory and Trish on this tour. Maybe a later one."

"They're not on the tour. But they were at the cemetery when you were there and now they're gone. I think they snuck on your bus."

"Impossible, ma'am. Nobody sneaks on my bus."

"They're just kids. They're good at sneaking places. Trust me."

"I promise you, nobody gets on that bus without John Archer knowing."

"Your name is Archer?"

"Sure is."

"I'm Archer too," she said.

"Not unusual around these parts to have the last name Archer," John said. "Name goes back to the Mayflower."

"That's my first name."

"Well, that is unusual."

"You think they're still on the bus?"

"Not on this tour, ma'am. Maybe a later one."

"No…," Archer sighed. "Can you check? Did you see them get off the bus?"

"Scary Salem Tours has strict policy. Every person who gets on and everyone who gets off is carefully noted right here," he raised the clipboard. "I was employee of the month for August. Trust me, I know what I'm doing."

"Can I check?"

"Check what?"

"The bus."

"No, ma'am. Company policy."

"Can you check?"

John raised the megaphone to his mouth, pointed it towards Archer and spoke through it. "Lady, your son and daughter are not on the bus." He put the megaphone down and smiled.

Archer walked away, bought a ticket and entered the museum—accosting employees, describing Rory and Trish to anyone who would listen, checking behind wax figures, looking in the men's and women's bathrooms, peaking behind doors. No Rory. No Trish.

She ran outside and watched the tour bus load then drive away.

Still no Rory. Still no Trish.

CHAPTER FORTY-THREE

Absolutely. She was absolutely crazy. Absolute. Absolut. She took another swig from the clear bottle with the black script on it. Reminded her of the Declaration of Independence. John Freakin' Adams signed this bottle. And Benjamin Go Fly A Kite Franklin too. She laughed. Took another sip. The clear liquid dripped from her lips. She wiped her chin then licked her fingers. Life, liberty and the pursuit of happiness, indeed.

With one hand clutched on the steering wheel and one hand wrapped around the neck of the bottle that rested between her legs, she drove past the Old Burying Ground, the wax museum, the witch museum, coffee houses, tourist shops, the old Salem clock, over and over and over again. The sights blurring, blending. No Rory. No Trish. Not even a miniature poodle eating ice cream. She really needed glasses. She couldn't see anything. She was tired of seeing life as an impressionist painting. She wanted life to be clear, sharp, unambiguous, free of conflict.

The moon was a cloudy sliver in the evening sky. Street lights domed over the road like electric candles, faux colonial style. Her cell phone rang. Again. She checked the number. It was Wayne. Again and again and again. Rory wasn't answering his phone and Trish wasn't answering hers. Only seemed right for Archer to ignore Wayne, and Campbell, and Kara, and her mother, and anyone else trying to reach her. Anyone but Rory, who didn't call, who never called.

She drank again, half way through the gallon jug. Wayne was a bastard. I hate his guts I wish he would die idiot asshole jerk of the world bastard. He can have Rory. Good riddance.

Archer circled the block again. The witch statue in front of the museum seemed to take flight. The white line down the center of the road focused, then blurred and distorted. She did want Rory. She just couldn't handle him. That's what Wayne had always told her. You're not fit to be a mother. It's your fault he's like this. But when she found out Wayne didn't want him either, well…it had all snowballed out of control. Rory in the middle. Rory the victim. She had always wanted Rory, or at least some version of him. A nicer version. One that respected her. And she didn't need that respect on a silver platter. She had earned it. Dammit. Maybe one that was predictable once in awhile. The one who raked leaves, who mowed the lawn, who built a crooked bookshelf and changed light bulbs. The one who wanted to learn sign language so he could communicate with Evan, his deaf friend at school.

What could she do for Rory? What had she ever done for him? Nothing helpful. Removed him from his biological mother. Saddled him with a librarian for a father. Wayne the pain from Maine. Rendered Rory the product of a broken home. Nagged him to clean his room, wear his bike helmet, take a shower. Don't kick the wall. Don't tear apart fans. Don't take alcohol to school. Don't punch your mother in the eye.

She put the bottle to her lips, tipped her head back and swirled the elixir like mouthwash, swallowed a big gulp. She coughed, choked on the liquid. Her eyes watered. A siren sounded. A quick alarm. She looked in her rearview mirror. The whirling red lights were unmistakable.

Shit. Would she lose her license to practice law if she were arrested for OUI? Are judges allowed to have OUIs? Could she be a judge if she were arrested for kidnapping? Hah. She had been a failure as a wife, a failure as a mother and as a friend and now she was going to be suspended from practicing law. Wouldn't even get the chance to be a failure at being a judge. She pulled over, braced to be arrested for operating a vehicle under the influence, already feeling the embarrassment of her peers and the legal community. She wondered if Wayne would be happy.

With the Subaru off to the side of the road, the police car slowly passed. She concentrated, waved, tried to look sober although at that moment she didn't know what sober was; knew all about slober, and slobber, and definitely about slumber, but sober—what was that? She watched the lights of the squad car dim in the distance then disappear as the car turned a corner. Drunk or clear-headed, it didn't matter, she knew one thing. She couldn't get arrested.

She put the car in drive and lurched forward, the vodka swishing against the sides of the bottle. She drove out of town, or so she thought that was where she was headed, over a steel bridge, up a hill, around a curve, to grandmother's house we go. She missed Grandma Rose, her mother, her friend. She would know what to do. She would know how to find Rory and Trish. She would tell Archer what a wonderful mother she was, what a wonderful person she was. Archer needed to hear those lies but they would only make her feel worse about how unkind she had been to her mother. Maybe she could channel Justice Hathorne. Maybe he could tell her some lies, sentence her to be hanged.

The road faded, disappeared. The ground no longer smooth, bump, bump, bump. She hit the brake. The pedal on the right? No, it's the one on the left. Jerked to a stop, she put the car in park, hopeful it wasn't in neutral or reverse, brought the bottle to her lips, sucked, so sleepy, if only Grandma Rose were here...no Rory...no Trish...

My name is Archer, an unusual first name. Does anybody love me? Does anybody care? If I were a witch, could I find Rory and Trish?

CHAPTER FORTY-FOUR

Percussions pounded, Rory's I-Pod screeched awful music, more like tires squealing and sirens blaring. Torture, deliberate aching, heart-wrenching torture. Archer opened her eyes, the right one first, then the left. She dug crust out from the corners. Her mouth was dry like sun-drenched leather. But it wasn't rap or hip-hop from Rory's I-tunes library drumming, boom-boom-boom, in her ears. It was her. All her.

She had never despised herself more than at this very moment. She should hang herself; save Justice Hathorne and the good people of Salem all the trouble.

She tilted the bottle, almost fully upside down. The vodka was warm and stale as it slid over her tongue and swished around her teeth. A couple more sips—drips more than sips—and the ruckus subsided. She smoothed her shirt and straightened her hair in the rearview mirror. Then, the sirens blared again.

The sound came from up the road, around a corner, Where? Nowhere. Everywhere. She started the car, backed onto the road and gently pressed the accelerator, moving cautiously forward, not looking back.

Three Salem P.D. police cars and Ellen's Camaro were scattered in front of the wax museum. It was early morning but the sirens still brought on-lookers and rubber-neckers. Archer parked a block away. She was OUI for sure. Her blood alcohol level had to be sky high.

From behind the steering wheel, she saw Rory and Trish being led out of the wax museum by a uniformed officer. The cops from the Old Burying

Ground leaned against their car, waiting. Ellen stood near-by, watching the kids as they walked toward her. The old clock chimed eight times. Ellen looked Archer's way. Archer sank low then raised her head slowly, peering over the dashboard. Ellen looked back at Rory and Trish, stepped toward them, her arms folded across her chest. The skinny cop had his hand on his holstered gun. The cop with the moustache pulled out handcuffs and grabbed Rory by the arm. Rory pulled his arm away. Ellen intervened, her body a fort between Rory and Trish and the officers. Wild gestures, finger pointing, an argument.

"No," Archer slurred, "leave them alone."

She started to get out of the car. Her head spun. She fell back in, still drunk, perspiring. Her sweat smelled like sweet rubbing alcohol, her breath like rotten eggs and—she looked at the wet spot between her legs—urine. She couldn't let them arrest him. Not here, not so far from home and Grandma Rose and Kara and Campbell and ... Ellen steered Rory toward the Camaro. He pushed the driver's seat forward and climbed into the back. Ellen put her arms around Trish's shoulder and pointed—toward Archer.

Archer sank low again. Looked for a place to hide. Shit. Shit. Shit. Nowhere to go. She made herself small, so small she could be stuffed back into her mother's uterus, so small she could disappear. Three raps on the window and she jumped. Her heart pounded. She looked up, her eyes wide like a child caught with matches. She rolled the window down.

"Is Detective O'Neill coming here?" Archer whispered.

"No," Trish said, "just me."

Archer sat up. "Where's Rory?"

"Detective O'Neill is taking him to his dad's."

"Let's go."

Trish didn't move.

"We need to go home," Archer said. "Get in the car."

"You can't drive, Mrs. Falcon."

Archer sighed, clutched the bottle of vodka, climbed over the console and fell deep into the passenger seat.

CHAPTER FORTY-FIVE

Trish merged the Subaru onto the highway. She stayed several car lengths behind Ellen and Rory.

"How'd you learn to drive?" Archer asked.

"From my Uncle."

"The same Uncle...?"

"Yeah. Since I was like nine I'd go to the Mobil To Go to get him and my mom cigarettes and when it was too cold to walk, he taught me how to drive. He's not really my Uncle, you know. He's my mom's boyfriend. They wanted me to call him Poppy after my dad committed suicide but I refused so we compromised on Uncle Raven."

"Uncle Raven?"

"He has a tat of a raven on his chest."

Archer cringed. "We need to call the police as soon as we get back to Bangor. That man needs to go to prison for a very long time."

"No."

The car swerved to the side, the right tires bumped over rumble strips.

"Be careful," Archer braced herself.

"Rory says I drive by Braille." Trish steered the car back into the lane. "No police. He'll kill me if the police find out."

"Okay, calm down. Do you want me to drive?"

"Maybe at the next rest stop we can switch. Rory says he's going to kill Uncle Raven. I don't want him to because Rory will go to jail. I can handle this." She patted her stomach. "Rory won't like jail. He'll feel claustrophobic and they won't let him have his stuff. I'm going to have an abortion and just forget about it. Rory says he hates being adopted so I'm not going to do that to the kid, and I'm certainly not going to raise a child. I'll just fuck the kid up like my mom fucked me up."

The vibrations from the rumble strips were making Archer nauseous. Or maybe it was the conversation. Or the alcohol. Or the fact that she was quickly sobering.

"Rory says he hates being adopted?" Archer asked.

Trish pulled onto the roadway again. "Don't take it personally, Mrs. Falcon. He'd hate it no matter who adopted him. I don't think it matters anyway. I wasn't adopted and my life sucks. I have gum. Do you want some?"

Archer took the stick and folded it into her mouth.

"There's the rest stop," Trish said. "I'm going to pull in, okay? I have to pee something wicked and maybe you can change your clothes."

"Is it that bad?" Archer asked.

"You smell worse than one of Rory's farts," Trish said.

"Why did you and Rory leave the cemetery?" Archer steered the Subaru onto the highway. Her hair was wet from a quick wash in the rest stop bathroom sink, her breath was fresh and her clothes were clean. She had stuffed her soiled pants, shirt, bra and underwear into the bathroom garbage pail.

"We saw the cops," Trish propped her bare feet up on the dash, made ten toe prints on the window. "Rory thought they were after him because he had climbed that tree to get the cat. I told him that wasn't against the law but he said we didn't know the laws in Salem and they were different than Bangor. So we snuck onto the bus. And then the bus started filling up so we stayed where we were. We got off at the wax museum and went in with everyone else."

"You were there all night?"

"The place closed and we hid. It's freaky, especially at night. Rory was scared. We slept in a cell. That's where the witches were locked up."

"Why didn't you call me?"

"Our cell phone batteries were dead. We figured we'd find you in the morning."

"I was worried sick."

"Sorry. You know, these people that they said were witches were regular people. The ones who wanted to hurt them said the witches had the devil inside of them so they jailed them and hung them if they didn't admit to being a witch. A bunch admitted it even though it wasn't true. They didn't want to die. But there were these three or four people who were too proud to admit to being something they weren't. They were hung and their bodies were left hanging from nooses for all the townspeople to see. Do you ever feel like the devil is inside you?"

"What kind of a question is that?"

"Rory says he feels like the devil is inside him. Makes him do things he doesn't want to do. He says he's going to stop talking so he doesn't get into any more trouble. Did Rory's dad really kill dolphins?"

"I don't think so."

"I know the devil is inside of me." Trish patted her belly.

CHAPTER FORTY-SIX

Archer focused on the highway, her hands tight on the steering wheel. Her thoughts jumped from Rory to Trish to the judgeship to Grandma Rose to Campbell's hands on her again.

"What?" Trish asked from the passenger seat.

"I didn't say anything."

"You didn't have to. You just got a big smile on your face."

Archer blushed. She breathed easier when her phone rang.

"Detective O'Neill," Archer said. She had programmed the woman's number into her phone, knowing her contact with O'Neill was far from over.

"You know Rory's with me, right?" O'Neill asked.

"I saw him get into your car at the wax museum."

"I'm taking him to his father's."

"That's fine. Trish told me. Thanks for helping them. Where's Rory now?"

"We're stopped at a gas station in Ogunquit. He's buying snacks. I only have a couple of minutes before he gets back but I need to tell you something." O'Neill was silent for a moment, then released a long breath. "I already told you I was there when Rory was born. What I haven't said is that when you couldn't pick him up right away because of the storm, he lived with me until you came and got him."

"What?"

"Rory was born in the storage room at The Crow's Nest during the storm.

Came like a week early. Kitty was alone. She wouldn't close the bar when the contractions started but then the weather got too bad and she couldn't get to the hospital herself. I responded to her 911 call because all the patrol guys and paramedics were busy. She went crazy, Archer. She thought he was the devil. She thought I was the devil and we'd been friends for years. When you picked up Rory at the airport, that was me. I handed him to you. You don't remember me but I remember you clearly. I can still smell his yellow blanket." There was a crack in O'Neill's voice. "Rory was supposed to be my son. I wanted to adopt him but Kitty wouldn't agree. She didn't want the devil living in Gloucester. It doesn't matter, I couldn't legally adopt back then since I'm gay."

Archer pressed two fingers to her left temple to stop the noise in her head. She looked at Trish who was staring out the window, uninterested in her conversation.

"Why are you telling me this now, Detective?" Archer asked.

"Rory's special. And it's time you started calling me Ellen. Here comes Rory. I have to go."

The call was disconnected. Archer closed her phone.

"She's right," Trish said after several seconds. "Rory is special." She leaned her head on Archer's shoulder. "Just like his bonus mom."

CHAPTER FORTY-SEVEN

Archer exited the highway on to Main Street in Bangor. She pulled behind an abandoned video store, its windows boarded with plywood, and parked near a trailhead into the City Forest

"What are we doing here?" Trish asked.

Archer hesitated. "I don't know what to do."

"About what?"

"About you. You won't let me call the police. I can't take you to your home. I guess you could come home with me but I would have to speak to your mother first and…"

"I want to go to my home," Trish interrupted.

"But I thought you said you weren't going home. What about your Uncle? I mean, your mother's boyfriend."

"I've been thinking about how you're always there for Rory. Maybe I need to be there for my mom."

Tears welled in Archer's eyes. She took Trish's hand. "Honey, it's not your responsibility to take care of your mother. She's an adult."

"Rory takes care of you."

"What do you mean?"

"He's always telling me how he cheers you up when you're sad and he makes you olive sandwiches. He says you can't fix anything in the house so he has to do it for you."

"That's all true but Raven is abusive to you. And your mom hurts you too."

"Rory's not always nice to you and you still love him."

Archer sighed. She was one of the best litigators in town but she couldn't win an argument with this teenage girl.

"As long as I'm home," Trish said, "Uncle Raven doesn't hit my mom."

"Your mother didn't even care you were gone." Archer said, feeling desperate. *How could she possibly let this girl go back to that environment?*

"She doesn't mean it. She just has a funny way of showing things. Please take me home."

"No."

"Fine." Trish opened the car door. "I can walk from here. The trailer park is on the other side of the woods."

"Wait."

"No."

Archer grabbed her wrist. "Don't…"

Trish wriggled free, her face quickly turning red. "Fuck off." She ran into the City Forest.

Archer reached for the door handle, debating whether to go after her. Archer loved the City Forest. Each time she ran its trails or biked its paths, she felt she was immersed in a perfect, peaceful world. If only she and Rory could complete the loop behind their house and through the City Forest. But Archer wasn't in the mood to chase after Trish. She didn't even know who this girl was. One moment nice and sweet, the other a monster. Besides, with Rory to worry about, she didn't have the time nor the energy to take on another troubled teen.

Rory. She knew she shouldn't go to Wayne's house but she had no choice. What was she supposed to do? Where was she supposed to go? Home and act like everything was fine and dandy? Go to work tomorrow like nothing was wrong? She drove back to Main Street, through downtown Bangor and into a residential area of neat homes, appropriately called Bangor boxes, four square rooms, few closets. Wayne and Marybeth did not live in the wealthiest part of town, but they were comfortable. She pulled into the driveway of the small, well-maintained home. Along the path to the front door, a limp scarecrow hung on a broomstick. Its arms and legs were stuffed with hay. It wore a red and brown flannel shirt and denim pants. Archer stopped. The shirt—she had bought it for Wayne for his thirty-fifth birthday. She pulled at the broom stick. The scarecrow toppled to the ground. Triumphant, she walked up three cement steps and knocked on the front door. Mary Beth answered.

"Where's Wayne?" Archer tried not to look at the start of her baby bump, but was pleased to note that Marybeth was dressed in the same outfit as the scarecrow, Wayne's shirt included.

Mary Beth took a step back. She was 13 years younger than Wayne and had decided that Wayne was the man for her while Wayne was still married to Archer. Having won the prize, Mary Beth now reminded Archer of a puppy being respectful of the older dog.

"If I wanted to hurt you, I would have done it a long time ago. Where's Wayne and where's Rory?" Archer barked.

"Who is it?" Wayne called.

Archer walked past Mary Beth, through the mud room, down a small foyer and into the living room. The house was clean and orderly. Fresh baked chocolate chip cookies cooled on a rack on the stove top. Pillows were neatly arranged on a brown couch in the living room. A love seat with a homemade quilt thrown over it was perpendicular to the couch. Books were alphabetically arranged by author on wooden shelves; no doubt with Wayne's handwriting on the title pages declaring the start and finish dates for each read, grading each book on a scale from one to five. Thimbles lined glass shelves, Mary Beth's prized collection. An upright piano sat in the corner.

Wayne walked in, his salt and pepper hair shaggy and falling into his eyes. He wore a University Of Maine t-shirt, ripped jeans and old sneakers, his typical Sunday attire.

"What do you want?" he asked.

"I want my son. Where is he?"

"You can't have him. I have a Court order that says…"

"That says you're a coward. You couldn't file in Bangor? You had to go to Portland where you could fool the Court into believing your lies."

"You know a lot of people here. I didn't want to get a biased judge."

"You're manipulating the system and you're using Rory so I can support your baby."

"That has nothing to do with it."

"Bullshit. Where is he?"

"Have you been drinking?"

"Of course not. Let's settle this now. You want money? I don't have any but maybe I can borrow from my mother. How about that? She was always so nice to you. I'm sure she'd be happy to give me blood money just to get rid of you."

"Talk to Finelli."

"I'm not talking to Finelli. He's a scumbag. How much of a retainer did he rip you off for? Correction, how much did he rip Mary Beth off? What are you trying to prove anyway? That you can be a better parent? How are you going to be in your plays, and work, and take care of little Ms. Princess and your baby? Where is Mary Beth anyway? Let me ask her how she's going to feel having a newborn and Rory in the house at the same time."

"Leave her out of this."

"Leave her out of this? Are you fucking kidding me? You wouldn't be doing this except for her. Does she know what it's like to raise Rory? Is this her idea? Maybe I'll have to pay enough child support so neither of you will have to work. Great idea."

"Calm down, Archer."

"Don't tell me what to do. You don't remember what it's like to parent him, do you? Remember how hard it was to discipline him, to get him to go to bed, to stop screaming, to eat, to stop holding his breath. Remember all the time outs, that stupid 1-2-3 Magic thing, the sticker charts? He's different, Wayne. Or have you forgotten? He doesn't respond like other kids."

"Mary Beth says . . . . "

"Mary Beth says? What the fuck does Mary Beth know? She's fifteen years old..."

"She's thirty."

"I don't care what Ms. Princess says. She may have gotten in the middle of my marriage but she isn't going to get in the middle of my parenting. Where's Rory?"

"He's not here."

"Ellen should have gotten him here by now. And where is Mary Beth?" Archer looked around the living room, the realization hitting her. "Oh, shit. I've been acting crazy and you haven't yelled back or kicked me out of the house. You're too calm. What are you up to?"

"Nothing," he said.

"Always the actor, aren't you? I'm going. Let me know when Rory arrives. It should be soon." She walked out the front door, kicking the toppled scarecrow as she passed down the walkway

As she was getting into her car, a police car stopped in front of the driveway, blocking her in. Campbell stepped out.

Archer walked to him. "What are you doing here?"

She looked toward the house. Wayne and Mary Beth stood in the doorway, his arm around her waist. Mary Beth leaned into him and smiled.

"Here," Campbell held out a stack of papers folded in thirds.

"What's this?" She opened them, read the title page. "Restraining order? I can't have contact with Rory? Are you kidding?" She leaned against the police car, flipped the pages until she got to the narrative. She recognized Wayne's handwriting. Archer read out-loud. "My ex-wife has a drinking problem which has affected her ability to care for our son. She has allowed him to take vodka to school. She lets him associate with kids who are troublemakers. He recently stole a car. She allows him to carry a bullet in his pocket, as well as other weapons such as pocket knives and large wrenches." Archer looked at Wayne and Mary Beth. "This is a joke, right?" She looked back at the pleadings, continued to read. "She recently removed Rory from the state of Maine without my permission or knowledge. His bedroom is unsanitary and dangerous. There are holes in the walls, electrical wires and discarded food scattered throughout. She doesn't make him do his homework. He put locks on his bedroom door because he is afraid of his mother. I am remarried and my wife is going to have a baby. We would provide a stable home for Rory and he would have a father figure." She looked at Wayne again. "You're married?"

"Eight days," Mary Beth said.

Archer looked back at the restraining order. "I have to pay temporary child support?"

Campbell touched her arm. "Do you want me to take you home?"

"No. I'll take myself."

"I'll follow you. Make sure you get home safely."

"I can't have any contact with Rory?" she asked, knowing the answer.

"None at all," Campbell said. "And you can't communicate with him through third parties or go to his school."

"Can I talk to Wayne?"

"Yes."

"Fuck." She said. "Life really does suck."

CHAPTER FORTY-EIGHT

Archer was relieved to finally be home, in her garage, with the Subaru in park. She wasn't really sure how she had gotten there. The drive was a vague memory except for the road that had been blurred by her poor eyesight and even further by her tears, frustration and rage.

A light shone in her rearview mirror. Rory? She turned quickly and saw Campbell's car pulling into the driveway behind her. She hadn't wanted him to follow her but now was glad he was there.

He came into the garage and opened her door. "Let me make you some tea."

He took her arm and led her into the house. She didn't resist his touch, his guidance. In the kitchen, he filled the teapot with water and put it on the gas burner. He took a Chamomile teabag and a mug from the cabinet. She leaned against the counter and watched him expertly navigate the kitchen like a sailor at sea. When he came close to her, she felt his warmth. She closed her eyes and ran her hands over his neck, back, shoulders and arms. He was soft and hard at the same time. She wanted to sink into him and disappear. Make the whole world disappear.

His mouth covered hers. Their tongues snaked together, their teeth gently touched. A soft kiss, then harder. She pulled him into her, her nails on his back, grabbing at him, wanting him closer. He placed his hands on her waist and lifted her on to the counter top. He fondled her with one hand, pulled at his zipper with the other, then reached for her.

At last. They fit together perfectly. She hung on, as tight as she could.

Her head tucked into his chest, safe, warm, hidden. She wanted to stay like this forever.

"I love you," she said as the tea pot let out a high screeched wail.

"What?" His lips brushed against her ear.

"Nothing. Don't stop. Ever."

CHAPTER FORTY-NINE

Almost midnight, dressed in pajamas, Archer fell into her cuddle chair, into the fabric of red poppies. Her eyes ached with exhaustion. Her muscles throbbed from the long day. She leaned to one side and felt underneath. She pulled out a wrench, then a screwdriver, finally a pair of pliers. Rory had been here.

She placed the tools in her lap and smelled him all around. Oil and gas, Axe cologne, noodles, olives and ketchup. She wished he were here in person. She wouldn't even mind if he was sitting in her cuddle chair.

A horn sounded, a quick toot, and Archer jumped up. The tools scattered to the rug. She ran to the front door. Rory? Was Rory home?

The front door was open, the screen door closed. She looked out and saw her mother limping—one leg shorter than the other due to a hip replacement – and rolling a flowered suitcase up the blacktop driveway. Archer hesitated then opened the screen door as the cab drove away.

"It's the middle of the night," Rose said. "You should lock your doors."

"Rory's not here," Archer said, unsure why this was her response.

He's not here and I'm waiting for him to come home? He's not here and he's the one who makes sure the doors and windows are locked each night?

"Where is he?" Rose stopped at the bottom of the three steps leading to the white porch.

Archer sprung out the door. "Let me get that." She grabbed the handle of the suitcase.

"I got it." Rose waved her away.

"I can help you."

"Don't treat me like an old lady."

Archer leaped back. Step-by-step, Rose lugged the bag up the stairs while Archer watched. Helpless. Again. Rose rested on the landing.

"Why are you here?" Archer asked. "How come you took a cab? Where's your car?" She lunged for the suitcase.

Rose pushed her hand away and reached for the door. "Who needs a car?"

"Wait," Archer put her hand on the screen. "I need some answers from you. Is everything okay?"

"Just fine. Where's Rory?"

"He's not here."

"I know that. He'd be down here already if he were home offering to make me popcorn. Is he with Wayne? That's good they're finally spending time together."

Archer opened the door and watched her mother roll in. "Wayne has temporary custody," she said to her back.

Rose turned sharply. "Temporary custody. Of Rory?" she laughed.

"I didn't expect you to laugh, mom."

"Wayne won't last long with Rory. What happened?"

"I don't want to talk about it. I'm tired. Just tell me why you're here."

"Guess I don't want to talk about that either." She left her suitcase at the bottom of the staircase and went into the kitchen. "Do you have any of that chicken a la king left over?"

"Rory ate it. I'll make you toast."

Rose looked her up, then down. "Is that what you're wearing?"

"To bed? Yes, mother."

"Take your bottoms off. They're too long. I can do a quick hem."

"They're pajamas. That's ridiculous."

"What's ridiculous is dragging those pant legs on the ground. What if you trip?"

"Mom, what's going on?"

Rose sighed. "My house is being foreclosed and my car was repossessed. And you?"

"Wayne got a restraining order. I can't have any contact with Rory."

Her mother's expression shifted like a grey, wilted flower. Tears filled her cataract eyes. Archer felt a tightening in her own throat. She focused on making toast.

CHAPTER FIFTY

Grandma Rose was asleep in the guest room. The sun was peeking in through the front door window and sending a beam of light up the staircase. Archer stood outside Rory's closed bedroom door; her cell phone jammed into her pajama bottom pocket in case Rory called.

It was quiet, way too quiet. No thumping bass throughout the house, no stomping feet, no uproarious laughter at reruns of *The Three Stooges*. Archer leaned against his door. She wanted to stay frozen in this spot until Rory came home but she couldn't think of any legitimate reason to skip work. She knew it would probably do her good to go to the office and be distracted from the mess of her life. But, if she was going to go, she needed to move now. Now, before she got back into bed. Now, before she shut out the world.

Her cell phone rang. She reached for it quickly.

"What time does he need to be at school?" Wayne asked.

"Why don't you ask him?" she snapped.

"He won't tell me."

"Eight o'clock." She hung up.

With no clients scheduled, she could dress casually. She pulled on jeans and a button down pink corduroy shirt and set out into the world.

In her office, Archer looked at the same files she had failed to work on last week, the same cases she hadn't worked on the week before either.

Delores walked in.

"I need a bigger desk," Archer said.

"You have a lot of messages."

"Anything good?"

"Some new clients."

"Anything bad? No, don't tell me. I'll find out soon enough."

She turned on her computer. The screensaver scrolled through pictures of Rory. She opened her e-mails.

My client does not accept your proposal. Why don't you give me a reasonable offer so we can negotiate for real? Sincerely yours, white, middle-aged male attorney with bad toupee and terrible breath.

How much does she want for spousal support? If it's too much, my client says he's moving to Brazil where his second cousin lives. Best regards, female lawyer with Napoleon syndrome.

Dick wants to take the children to his mother's house in Ohio for Thanksgiving. Last time he took them on a trip, my thirteen year old daughter came home with a belly button ring and my nine year old son shaved his head. What do I do? From, freaked-out soon-to-be ex-wife.

It never ended. Other people's problems. She knew that was what she was paid for and she was good at resolving *their* issues. Archer deleted e-mails. Saved others. They blended together. Complaints about this, objections to that.

Her cell phone rang. Wayne again.

"Did you get him to school?" Archer asked.

"Yeah. You know, he wears a black sweatshirt and pulls the hood over his head and face all the time."

"I know."

"And everything he wears has a skull on it. You think that's okay?"

"I don't know how to stop him."

"He looks creepy. When I dropped him at school, I suggested he try out for the football team or audition for the drama club."

Archer sighed, deeply. "Why are you calling me?"

"Should we be worried about him? He wouldn't talk to me all night. Just kept writing notes."

"What do you mean he wouldn't talk to you?"

"Just like I said. The last thing he said before he stopped talking was that he was tired of getting into trouble all the time. That's not normal."

"Of course it's not normal. Haven't you been listening to me for the last several years?" She shut her office door.

"What do the doctors say?" Wayne asked.

"About how to get him to wear Abercrombie & Fitch and play football and take a girl to the movies?" The words rocketed from her throat. "They don't say anything. Okay? Nobody knows what to do."

"Mary Beth's brother plays football at the University of Maine. We're going to take Rory to a practice this weekend. Maybe he'll take an interest in football."

She sighed again; reminding herself to breathe. "I have work to do. What do you want from me?"

"I need to fill out these forms for health insurance and life insurance. Should I add Rory?"

"What are you talking about?"

"I quit my job at the library."

"What?"

"Mary Beth's working and she has health insurance for us."

"Why did you quit your job?"

"I'm going to try again. I got that part in the play in New Hampshire. I really think I can make it this time. I need to be able to focus on that."

"Are you serious?"

"Mary Beth makes enough money. She can support us."

"Why are you doing this?"

"Everybody at the repertory says I have real talent."

"I mean why are you doing this about Rory? You don't really want him."

"Mary Beth says…"

"Do me a favor," she yelled. "Never mention that phony June Cleaver to me again."

She threw the cell phone across the room, hitting a hanging photo of five-year-old Rory beaming over the first fish he ever caught. The frame crashed to the ground. The glass shattered. Her cell phone lay on the floor in two pieces.

Archer put the battery back in her phone and turned it on. It still worked. She tried to focus on the stacks of files on her desk. The blue files indicating divorce meshed with the green ones for paternity cases. She looked back at her computer.

Lou hasn't paid the mortgage for three months. The bank called and said they are going to foreclose. The kids and I will have to move out. I don't know where to go. Help me Archer. Jessica Stroud.

Sometimes, it was scary to Archer how much her clients relied upon her to save them from the mess of their lives. Archer quickly shot back an e-mail to Jessica: *Sit tight. Don't panic. I'll take care of it.* She pressed send.

"Delores," Archer called. The office walls were so thin they didn't need an intercom. "Finelli is supposed to deliver the discovery in England by two this afternoon. Give him until five after and if he doesn't show up, file a motion to show cause."

Delores walked into her office. "He's already called. He needs until tomorrow. Said something about his dad being sick."

"Of course." Archer rifled through an appraisal of a cute little house on the west side of Bangor. It too would probably get foreclosed upon. She pushed the file aside. Her eyes grew wide when she looked underneath and saw a Notice of Hearing. "Shit. I have to be in court for the Marchwinski Final Hearing in….," she looked at her watch, "…five minutes. Do I still have those black pants here? I can't go to court in jeans."

Delores spoke quickly. "Your black pants are hanging in the closet. I'll grab her file and get tea for Judge Murphy's bailiff. You know Joe enjoys his Monday morning tea from you. I never saw that notice of hearing otherwise I would have docketed it. I'm sorry, Archer. I'm really sorry, I must have put it in a wrong pile and…"

Archer knew all about mistakes. "No problem. Your boss is high-maintenance. I hope she's paying you well."

Delores smiled. "Not bad, but she can make up for it with a nice fall bonus."

"Yeah, don't I know it," Archer said as she changed pants. "Hey, can you order one of those rolling carts I can use to carry files to court? I keep meaning to ask you."

"Sure."

"Excellent." Archer ran out the door, pleased she had at least remembered to ask Delores about the cart.

CHAPTER FIFTY-ONE

Cheryl Marchwinski was thirty-five years old. She had discovered her husband was having an affair with an eighteen-year-old girl when she found the tassel from the girl's high school graduation in his car. Out of guilt, he had agreed to everything Cheryl wanted in the divorce. Unfortunately, there had only been debt to divide.

"Sorry I'm late." Archer saw Cheryl huddled with her three sisters. Their wide grins lit the dim hallway.

"That's okay," Cheryl said, "we're planning a few hours of freedom. After this, we're going to the mall and then to Chili's for lunch. "

Archer's phone vibrated. Bangor High School. Shit. She walked away from the women. "Hello?"

"Hey, it's Kara. How are you?"

"Is Rory okay?"

"I was going to ask you the same thing. He's allowed to come back to school today."

"I know."

"He's not here."

"What? Wayne said he dropped him off this morning."

"No one has seen him."

"You're kidding. Did you call his dad?"

"Why would I call him?"

"He has temporary custody."

"No way. How did that happen? Why didn't you tell me? Are you okay?"

"Yeah, I'm fine. A lot has happened. Sorry I've been out-of-touch. It's been crazy. I'll tell you later. I'm in court right now. Can you call Wayne?"

"Sure."

"I'll check back with you after my hearing." Archer hung up. She counted down from ten, timing it perfectly. 5 – 4- 3- 2- 1 – her phone vibrated again.

"Kara just called me. Rory's not at school," Wayne said. "I dropped him in front. I swear. What are we going to do?"

"Marchwinski v. Marchwinski," the bailiff called.

"I'm going into a hearing," Archer watched the three sisters, grinning, their arms interlocked. A twinge of jealousy settled in Archer's stomach.

"You're going into a hearing? What about our son? You don't care about him. It's so obvious. Work, work, work, that's all you care about."

"Me? That's all I care about?" she seethed, keeping her voice low. "You're the one without a job, remember? You're the one who has temporary custody. Find him, Wayne. Look in his favorite places."

"His favorite places? What are his favorite places?"

"You're pathetic."

"If you hadn't alienated him from me…"

Archer saw Cheryl and her sisters high-five each other as they walked into the Judge's chambers. Cheryl looked at Archer and gave her a thumbs-up sign. Cheryl's words reverberated in Archer's head. *We're planning a few hours of freedom.*

"I have to go. The hearing is starting." she headed toward them.

"Wait. What about Rory?"

"Find him, Wayne."

"You're not going to help?"

A few hours of freedom.

"Of course I am."

"When?"

"As soon as I can." She snapped the phone shut wondering if she would dare take a few hours of freedom for herself.

CHAPTER FIFTY-TWO

Archer looked up from the brief she was writing, amazed she had been able to engross herself in work. Wayne hadn't been able to locate Rory. After leaving the courthouse, Archer had driven by the Mobil-to-go and the trailer park where Trish lived. No Rory. She had left several messages on his cell phone and had texted him repeatedly; even though she knew this was in violation of the restraining order. No response. Even Grandma Rose wasn't returning her calls. Wayne had told her not to worry, he would find him. But worrying about Rory was her specialty. That, and solving other people's problems. She had been able to successfully negotiate with the bank on behalf of Jessica Stroud, giving her at least two months before the bank would foreclose on her home; plenty of time for the divorce to be resolved.

An e-mail from the judicial selection committee appeared in her in-box. She opened it, pleased the interview had been rescheduled for the following day. With so much going wrong, it was nice that one thing could go right.

It was already four o'clock. She had given Wayne enough time to locate Rory. She was no longer letting Wayne run this show. He had done enough damage. Starting when Archer had said "I do." It was time for her to get out there and find Rory.

"A Detective O'Neill is on the phone." Delores yelled through the walls.

Archer lifted the phone to her ear and took a deep breath. "Ellen?"

"I have Rory."

She exhaled. "Thank God. Is he under arrest?"

"No."

"Is he okay? Where is he? I can't pick him up. You know his father has a restraining order that prevents me from having contact with Rory. The hearing isn't for another week."

"He's fine. He's in Gloucester."

"Gloucester? How'd he get there?"

"Your mother brought him."

"You're kidding?"

"No, here, you talk to him."

"Wait. What about the restraining order?"

"I won't tell anyone."

"But…"

"Hi, Mom." Archer was cut off by Rory's greeting.

"Hi, Sweetie. What's going on?"

"I need to meet her. I need to know what she's like and why I have all these problems. I'm not coming home until I meet her. Grandma Rose says everyone should know where they come from."

Archer sighed. "Does daddy know where you are?"

"No, and I'm not telling him. He wants me to play football like Marybeth's brother and be in plays like him. I'm not like him. Or anybody else. I had to leave or I was going to explode. Too much stress. And you better not tell him where I am or else I'm never coming home. Ever."

"Where's Grandma?"

"Right here, with me."

"Why did she take you there?"

"Cause I asked her to, that's why."

"Where are you going to stay?"

"Detective O'Neill said she took care of me when I was a baby before you and dad picked me up. Did you know that? She said Grandma and I could stay here if it was okay with you."

"Let me talk to Detective O'Neill." Archer picked up the restraining order from her desk, viewed the cover page. Wayne Falcon vs. Archer Falcon. *Give me a break.* She crumpled it into a ball. She didn't need to read it again. Especially the one line that killed her the most: *No direct or indirect contact with Rory.*

"Yes," Ellen said.

"You need to call his father. Rory knows the number."

"Rory begged me not to call him. And I have to tell you," she lowered her voice, "I don't know if Kitty will agree to meet him under any circumstance."

"Please call his father. Let him handle this."

Ellen continued speaking as if she hadn't heard a thing Archer had said. "I can't believe how big and handsome he is. I was the first to see him. He had a thick head of black hair. Kitty was screaming like I'd never heard. I caught him, Archer. I actually caught Rory in my hands. It was the most amazing experience I've ever had. She didn't want him and I wanted him so badly. I never thought she'd reject him like that. How can you hate a baby?"

The little baby with Down Syndrome in Texas flashed in Archer's mind but she knew Ellen's question was rhetorical. Archer hadn't hated that baby—just herself. She glanced at her computer, clicked on a new instant message.

Archer, Thank you so much. The bank just called. I don't know what I would have done without your help. You're the greatest lawyer I know. Jessica had inserted several smiley faces at the end of the message.

"Archer, are you still there?" Ellen asked.

Archer typed back, *I am glad I could help.*

"Archer? Do you want to talk to your mother?"

Rose got on the phone before Archer could respond.

"I know you're mad but he was so insistent and you know it's impossible to say no to Rory and…"

"It's okay, Mom."

"Huh?'"

"It's okay. We'll talk about it later."

"You're not mad?"

"Of course I am. I'm furious that you drove him to Gloucester but I'm also ecstatic that you're both safe."

"You're a great mother, Archer."

Archer sighed, wishing she believed that were true.

"Mom, give the phone back to Ellen."

"You coming to get him?" Ellen asked.

"No, I can't. Call Rory's father," Archer said. "There's nothing I can do. I'm not violating the restraining order." She took the crumpled document from her desk and tossed it into the waste paper basket.

CHAPTER FIFTY-THREE

"What is the most important constitutional amendment?" Jude Chisolm asked.

Archer looked across the table at Jude. She was a few years older than Archer, wore her salt and pepper hair cut short around her ears and spiked on top and was a partner at a large insurance defense firm in Orono. She and Archer had been opponents several times and had always gotten along well. One time, between hearings, she remembered speaking to Jude about how difficult it was to raise Rory.

But this? Talk about lawyering 101. Archer looked to the remaining five members of the Governor's Judicial Selection Committee. No one else seemed to feel the question carried with it a patronizing tone.

Archer had been pleased the governor had allowed her to quickly re-schedule this interview. And after almost twenty minutes into the interview, things seemed to be going well. She mulled the question over. *The most important constitutional amendment?* She thought about Wayne's accusations against her. She considered Justice Hathorne sentencing people to death who wouldn't admit they were witches. She thought of all the people falsely accused throughout history simply because they were different.

As she was about to speak, her cell phone vibrated in her pocket. She should have gone with her first instinct and turned it off but she had left it on in case Rory needed her. A sinking feeling lodged in her gut.

She spoke quickly. "The Sixth Amendment right to confront one's accuser is a very important amendment intended to guarantee that truth be discovered and justice done."

Jim Smith nodded in agreement.

Archer glanced down into her pocket and looked at her phone. It was Ellen.

She held the phone up for the committee to see. "I'm sorry. I have to take this."

Without giving them the opportunity to protest, she ran out of the large courtroom where the interview was being held and into the lobby. It was five thirty in the evening and the halls were empty.

"Is Rory okay? Have you talked to Wayne?"

"Everything's okay now," Ellen said. "Rory was cited for vandalism about an hour ago. I had to run an errand. I didn't think it'd be a problem leaving him alone with your mother. He told your mother he was bored and he went for a walk. An officer caught him spray-painting a wall."

"Like graffiti?"

"He was spray-painting over a swastika on the side of an overpass. We've been getting complaints about that swastika all week. I had some spray paint in my garage. While he was walking, Rory saw the symbol, came back and got the paint. It's illegal to deface state property, even if it's something despicable. I wouldn't have arrested him but this officer was a rookie and… I can get the charges dropped but Rory is really upset."

"I can't talk to him, Ellen, remember?"

"I know the restraining order's in effect but he won't talk to his dad. I've tried. I've spoken to Wayne on the phone like five times. He wants to come here but Rory says he'll run away if he sees him. I don't know what else to do."

"All right," Archer sighed, weighing the risk of jail for violating the restraining order versus Rory running away. Again. She'd rather go to jail. "Let me speak to him."

Archer heard shuffling, then Rory's panicked voice jetting through the receiver. "Mom, I hate that swastika thing. It means killing and hurting people and I don't know why anyone would want to paint it there. Did you know that the swastika dates back to Ancient India and it meant good luck? Like a lucky charm. It wasn't until Hitler did all those really bad things to the Jews that the swastika came to mean something really bad. When I saw it on that overpass, I couldn't get it out of my mind. Over six million Jews were killed. And not just Jews but gay people and poor people and people with diseases. I bet they killed people just because they had Asperger's Syndrome. Do you think I would have been killed? I'm not Jewish but I do have Asperger's. I had to cover it up, mom, to get it out of my thoughts. Then the cop came. I told him that covering it was good but he was mean, just like those Nazis were."

Maybe she should have told the Judicial Selection Committee that the First Amendment, the freedom of speech, was the most important constitutional amendment. It certainly was to Rory.

"Rory," Archer began, "if you have thoughts like that you need to talk to someone before acting on them. I know you were doing something good but just because it's good doesn't mean it's legal. You need to let adults handle things like that." Blah, blah, blah. Archer felt stupid, lecturing him about covering up a message of hatred and death. What she wanted to do was beam herself to Gloucester, wrap her arms around her son, and take him out for a celebratory olive pizza.

"I'll try," Rory said. "I'm going to talk to Kitty tomorrow. Bye." He hung up.

Archer looked at her phone and slowly closed it. She returned to the courtroom, hoping the interview would soon be over. Restraining order or not, she needed to get to Gloucester.

As soon as Archer was seated, Jim Smith spoke. "We know your work day is sometimes cut short to deal with family issues. Can you commit to the regular hours of a judge?"

Archer shifted in her seat. This interview was long from over. She wondered if she could refuse to answer the question, claiming her Fifth Amendment right to be free from self-incrimination.

CHAPTER FIFTY-FOUR

Archer drove home. Despite Ellen's phone call and Rory's latest debacle, Archer was content. It seemed like the committee had liked her. She even felt she had handled the Rory question well. And now, she was taking control again. She was going to Gloucester to be with her son. Fuck the restraining order.

Her phone rang. She didn't recognize the number.

"Hello?" She asked tentatively.

"Archer Falcon?"

"Yes?"

What has Rory done now?

"This is Kitty Warren."

The Subaru swerved onto the shoulder of the road. Archer turned the steering wheel to the left. The overcompensation sent the vehicle to the opposite lane. She slammed on the brakes and stopped perpendicular to the two lane roadway.

"Hold on, hold on," she yelled, her heart beating wildly.

Grateful for the rarely traveled roads, Archer pulled the car to the side and parked, her hands shaking. She put the phone back to her ear, breathed heavily.

"I need to talk to you about your boy," Kitty said. "Tell him not to contact me anymore."

"Why?"

"Don't you get it? My mama was right. He shoulda' never been. The devil put him inside of me and the devil took him out."

"I don't understand."

"Witches shouldn't have children," Kitty said. "I know I agreed to have the baby and all but I thought I was in love. I thought we could make it work. Witches shouldn't fall in love either."

"Witches?"

"Rory keeps calling the Crow's Nest, saying he wants to know why he is what he is. Tell him to leave me alone."

Archer stared at her phone. It read, call ended. She wasn't sure why but she thought of little Rory, twenty-two months old or so, bopping about the living room on Maple Street, running gleefully from their golden retriever, to Archer, and back to the dog again. Rory was her monkey, crashing into the cushions of the couch, laughing with proud hilarity at his escapades. She remembered the dog, so patient with the screeching and movement of the bouncing ball of boy energy. Back then, she could sit on the sofa all day and watch them. And when Rory finally tired, he would come to her with his dinosaur blanket, his "gacket", and crawl into her lap. He would fall asleep as soon as he had burrowed in. He had only two gears back then – frenetic and sleeping. Now, it was only frenetic.

She dialed Wayne. "I need to go to Gloucester and talk to Rory. He's not safe. I'm afraid without intervention he'll end up back in the hospital. Maybe he needs his meds adjusted. The signs are all there."

"What do you want me to do?"

"Drop the fucking restraining order," she screamed.

"This isn't my fault," he yelled, "if you took better care of him and didn't disappear at the end of the work day . . . ."

"What?"

"I called Delores this afternoon. She didn't know where you were."

"Give me a fucking break. I haven't been out in years and you know that. My life is Rory 24/7. Everything else I do fits in around him. I barely have time to work. I can't tell you the last time I saw a movie. If you were a better father…"

"I'd be a better father if you'd stop alienating him from me. That's why I filed the protection order."

"You need to drop it so I can take care of our son…"

"Okay."

"…you're making everything worse. You and Mary Beth think life fits into a neat package. With Rory, nothing is neat, nothing is as expected, nothing is…"

"I said, okay," Wayne yelled. "If you would stop talking and listen to me for a change, I said okay. He won't talk to me anyway. He didn't sleep at all last night. He spent the whole night pacing and talking to himself. Not saying anything that made sense. Something about a tree and leaves. I can't do it, Archer. I'm going to drop the protection order."

Archer wasn't sure whether the dread she felt in her chest and throat had come from Wayne's admission of defeat, from her fear for Rory's future, or from the actual confirmation that she was going to parent Rory alone.

"Drop it tomorrow. I'm going to Gloucester first thing in the morning."

"Fine. You know, Archer, I'm not the bad guy. I want what's best for him. I'll show you with my new baby what a good father I can be."

She didn't let him finish, hung up and speed dialed Campbell. "Can you take me somewhere tomorrow? I can go myself but…I don't know. I guess I don't feel strong enough. I want a ride to Gloucester."

"You were just there. What's up with that place that you want to go there again?"

"Rory's there."

"By himself? I thought he was with Wayne."

"He ran away."

"How'd he get there?"

"My mother drove him."

"You're kidding?"

"No. I haven't gotten the details yet of why she took him. I don't know what she was thinking. All I know is Rory wants to meet his birth mother who lives in Gloucester but I think she's a nut and it's just going to make everything worse for Ror. I need to go get him."

"What about the protection order?"

"Wayne is going to dismiss it. He's giving up. I told him he could have Rory and he changed his mind. Suddenly paying child support doesn't seem so bad to him."

"Where are they staying in Gloucester?"

"With Detective Ellen O'Neill."

Archer waited for a response.

"Are you there?" Archer asked.

"Yeah. What's he doing with her?"

"She was at Rory's birth. She delivered him during a storm. She had wanted to adopt him but I guess decided against it. I don't know what I'm going to do." She let the tears flow. "I know I can't save him but I have to find a way to help him. I feel so bad for him. I mean, how is he going to finish high school, get a job, have normal relationships?"

"I hate Gloucester."

"Did you hear what I said?"

"Yes, I'm sorry. I know the situation with Rory is hard. I wish I could help him too. You know he's very special to me. I'm sorry. I can't take you to Gloucester."

"Why do you hate that place so much?"

"It's an old smelly fishing town that isn't even making any money off of fishing anymore."

"What do you know about Gloucester or about fishing? And who cares? I just want to go there, get Rory, bring him home and have things go back to normal." She laughed at the irony, the impossibility of anything every being normal.

"I have to work," Campbell said.

"24/7?"

"No, but...okay, we'll pick him up and bring him right home. I'm on duty until midnight. I'll be at your house around eight in the morning."

"Thanks."

"You'll owe me big for this."

She pictured his impish grin through the phone. "I know," she said, hoping to pay him back soon.

CHAPTER FIFTY-FIVE

Pulling into her driveway, Archer saw the familiar shape of a hooded, hunched-over teenager on her front stoop. For a moment, she wondered if Rory had come home. But it wasn't Rory. It was Trish, wearing Rory's University of Florida sweatshirt. She pulled into the garage and walked to Trish, huddled like the runaway she probably was.

Archer sat next to her. "Are you okay?"

"Yeah," Trish's hands were stuffed in the front pocket of the sweat shirt.

"Does your mom know you're here?"

Trish shrugged.

"What's wrong?" Archer asked.

"Can I have something to eat?"

"First tell me why you're here."

"Forget it. I'll walk to the Mobil-to-go," Trish got up.

"No, come in."

They entered the house; Archer flipping lights as they walked to the kitchen. She opened the refrigerator.

"There's yogurt, apples, bacon. I can make you a peanut butter and jelly sandwich or Rory's specialty – noodles, ketchup and black olives. There might be some left over in this container..."

She turned toward Trish who leaned against the counter, her hood lowered, her face revealed. Under her left eye was a gash about two inches long. There was clear tape over it to keep the wound shut. Surrounding her eye was the purple and red beginnings of a shiner. Her right cheek was bruised.

Archer ran to her. "What happened?"

"I told my mom I was pregnant. I don't know why I told her; I just did. She hit me in the eye and I fell and hit my face on the back of a chair." She rubbed her cheek. "It really hurts."

"We need to put ice on it." Archer gently lifted Trish's chin and looked at her eye. "I think we need to get that looked at. You'll probably need stitches."

"No way. I'm not going to the hospital." Trish pulled away.

"Do you want to talk to the police? I can call Officer Campbell."

"No, she'll kill me. And if she doesn't, he will."

"Who? Your uncle? I mean, her boyfriend?"

"It doesn't matter. Can I just have some ice?"

"Sure." Archer leaned into the freezer, wondering why she was once again following the instructions of a demanding teenager. As the adult, wasn't she supposed to take control, wasn't she supposed to make good decisions for Rory? And now, for Trish?

"You know," Trish's voice wafted from behind Archer. "No one's ever been nicer to me than Rory. I really love him."

Archer turned to Trish and raised her eyebrows.

"Not like that. In a brotherly way." Trish took the ice pack from Archer. She walked toward the cuddle chair. "Is it okay if I sit here?"

Trish sank into the chair without waiting for an answer. Her legs curled under her. She wrapped her arms around her chest, Rory's big sweatshirt was her cuddly blanket. She had black nail polish on her toes, purple polish on her fingernails. The left side of her face lay on the arm of the chair. The ice pack rested on her right cheek and eye. Trish fit perfectly in the cuddle chair. Before Archer could say anything else, offer some motherly advice maybe, she heard the steady breathing of sleep.

Whoever said the twos were terrible had never experienced fifteens.

CHAPTER FIFTY-SIX

Finally in the tub, hot water wrapped around Archer like silk. She toyed with shutting her phone off. Not just putting it on vibrate, shutting it down completely. But she couldn't do it.

She leaned her head on an inflatable pillow. Enjoying the silence, the solitude, visions of a black robe. Could she do it? Could she meet the needs of Rory and the State of Maine? If she received a call during a trial that Rory was drunk at school again, or got into another car accident, or a million other scenarios could she stop the trial and run to her son? She knew the answer. She was the Judge, of course she could. She could do anything she wanted. But how would that make her feel? She had always disliked the judges with black-robe fever; egos bigger than the courthouse. The ones who felt they were not subject to any rules or laws; or just common courtesy. She certainly did not want to be *that* kind of judge.

The phone rang. She jumped, water splashed in the tub and over the sides like a mini wave pool. She grabbed for her phone on the tile floor.

"Archer, Is everything okay? Why haven't you called me or answered my calls?"

"Mom, what were you thinking? Kitty doesn't want to meet Rory. How is that going to make Rory feel? She's crazy; like clinically crazy. If he meets her, it will flip him out. And how could you drive him all the way to Massachusetts without checking with me?"

"I couldn't dissuade him. I really tried. He walked home from school. He didn't know I was going to be there. He was going to ride his bicycle to Gloucester."

"You should have called me."

"I didn't want to bother you. I figured we would go to Massachusetts, he'd meet Kitty and that would be that. I thought we'd be back before you got home from work."

"What car did you use?"

"Martha's minivan. She was going to be watching her grandchildren all day so she didn't need it. I just had to run over with her to get her blood pressure checked at Walgreens first, and then . . . ."

"Mom," Archer interrupted, "have I been kind to you?"

"Of course you have, honey. I love you."

"I know you love me but when I was a kid, was I kind to you? Like when we redecorated my room when I was a teenager, I remember the carpet was different colors; oranges and yellows. When we picked it out, was I kind to you?"

"Of course you were, sweetie."

"But are you just saying that? I feel like you only say positive things to me. I can't be perfect."

"No one's perfect. Does this have to do with Rory? Teenagers are supposed to be unkind to their parents."

"No, it has to do with me. When I was growing up, if you were sad, did I know you were sad? Did I ever ask how your day was?"

"Why are you asking all these questions? You were always sweet. You cried at Lassie.

"That really doesn't answer my question."

"I'm sorry. I don't know what you're looking for."

Archer sighed, tried to identify how she was really feeling. Like everything else in her life outside of the law, she felt like she had no clue. "I guess I don't know what I'm looking for either. Don't worry about it."

"I'm here for you anytime."

"I know."

Archer felt her throat restrict, tears build. Why did needing her mother make her feel so bad?

"I'll be in Gloucester tomorrow morning. We'll talk then." She hung up and sunk into the tub, knowing she was shutting her mother out, wondering why as an adult she continued to be unkind to the person who had always treated her the best.

CHAPTER FIFTY-SEVEN

The alarm radio woke Archer at seven. *Don't go changing, to try and please me.* She had slept well. A Great Dane with a fluffy tail had monopolized her dreams, trotting to work with her, through the City Forest, to Bangor High School.

Her phone beeped. She sat up quickly. Had Rory contacted her? There was a text message and a voice mail.

She read the text message. *If ur coming here 2 git me Im not going home until I talk 2 Kitty I mean it dont waste ur time.*

The voice mail was from Wayne. Detective O'Neill called. Rory's in Gloucester. I can't pick him up today. Are you going to get him? I told Finelli to drop the protection order.

Of course, Archer thought, you can't go pick him up; you're too busy and we had already decided you were going to drop the injunction. Why was he presenting it like it was his idea? She kicked thoughts of Wayne out of her head like a rusted and bent tin can.

Archer took a quick shower, dressed, went downstairs and made coffee. Even when Rory was around, her mornings were generally peaceful. While Rory slept, she enjoyed a cup of coffee; hot, sweet and creamy, along with the Boston Globe and the Bangor Daily News. Hell broke loose when it was time to wake him for school.

But it wasn't Rory sleeping in today. It was Trish, who was bent like a question mark on the cuddle chair. She recalled that Trish had a doctor's appointment set for today. Archer put three one hundred dollar bills on the counter and a note.

I hope this works out for you. Fondly, Archer Falcon.

Archer heard a car horn and stepped outside. The air was crisp and clean, the sky aqua blue like a sleepy ocean. It was going to be a good day. She was going to bring Rory home. She waved to Campbell then lowered herself into the revamped 1975 fire engine red Volkswagen Scirocco.

"You're twenty minutes late," she smiled.

"This is the last time I save your ass. I stopped by the station and picked up the dismissal of the protection order."

"Thanks." She kissed him on the cheek then drew herself back.

"I'm going to require more of a thank you than that," Campbell said. "I hate Gloucester. Goddamn fishing town stinks."

"How come you're so grumpy this morning?" This was not the feigned, playful belligerence Archer was used to from Campbell.

"Long night, that's all. Where are we going in Gloucester?"

"To Detective O'Neill's house."

"He's with her?"

"I told you that yesterday."

"Why doesn't your mother just bring him back?"

"I need to be there. She won't know what to do if he flips out." As if Archer did. "If you don't want to go to Gloucester, I can go myself."

"I said I would take you. Do you know where she lives?"

"Russell Avenue, I think. I have it written down. She gave me directions. Take 95 to exit…"

"I know how to get there."

"How do you know?"

"I just do, okay?"

Archer looked at Campbell, then back out the window. She didn't know what was bothering him but didn't care. She was on her way to Rory.

CHAPTER FIFTY-EIGHT

Archer and Campbell drove along the Gloucester waterfront, past the police department and the hotel where she had stayed with Rory and Trish. It was hard to believe that had happened only ten days ago. It seemed like another lifetime.

"There's the Gloucester Fisherman," Archer said. "Do you know about him? It's a tribute to the fishermen who died at sea." She flipped through a guide book she had thrown in her purse. "They that go down to the sea in ships. 1623-1923. Let's stop. I want to look at the names of the people who died on the Andrea Gail. I think Rory would like that. I wonder which one was his biological father."

Campbell pulled over and parked. He shut the car off and handed the keys to her.

"Where are you going?"

"To get coffee. Or maybe a beer. Call my cell when you and Rory are ready to leave. I'll tell you where to pick me up."

"Can't you drive me to Ellen's house?" She looked at the stick shift. "I don't know if I can drive this car."

"You drove it when I first got it, remember? Rory thought it was hysterical when you rolled backwards on Sawyer Hill Road. He pulled the emergency brake to stop us."

"This is the same car? You're kidding. You can add air conditioning to a car? And cushioned seats? This isn't the same radio, is it?"

"No, I replaced that. The engine too. You know, for such a smart woman you're ignorant about important things in life, like cars. You're going to have to drive it. I'm leaving. Can you grab my sunglasses from the glove compartment?"

Archer opened the glove box and handed the mirrored shades to him. "Are these standard for cops?"

He put them on. She looked into the lenses, hated that she couldn't see his eyes. She needed eyes to talk.

"Why didn't you tell me I needed to brush my hair?" She made a joke.

Campbell kissed her quickly, grabbed a Bangor P.D. baseball cap from the back seat and slung it low on his head.

He stepped out of the car. "Russell Avenue is up that way off Poplar Street." He pointed vaguely out beyond the memorial and walked off.

The fisherman looked out toward the sea. A semi circle of plaques with names of those who had failed to return from the sea surrounded him. Archer strolled around the statue, not focusing on any of the names. She knew it was disrespectful but she couldn't get the old jingle out of her head. Trust the Gorton's Fisherman. She faced the man at the wheel. He was a determined Captain, unwavering in his desire to get his ship and crew home safely. She walked toward the car. She would be Rory's Captain, resolute in her desire to get him home despite the turbulent seas.

Russell Avenue was a dead end street. Just beyond the last house and woods was the hustle and bustle of Route 128. Archer figured that was the path Rory had taken to get to the highway to spray paint over the swastika. Rory certainly had experience navigating through woods, like he had a GPS implanted in his brain.

Ellen's house was ranch-style, modest in size with a yard that looked freshly mowed. Archer parked the Scirocco in front. A black Camaro with dark tinted windows sat in the driveway. It looked like a confiscated drug dealer's car. A perfect match for Campbell with his baseball cap and mirrored sunglasses. Martha's grey minivan was in the driveway.

Archer sunk her forehead to the steering wheel, suddenly overcome with nerves. What if Rory refused to come home? What if he wanted to stay with Kitty? Or Ellen? She took a deep breath and faced the world again. She stepped out of the car and to the front door. Ellen greeted her before Archer could ring the bell.

Ellen looked at the Scirocco. "That's a great car. My brother had one of those when we were growing up. Have you had it long?"

"It's not mine. It belongs to a friend."

"Cool. Come on in."

The front door opened revealing a wide set of six steps leading up to an open living area. To the right of the front door was a den with a couch, rocking chair and television. The walls were covered by wood paneling. Archer followed Ellen up the stairs and beyond the living area to the kitchen. The house was tidy with little attention paid to décor; it was very stylish for the seventies. A police type radio sat on the kitchen counter. Voices crackled over the sound waves. A wrapped Subway sandwich was next to the radio.

"Hi honey." Her mother sat on a stool by the counter.

Archer couldn't look at her. Not yet.

"Rory told me you like Subway," Ellen pointed to the sandwich. "I already ate mine. This is yours. Turkey and cheese, no onions. That's what Rory said you liked."

"Thanks. Is he here?"

Ellen hesitated. "He left this morning around ten. Said he was going to see Kitty. I tried to distract him until you got here but after he mowed the lawn, he took off. When he's determined to do something, there's no stopping him."

"We tried, Archer. Rory was having none of what we were saying." Grandma Rose added.

She faced her mother. "Why didn't you go with him? Did he know how to get there? Have you heard from him? Or Kitty? And why does everyone think it's okay not to inform me of these things when they happen?" Archer tried to control the panic rising in her gut and in her voice.

"He knows the way," Ellen spoke quickly. "He's good with directions. I've learned a lot about him in the last day. I haven't heard from either of them. I called Kitty at home and at The Crow's Nest. No answer. I was going to go there, see if I could check on him without him noticing me. And we didn't tell you because we didn't want you to worry."

Archer glared at Grandma Rose, knowing that was her doing.

She looked back at Ellen. "You were adamant they shouldn't meet. How could you let him go?"

Ellen looked away then back at Archer, as if she had been slapped. "He was going to go no matter what I said or did. And he said if I followed him or showed up, he was going to run away. I'm sorry. I didn't know what to do."

"You think she could hurt him?" Archer sat on the stool next to her mother.

Rose took her hand. Archer didn't resist.

"No, Kitty's not violent. Just, um…" Ellen said.

"…crazy?"

"Off. She thinks she's a witch."

"I heard."

"Her great great great - I don't know how many times - aunt died during the Salem Witch trials. Kitty's mother Margaret thought she was a witch too."

Archer's stomach grumbled as she slipped her hand from her mother and unwrapped the sandwich. A black cat jumped up on the counter then into Archer's lap.

Ellen removed the cat. "Sorry, this is Miss Purrchance. I got her in my divorce."

Archer returned her hand to her mother's grasp, intertwining their fingers. "You're divorced?"

"Well, not a real divorce, a break up with my girlfriend. Tori got all the furniture, the money, the house. I got Miss Purrchance." She hugged the cat to her chest. "Frankly, I think I got the better deal." Ellen sat on the couch, pulled her legs under her and absent mindedly stroked Miss Purrchance who purred, loving the attention.

Archer took a bite of the sandwich as her phone chimed, indicating she had a text message. She looked at it, froze wide-eyed.

"What?" Ellen asked.

"What?" Rose asked.

The bite of her sandwich lodged in her throat. Archer gurgled, unable to speak, cough, make a sound; unable to uncoil the food stuck in her throat. Ellen jumped up, hit her on the back. Once, twice, three times until the bread and meat dislodged. Archer coughed wildly, spit into the sink. Finally catching her breath, she looked at the text message again.

Kitty is ded.

CHAPTER FIFTY-NINE

Archer called Rory. No answer.

Where r u? she texted.

"Where is he?" Rose stood on her tiptoes and looked over Archer's shoulder.

Ellen's radio cackled. "White female deceased. The Crow's Nest. Cause of death unknown, possible murder."

"Let's go," Ellen grabbed a leather strap key chain from the counter.

Archer followed her to the Camaro, watching her phone as she hurried to keep up. Still no response from Rory. She hoped he wasn't at the Crow's Nest. She hoped he wasn't the one who had found Kitty. She hoped he wasn't somehow involved.

Kitty is ded, his text had read.

She texted him again. *Answer me. Where r u?*

"Is that from Rory?" Rose followed close on Archer's heels.

Archer whipped around, unable to control herself. "Mom, please go away."

"Really?" Rose stopped walking.

"Mom, please." Archer got into the passenger seat of Ellen's car.

As the Camaro started to pull away, Rose stood on the sidewalk, her face grey, forlorn. Archer motioned for Ellen to stop the car.

She rolled down the window."Please stay here, Mom. In case Rory comes back. Okay? I *need* you to be here."

With a job to do, determination and fortitude washed over Rose's face.

"Let's go," Archer said.

Ellen rolled down her window, reached under her seat and pulled out a portable siren. She attached it to the top of the Camaro and they sped off, the blaring siren thankfully drowning out Archer's thoughts.

Three Gloucester police cars were parked in front of the Crow's Nest. An ambulance was on the side street. People were lined up on the sidewalk across the street, their collective gazes - usually focused on the fishing boats in the harbor - were fixed inward to Gloucester and the show at the run-down bar. Rory was seated on a bench in front of the restaurant. Police officers surrounded him. Archer opened the Camaro door and jumped out before the car stopped.

She ran to Rory, skidding to a stop to allow the body bag to pass in front of her. Rory's eyes were intent on the body as it was wheeled out.

"Rory!"

"Mom! I saw my real mom!"

Archer flinched like she was afraid of a punch. She wanted to shake Rory, convince him she was his real mom. Not a bonus. The real thing. But this wasn't the time. This certainly was not the time.

Rory was pale. His voice and hands were shaking. "She looked like she was asleep. They covered her with a sheet but not her feet. I asked them to cover her feet." He jumped up, walked five steps forward, five steps back.

An officer put a hand on his shoulder. ""Sit down, son. I want to talk to your mother."

The police officer took her aside. "That's the first thing he's said since we got here. He won't talk to us. He'll only write. I gave him a pad. He wrote that Kitty was saying weird things about frogs and fish and the moon and then she got really upset so he hid behind the bar. I think he's delusional, maybe in shock."

"Is he a suspect, officer?"

"Not right now. We're still trying to sort things out."

Ellen walked up. "What's going on, Flannigan?"

He opened a flip pad. "The deceased is Kitty Warren, fifty six years old. Cause of death unknown. She's on her way to the ME's office. No witnesses except for the boy but he's not talking. He's written a few things but that's all. He seems out of it."

"He's been in a traumatic situation," Archer said. "Let me talk to him."

"I don't know," Flannigan said.

Archer stepped toward the officer. "He's a minor and he's my son. And he's not a suspect. And if you think for one second…"

Ellen got between them. "It's okay. She can talk to him."

Archer sat next to Rory, who stared at the lights on the ambulance and watched Kitty's body being driven away. The officers and Ellen stood over them.

"What happened?" Archer put her hand on his knee.

Archer watched Rory scribble on the pad; horrified as she read. It was not what she had expected. She reached for the pad but the officer was quicker. He showed it to Ellen. Time seemed to stand still as Ellen looked at Rory, then at Archer.

"Arrest him," she said softly.

The officers roughly grabbed Rory, turned him around and cuffed his hands behind his back. Rory didn't fight, kept his eyes on the fading lights of the ambulance, not saying a word as they led him to the police car.

Dangling from Ellen's hand was the note Rory had written.

I kilt Kitty.

CHAPTER SIXTY

Archer stared as the police officer guided Rory to the patrol car. She wondered what she should do. Stop them, ask to go in the car, grab him and run? As a lawyer, her response would be obvious. As a mother, she never knew the right thing to do.

The officer held the top of Rory's head as he bent into the back seat. It was like a scene from a movie, only this was real.

The lights on top of the police car whirled as it drove away. In the back seat, Rory's head bent forward. Archer imagined he wished his hands were free so he could pull his hood over his head.

The ambulance followed the police car. Archer stood silent, shocked, wondering what Kitty had thought of Rory and his black wind pants, black t-shirt with tiny white skulls patterned across it—one hundred and seven as Rory had counted—and his homemade necklace of blue lanyard with several shiny bolts as charms. After meeting Rory, had she still considered him the devil?

Ellen grabbed Archer's arm and dragged her to the Camaro. Archer stumbled as she continued to look backward, watching the ambulance and police car until they turned a corner and were out of her sight.

"We have to find out how Kitty died." Ellen opened the front passenger door and, just like the officer with Rory, guided Archer in.

"Maybe Rory didn't have anything to do with her death." Ellen started the car. "Why'd he have to write that he killed her? Why'd you let him come back here?"

"Why'd you let him go to the Crow's Nest?" Archer screeched as if she were talking to Wayne. "And I didn't let him do anything. You think I can control him? You think anyone can control him? You don't know him. Rory controls every situation he's in. He's not the prisoner. We're the prisoners of his moods and whims."

"Okay, okay. Calm down."

"My son has just been arrested for murder. I will not calm down."

"Maybe you need to act more like a lawyer and less like his mother."

"Maybe you need to act more like a cop and less like his mother."

Ellen parked in front of the police department and looked at Archer. Tears filled Ellen's eyes.

"I'm sorry," Archer said. "I didn't mean to make you cry."

"No, I'm sorry. You're right. I don't know Rory. I wish I did. This is like a gift for me, a second chance."

"At what?"

"To get to know him."

"If you want to know him so badly, why didn't you keep him? A lot of gay people raise children. I know, I represent them and trust me, gay or straight, we all screw our kids up."

Ellen laughed. "Being gay was only a partial excuse. I mean, it was a factor. I knew it would be hard for me and Rory but that wasn't the only reason. Kitty asked me not to keep him." She hesitated. "One of her relatives was hung in Salem during the witch trials. I don't know all the details. I know she kept a family tree. She showed it to me once. She was so happy when she got pregnant but then as the baby grew inside of her, she started to fear it. She loved him and hated him at the same time. And she didn't want to be reminded of..." Tears streamed from Ellen's eyes.

Archer watched, waited, wondered: how did this stop being about Rory? How did this become about this teary-eyed cop obsessed with my son?

"I'm sorry," Ellen said as if reading her mind. "I know this isn't about me. I know Rory could be in serious trouble. We can talk about this later."

"No way," Archer said, "now or never. As far as I'm concerned there is no later for me and Rory and Gloucester. Once we're out of here, we will not be coming back."

"Please don't say that."

"Detective, you have been very kind to Rory and I appreciate it but right now, I am going to take your advice. I am going to act like a lawyer and not like his mother. I suggest you do your job and act like a cop. So," she pulled the latch to open the door, "I need to speak to my client. Alone." Archer placed her foot on the curb.

"Wait." Ellen took a deep breath, released it. "I know I'm not Rory's mother."

"That's a good start," Archer said.

"I'm his Aunt."

CHAPTER SIXTY-ONE

Archer saw Rory through the glass partition before he saw her. He was pacing. Five steps forward, five steps back, repeat. His head was down, head phones plugged in, his hand grasping his I-pod. His lips were moving.

Archer looked at a young police officer. "I'm his attorney."

He opened the door and she walked in. Rory's back was to her. He was singing his favorite verse from his favorite Eminem song.

She sat down, waited for him to notice her. When he did, he took the buds out of his ears and let them fall around his shoulders. Through the earphones, Eminem's demands for success were muffled but audible. Rory sat across from her at the table.

"Have you ever gone to church?" he asked.

"I went one Palm Sunday with friends before you were born. And I've been to church for a couple of funerals. I'm not Christian, Rory. I used to go to synagogue when I was young. Why?"

"I've never been to church. I went to Hebrew School for a little bit. I get Hanukkah presents *and* Christmas presents. Grandma Rose takes me to synagogue every year for Rosh Hashanah. And when I was little we'd go on Easter egg hunts. I don't know what I am."

Archer froze. Wayne was right. This was her fault. He had wanted to raise Rory Catholic but Archer has thought since they had different religions, Rory should experience both. Had she messed up her son by not exposing him to one religion?

"Sweetie, why are you talking about this now? Shouldn't we be talking about other things?"

"Kitty told me about church." Rory got up, paced again. Eminem's verses bounced off his shoulders.

"What did she say?"

"She said Puritans fear God. She asked if I go to church and if I read the Bible. When I told her I didn't, she called me the devil."

"You're not the devil, Rory."

"Sometimes I act like one."

Archer sighed. "Most people don't believe in the Puritan religion."

"At first I thought she was taking drugs. I mean, she was acting real weird, talking one moment, quiet the next, then saying all these crazy things. But then I thought it was just her religion making her say those things. What do you think?"

"I don't know, Ror."

"Maybe if I feared God I would make better choices."

"I don't think it's about that."

"I just think I should go to church."

"Your father would love to take you."

Rory stopped pacing. "When's the last time *he* went to church?"

"I don't know."

He paced again, rapped along with Eminem. "Failure is not an option." He sat next to her. "Do you want to hear what Kitty told me?"

Archer blinked, took a moment to figure out what he meant. "You recorded the conversation?"

He took his phone out of the side pocket of his wind pants, held it up. "Yeah. She didn't know."

"I would like to hear it. But first, I need to know something."

"What?"

"Did you kill her?"

"Not really."

"I don't know what that means."

He placed his phone on the table, pressed a few buttons. "Listen."

On the recording, Rory's voice was clear. Kitty's was more distanced. Archer strained to hear her.

"You're a handsome boy," she said. "You're lucky. You got your looks from your father."

"My father died in The Perfect Storm."

"I know. Why are you here, Rory? Your name is Rory, right?"

"Yes."

"I'm Kitty."

"I know."

"I told your mother I didn't want to speak to you."

"She doesn't know I'm here. If she did, she'd be really pissed. Probably ground me for a million years."

"Is she a god-fearing woman?"

"I don't think so. She doesn't talk about God much unless she's mad at my dad."

"Do you go to church? Do you read the Bible?"

"No."

"If you want to save your soul, you should. You came from the devil, boy. As far as I can tell from looking at you, he's still in you."

A loud thump sounded from the recorder.

"Are you okay?" Rory sounded concerned.

"Yeah, I just tripped."

"Are you sick or something?"

"These pills make me sleepy."

"I take pills too. They make my hands shake."

"Why are you here, boy?"

"I have questions."

"You can ask ten."

"Only ten? How come?"

"Because that's all I have time for. What's your first one?"

"I should have written them down. That's what Mrs. K would have told me to do. She was my history teacher. Now she's my principal. She's my mom's best friend. They've been friends forever. Mrs. K's always telling me to write things down so I don't forget. I have so many things going on in my mind that I can't keep track of stuff."

"I know what you mean."

"You too? That's fuckin' wicked."

"I wish you wouldn't use that word."

"Sorry. My mom is always telling me not to curse."

"I don't mind the cursing. It's the word wicked. It has a bad connotation."

"Where I'm from, wicked is good."

"Where I'm from," Kitty said, "wicked is bad."

"Where are you from?"

"Is that one of your questions?"

"I guess."

"I'm from Salem."

"Is that why my grandmother, I mean your mother, was buried there?"

"Yeah."

"Salem's really old, right?"

"It was founded in 1626. It was originally called Naumkeag because that was the name of the river. One of my relatives was one of the founders. My family has lived there or in the area ever since."

"Wicked cool. I mean, cool. How did it end up being called Salem?"

"In 1629, the name was changed. Salem is related to the Hebrew word Shalom which means peace."

"My mother is Jewish and my dad is Catholic. I think that makes me Jewish but I don't feel like anything. What religion are you?"

"Puritan Catholic."

"I know about that," Rory said. "My dad read this play to me called The Crucible by Arthur something. Are you a witch? You say spells and stuff."

"I am a witch."

"For real? Can you be a Puritan and a witch? Are you a good witch or a bad witch?"

"Those are difficult questions to answer."

"Is that why you don't like the word wicked?"

"Yes. That was your last question."

"No way."

"That was ten. Actually, more than ten. I was counting."

"But they weren't real questions. They were mostly follow-ups."

"I said ten questions and you asked ten."

"One more, please."

"I have things to do."

"Please."

"No."

"How about another time? I can come back later or tomorrow."

"There won't be another time."

"You don't know me," Rory said. "I get whatever I want. Ask my mom. She'll tell you. I'm very persistent."

"Like your father."

"He was persistent too?"

"Got whatever he wanted."

"I wish I could see him."

"Me too."

"One more question. Please."

"Okay," Kitty said. "One more. Make it good."

There was silence, then Rory cleared his throat: "why didn't you want me?"

In the interrogation room, Rory leaned over the table and shut off the recorder.

"Why'd you do that?" Archer asked.

"I need a break." He put the buds in his ears and circled the room like it was a mini track.

CHAPTER SIXTY-TWO

Archer stepped out of the interrogation room and into the hallway. Rory had refused to play the recording again and she was tired of listening to him recite angry rap lyrics. She watched him through the one-way glass. He was circling the table. She checked her phone. Five missed calls from Campbell. She called him back.

"Where are you? I've been trying you for over an hour." he said.

"At the Gloucester P.D. Rory went to visit his birth mother without me knowing. While he was with her, she died."

"She what?"

"She died. He might be a suspect."

"A murder suspect?"

"Yes. Where are you? What's all that noise??"

"I'm at the Amtrak station. I'm going home. My train leaves in ten minutes."

"What? Why? What about me and Rory? I need you. *We* need you."

"I'm sure he had nothing to do with her dying. You'll clear it up. And you have the Scirocco. You can drive home."

"Campbell, I need you."

"I'm really sorry. I have to get back to work. Did you say Kitty is dead?"

"You remembered her name. Yes, she's dead."

"Rory didn't do it. He couldn't have."

"I know. I just have to convince the police so they don't charge him."

"What did Rory say happened?"

"You know how he records things with his cell phone? He recorded their conversation. I listened to some of it before he shut it off. Kitty called him the devil. I'm going to go back in and hear the rest. I don't really want to hear it. I mean, what if he…Can you come here? Please."

"It's too much," Campbell said.

"But we're friends. Why'd you drive me here anyway if you weren't going to help me? I need you."

"I can't do it, Archer. I have to go to work."

She waited for him to continue, to explain his feelings. She had never understood him. One moment hot – sizzling hot with his hands all over her body – the next minute colder than a blizzard. But never one to share his emotions. The strong and silent type, she always called him. But now, she needed more strong than silent.

"I'm sure your Captain will understand if you miss another day of work…"

She looked at her phone and sighed. *Call ended.*

Archer peered into the interrogation room. Rory was seated at the table fingering his cell phone.

She stepped inside and sat across from him. "Are you ready to play the recording?"

He stared stonily at his cell phone.

"I'm ready to listen again if you are," Archer said.

"Can't."

"How come?"

"I erased it."

"You did? Why?"

"I don't know."

"Why would you erase it? Was it incriminating? I need to know what went on between you and Kitty. Did you hurt her?"

"Leave me the fuck alone. Okay? Kitty said my ancestors were witches and she wanted to end the bad blood. She started saying this thing over and over about evil and frogs and shit. I got scared, Mom. I crawled under the bar. She kept saying the same thing, over and over." He stood and walked in small circles; his hands gesticulating in expanding circles. Then he cried, ignoring the mucus dripping from his nose. "She took pills and then stuck her head in the oven and I was too scared to stop her. I killed her because I didn't stop her. I could have pulled her out. I could have done something."

He sat on the floor and pulled his knees into his chest, head tucked down. She reached for him but he flailed his arms. She stepped back and watched as he spin on the floor. Just like when he was a little boy.

CHAPTER SIXTY-THREE

Ellen stuck her head into the interrogation room. She motioned for Archer to go out in the hallway.

"Good news for Rory," Ellen said. "The M.E. ruled out homicide. He thinks Kitty killed herself. Overdose and carbon monoxide poisoning. She took pills then stuck her head in the oven at The Crow's Nest. Has Rory told you anything?"

"Nothing." She kept her expression stoic.

"Doesn't matter. He's free to go."

Archer moved to step back into the interrogation room.

"Wait," Ellen said. "Your car is at my house and it's getting late. Why don't you, Rory and your mom stay over?"

"I don't think that's a good idea."

"Why not?"

Archer glanced back into the room. Rory was on the floor, motionless, staring straight ahead.

"I haven't told Rory about you. And I'm not going to."

Ellen looked away, then back at Archer. "I guess that's your choice."

"He's been through enough." Archer stopped. "How are you his aunt?"

"His father was my brother." Ellen spoke softly.

Archer looked into Ellen's eyes. She spoke just as softly. "His experience with his birth mother was not a positive one."

"I can tell him about Jib."

"Was that his father's name?"

"Jib Pero."

"How come you and Jib have different last names?"

"Same mother, different fathers. We were raised together."

Archer looked in the room through the glass partition. She didn't see Rory. She rushed in, Ellen close behind. Rory was in a corner, spinning on his bottom.

CHAPTER SIXTY-FOUR

"Spin, spin, spin," Rory said.

Archer knelt next to him. "What are you doing, Big Guy?"

He turned to her. "Spinning."

She retrieved a crumpled tissue from her pocket. When he stopped, she wiped the tears from his face.

"All done now," she reached out her hand. "Let's go."

He didn't take her hand but stood, clutching his I-pod, his cheeks red from exertion. He followed her out of the interrogation room, pulled his hood up. As they walked down the hallway, he became mesmerized by a display of shiny badges. Ellen came up behind them.

Archer turned to her. "I need to get my car. I mean, Campbell's car. Rory and I are going back to Bangor. Can you take us to your house?"

"Sure. I'll follow you to Maine. Make sure you get home safely."

Archer searched Ellen's face for a resemblance to Rory's. Did they have the same nose? Similar cheekbones? Matching chins?

"I need to make sure he's okay," Ellen offered.

Archer stepped closer to her. "That's my job, Detective." She kept her voice low so Rory wouldn't hear. "Not yours. I've been taking care of him for fifteen years. Where have you been? Where were you when he was throwing light bulbs at my garage door, or crying because of a commercial for abandoned pets that made him sad, or refusing to eat anything but peanut butter? He's okay and it's because of me. Not because of you or his father—biological or otherwise; or anyone else. You think you can just step back in his life? Think again."

Archer paused long enough to see a tear drop from Ellen's eye. Ellen and Rory didn't have the same noses or cheekbones or chins. But they did have the same sad blue eyes that stole Archer's heart like a brazen thief, suddenly and without warning. Archer looked away. She didn't want Ellen to see the tears in her own eyes, the guilt she was feeling over her latest tirade. But there was no way she was going to let this woman step into Rory's life like some knight in shining armor. If anyone was going to save Rory, it was going to be Archer. Hadn't she earned the right to be his hero?

At Ellen's house, Rory jumped out of the backseat of the Camaro.

"Where are you going?" Archer called.

No surprise, Rory didn't answer. He hadn't said a word since the interrogation room. She watched him run into Ellen's house.

Ellen turned to Archer, the two of them seated close, still in the tight front bucket seats of the Camaro.

"I think he's going to get his things." Ellen said.

"His things?"

"When he and Rose came he had a bag of drinks and snacks and…"

Archer quickly searched the driveway and the street for Martha's minivan. Archer had forgotten about her mother. The car was gone. She reached for her cell phone to call her mom.

"What is that?" Ellen asked.

Archer put her cell down and turned to Ellen who was looking at the front door to her house. Archer followed her gaze. On the front stoop, Rory stood encased in his ghille suit, looking like Bigfoot's little brother. Ear phones and wires hung below the leaves and grass. He juggled two hacky sack balls in his right hand.

Archer got out of the Camaro and into the Scirocco. Rory sat in the backseat still wearing the ghille suit. Archer couldn't wait to get home.

CHAPTER SIXTY-FIVE

Archer drove by rote, enjoying the mindlessness of highway driving. Rory was in the backseat, surprisingly at ease. She checked on him often in the rearview mirror, watching his head of leaves and branches—held together by chicken wire, tape and string—bent forward. Music streaming into his ears, calming him—or so she hoped.

She looked at the road again. They were halfway into the four hour trip. It would be good to be home, good to get back into their routine. So what if he wasn't like other kids, so what if they had bumps in the road together, at least Rory wasn't the father of Trish's baby, at least he cared about things like animals and the environment, at least he wasn't charged with murder. It was all relative. Yes, that's how she would view life from today forward. A renaissance. Their new beginning. Their fate.

She looked at Rory again. His head was still bent forward.

"You okay?"

He didn't answer.

"Rory," she spoke louder. "Are you okay?"

She eyed the road again. Then the mirror. Road. Mirror. Rory wasn't moving, wasn't even chastising her for interrupting his favorite song. His hands were still, his legs not bouncing, his head down. Her heart skipped several beats.

"Rory," she screamed.

He picked his head up.

"You okay, Big Guy?" she asked, trying not to sound panicked "If you want to talk about anything, I'm here for you."

His chin dropped to his chest.

She took the risk. "Kitty didn't want to live any longer. You didn't do anything to cause it. Do you know that?"

He reached under his suit, fumbled. She waited to see what he was doing. The Maine towns of Kittery, then Kennebunk, flew by. One arm finally emerged from the ghille suit with a sheet of paper. She reached back to retrieve the note.

I know, it read.

He bent his head down again, concentrated on pen and paper. More scribbling. They drove past Biddeford and Saco. Rory handed her another note.

Kitty sed my fathers name was Jib.

Archer nodded, reached back for another note.

He's alive.

Heart pumping wildly, Archer pulled off the interstate at Topsham and stopped at a gas station. The black Camaro stopped behind her at the pump.

Archer stormed out of her car. "I told you not to follow us."

"And I told you I was going to. Look," Ellen pointed to the rear window of Archer's car. Rory was staring out the back window. His eyes were partially camouflaged by twigs and leaves, but not so much that Archer couldn't see they were wide open with fear and sadness. Archer turned away from Ellen not wanting to cause a scene in front of Rory. After filling the Scirocco with gas, she drove off, the Camaro close on her tail.

"I'm sorry," she looked in the rearview mirror. "You have to understand. Kitty was sick. Your birth father isn't alive. He was killed in the storm."

"How do you know?" he screamed.

"He was declared dead. Nobody could survive those seas. He was in the middle of nowhere. I'm sorry."

"He's alive. He's alive. He's alive." Rory yelled.

His screams became heckles, then laughter, giggling, cackling. He pulled leaves and twigs from his suit, tossed them in the air like a celebration. At first, he picked at the suit slowly. As his laughter grew louder, the pace quickened. He threw leaves in the air, twigs out the window. He found pebbles amongst the greenery and threw them at the rear window, then at the front window.

Two hacky sack balls hit Archer in the head. She turned around. Rory was shoving dirt and leaves and ground cover into his mouth.

"Rory. Stop." A knot filled her stomach and throat. Traffic whizzed by at seventy miles per hour. She didn't know where to go, what to do. Kept her shaking hands as steady as she could on the wheel. She searched for a safe place to pull over. No, she wanted to keep going. Couldn't stop. What good would that do? Give Rory the chance to run into traffic? She had to keep going. They were almost there.

She turned around again. Saw the flashing light on top of the Camaro and Ellen's exaggerated hand movements. No, Archer wasn't pulling over. It was not what was best for Rory. She looked at the backseat. The ghille suit was torn apart. Rory threw a black DC sneaker at the front window, took the other shoe off and banged it against the side window; the red laces berating her like flopping tongues.

As quickly as the tantrum started, it ended. He stopped laughing, spread himself out on the rear seat then curled into a ball. Parts of the suit covered him. The rest blanketed the car seats and floorboards like leaves on a fall day.

Rory began to rap. Eminem. *Failure is not an option.*

"What are you doing?" She asked, gently.

Among the mess, he found the pad and pen, wrote something, handed it to Archer.

Spinning.

CHAPTER SIXTY-SIX

Twenty minutes later, Archer turned toward Bangor Hospital. The Scirocco bottomed out as she raced down the long ramp which ran along the cement garage and led to the Emergency Room. Ellen was behind them, a single police light whirring and flashing on top of her car.

No ambulances in the entrance bay. *Good. Maybe our wait won't be long.* Archer found a parking place by the front door and marveled at how she could feel lucky nabbing a close parking place to evaluate her son's emotional breakdown. Ellen parked in a no parking zone, the earned priority of a police officer.

"Let's go, baby," she turned to Rory.

Curled on the backseat, he looked up at her. She tried to gauge his reaction. Would he cooperate? Fight? Run? He sat up, wrote on the paper.

Ok.

He followed her out of the car and shuffled beside her, head down, ear buds plugged in. Remnants of the ghille suit dangled off his wind pants, shirt and hair. The automatic doors to the emergency room slid open.

No longer feeling lucky, she approached the registration desk. Rory wandered to the kid's corner where a cartoon was playing. Ellen ran up and stood next to Archer.

The nurse looked up, judgmental behind Dolce & Gabbana imitation glasses. "Hello, Mrs. Falcon. Is he hurt again?"

"Not physically."

The nurse frowned. The hospital staff always seemed friendlier when she and Rory were there for the physical mishaps, not the emotional ones.

Archer watched Rory leave the kid's area and go to a nurse's station. He reached over the desk and fiddled with something, emerged with a pencil. The nurse handed him a small pad.

"Is he a threat to himself or others?" The registration nurse asked.

"Yes. No. I don't know."

"Do we have all of your updated information?" The woman tapped on a keyboard and looked at her screen. She stifled a yawn. "Oh, that's right. He was here recently for head trauma and minor burns. Do you think this is a result of his concussion?"

Archer wished. "No."

Rory paced, holding the pad and paper like a nervous journalist.

"Follow me." The nurse looked at Ellen. "Rory and his mother only."

Archer and Rory followed the nurse through a door, down a corridor and to a room segregated from the others. Clearly a different set-up from the triage space cordoned by curtains and designed to aid those that were physically, not mentally, ill. The room was hot and sparse with a metal gurney with tissue paper on top and one white plastic chair. The walls were white. The floor was covered by white linoleum. The room had two entrances, one on either side. Each door had a small, square window; the only windows in the room. The nurse stood at one door, observing Rory. The other door was guarded by a short, barrel-chested security officer.

The nurse looked at Archer. "You okay?"

"Of course."

"A doctor will be with you soon."

The door swung closed with a resounding thud. Archer looked at her cell phone. No service.

Rory paced, then sat on the gurney. Archer reached for him. He flinched.

"I just want to get the leaves out of your hair."

His non-response was his concurrence. She picked at his hair and his shirt. She brushed his pant legs and by his feet, enjoying the connection. She knew it wouldn't last long. A small pile of outdoors landed on the floor. Rory pulled away, grunted. He had reached his limit of physical contact.

They waited. Archer wondered what Ellen was doing. She hoped she was on her way back to Gloucester. Rory methodically shredded the tissue paper on the gurney then threw it on the floor like confetti. He jumped off the table and twirled then paced like a hungry, caged animal. Archer also felt caged but there was nothing to do but wait. She sat in the plastic chair.

The heat in the room and Rory's repetitive pacing made her tired. She leaned her head against the wall and closed her eyes. She saw visions of Rory, unable to wait in the pediatrician's office as a child without rolling and spinning on the floor. She saw him pushing chairs into walls and tables then laughing. She remembered the other parents protectively hugging their own children.

A loud rap on the door startled her. Even more startling was Wayne's face in the window of the locked door. She directed him to the other door where the guard was.

"How're you doing?" Wayne's voice boomed theatrically as he greeted the guard.

Rory's eyes widened. His mouth gaped. "Dad's here?"

Archer heard another voice, a woman. Mary Beth? Had he actually brought Mary Beth with him? Archer listened. No. It was Ellen.

"Sorry," the security guard said, "I can't let you in if you're not a parent."

The door opened then shut behind Wayne. He stood still for a moment, looking between Rory and Archer. *Comfort your son*, she thought. But instead, Wayne rushed to her, drew her into him. Archer flinched, his touch unexpected, odd but then quickly familiar. She relinquished in his embrace to all the years of suffering with Rory and buried her head in his chest. She wanted to pull away. She wanted to present a strong front but the tears flowed. She couldn't stop them.

Finally, he pushed hair from her face.

"Are you okay?"

She nodded and wiped her eyes on his flannel shirt. He was always cold when she was hot. She looked at Rory who was pacing, his circle getting smaller and tighter.

"I missed you, Big Guy," Wayne reached out a hand to him.

Rory shrugged and shoved his hands into his pockets.

Wayne dropped his hand to his side. "I was worried about you."

Rory pulled out the pad of paper and a pencil from his pocket and wrote. *Why?*

"Because I love you. I don't want you to get hurt or feel bad."

Did my real dad love me?

Wayne looked to Archer, who shrugged just as Rory had. *Let Wayne handle this.* She was tired of trying to figure out the right answers and the best responses.

"He never met you," Wayne said. "He died before you were born. But he would have loved you."

Archer was impressed. *Was this a new Wayne?*

Rory scribbled frantically. His fingers poised close to the nib of the pencil, his strokes hard and dark. His brow furrowed.

The door opened. Rory tossed the pad onto the gurney like he was getting rid of evidence at a crime scene. Wayne extended his hand to the man who walked in. He was dressed like Wayne in the uniform of Northeastern men as winter approached—jeans and a flannel shirt.

"Hey, Luke," Wayne said. "I didn't know you worked at the hospital." He turned to Archer and Rory. "This fellow here is the greatest jazz guitarist in the area. We performed together for several weeks and he was amazing. Able to follow my lead and improvise. He's attending the University of Maine. You're in the medical program, right? Getting your degree in social work..."

Rory turned his back. Archer stopped listening. Not a new Wayne, the same old one. She tuned out the mutual stroking between the men and glanced at Rory's pad which lay sideways on the gurney.

My real dad is not ded.

CHAPTER SIXTY-SEVEN

Rory stood in the corner, a self-appointed time out. He looked toward Wayne and Luke who were laughing and playfully hitting each other but Archer knew Rory wasn't seeing them. Outside the room, Ellen's muffled voice grew louder, mixing rhythmically with words from the security guard intended to calm and diffuse.

"You need to let me in now. I'm a police officer." Ellen demanded.

Rory looked toward the door, then back at his father.

"Wayne, shouldn't we be talking about Rory?" Archer asked.

Wayne played air guitar, "Smoke On The Water is the greatest guitar riff. No one beats Deep Purple."

"Iron Maiden by Black Sabbath is better by a mile," Luke said.

Rory walked toward the door, toward Ellen's voice.

"You okay?" Luke asked him then addressed Wayne. "He seems stable."

Rory sat on the plastic chair, put his head down and shoved the buds in his ears. His feet bounced. His hands shook.

"Let me in now," Ellen said. "Don't make me go over your head."

Rory rapped under his breath. "Success is my only mothafuckin option, failure's not."

"I don't think Rory is doing well," Archer said softly.

"Detective," the guard said, "you are not family. I cannot let you in."

"Yes, I am. I'm his aunt."

Rory stopped singing, looked up then down again.

Archer walked out of the room, left the door open so she could see and hear Rory. Wayne and Luke were discussing local politics.

"This isn't your jurisdiction," Archer folded her arms across her chest. "It's time for you to leave."

"I need to see him."

Archer pulled Ellen to the side but not too far that she couldn't observe Rory. "He can hear us. What is your problem?"

"I'm sorry. I really am. I know you're going through a lot right now. But I've been trying to find Rory since the day I handed him to you at the airport. Kitty wouldn't help me and the adoption agency wouldn't give me any information without Kitty's consent. Don't you understand, I lost my brother fifteen years ago. Rory is my only connection to him."

"No, I don't understand. You're selfish and you need to go home. Rory has enough problems without you adding to them."

"I'm not adding to them. I'm going to help him. I can help you. I can be his family."

"He has a family," Archer said.

Ellen's face sunk, her eyes teared. "You know, when Rory was with me, he told me all about his love of lawn mowers and snow blowers. He is just like Jib. Jib loved tinkering with engines. He loved lawn mowers. One time he drove a riding lawn mower to school and back. Left at like four in the morning so he would get to class on time. I don't think he got home until nine o'clock that night. Those things don't top five miles per hour unless you tinker with them. And Rory told me about his gas can collection. Jib collected gas globes."

"I don't give a fuck, okay, Detective? Either you leave right now or I'm filing a restraining order to keep you away from *my* son. And I guarantee, not only will you never see Rory again, but you will lose your job. Any questions?"

"Rory. You can't leave," Wayne said.

Archer looked quickly at Rory, then back at Ellen. "Good-bye, Detective." She folded her arms across her chest.

Ellen placed her hands on Archer's shoulders. "You don't have to go through this alone. Let me help you with Rory."

"I don't need your help."

"Nobody's perfect and that's okay."

"I don't need your psycho-babble, Detective. I need to get back to my son and you need to leave."

"Fine." She dropped her hands to her sides. "But if Rory ever needs me for anything…"

"Rory, no," Wayne said.

Archer ran to the room. Rory stood at the un-guarded door shaking the knob. The door wouldn't open. He kicked the door and threw his body against it. Luke called for help on an intercom. Wayne grabbed Rory in a bear hug. Rory pushed Wayne aside and ran to the opened door where the guard stood. Despite the guard's short stature and beer gut, he was too strong, too skilled for Rory. He flipped Rory around and held him from behind with Rory's arms crossed over his chest.

Archer turned away, recognizing the hold as a restraint used in psychiatric hospitals, remembering the papoose technique first used on Rory when he was eight years old and first committed to a hospital. The morning after he had been admitted, she had gone to the hospital to bathe him and read to him when she found him cocoon-like on the floor with an attendant by his feet. They had wrapped her son in a piece of large canvas with wings extending out of the center. The wings were wrapped around him and strapped closed with belts. Only his face was visible. His perfect little boy face gazing at her from deep sorrowful blue eyes. From that moment on, she had never let go of the fact that she had failed him.

Archer looked back, saw Rory struggling with the guard who tightened his grip. She wanted to scream. *Stop, stop, stop, you're hurting him* but she felt immersed in a thick fog, like a boat lost at sea. Three men wearing hospital scrubs rushed in. Two grabbed Rory. One held a syringe, aimed, stuck the needle deep into Rory's thigh. Rory fought, yelled, spit flew from his mouth, snot from his nose. His buds, out of his ears, flung like a wild carnival ride.

A few seconds later, Rory's knees buckled. The men gently guided him to the floor. He curled into a tight ball, a caterpillar in a cocoon that would never become a butterfly.

Two of the men lifted Rory on to the gurney. They strapped his wrists and ankles to the stretcher. Someone spoke, said something about taking him to a room where he would sleep the rest of the night. Archer wanted to ask why the need for restraints if he was sleeping but her voice was gone, stolen sometime between Ellen leaving and Rory being restrained, sometime between the day she had realized she wanted to become a mother and the day she actually became one.

They filed out of the room like a funeral procession, Rory's gurney the casket, men on all sides, Wayne in the rear.

Wait, she wanted to say to Wayne. *Let's discuss our son. What do we do now?* But the words were again missing. Wayne walked down the hallway, not looking back.

They were gone and she was alone. The silence surrounded her, too thick to break through. She was stuck, backed into the corner. Alone. So alone. *Rory. Come back, baby. We'll reverse time. No vodka in the house. You can have a million lawn mowers. Keep them in the guest room, in your room, I don't care. Anything to make you happy. Anything to keep you safe.*

Her heart ached and she knew, really knew for the first time, that she was many things: Mother, Daughter, Former Wife, Attorney, Boss. But none of that mattered. She was nothing without Rory.

She felt soft hands on her shoulders, turned, fell into Ellen's embrace.

CHAPTER SIXTY-EIGHT

In the same hospital room where Rory had just been restrained, Archer leaned against the wall in the corner, her own timeout. The room was empty. The gurney was gone. Rory had been taken away. Archer had convinced Ellen she was okay and Ellen had left, reluctantly. Said she would return to Gloucester but was only a phone call away.

Torn tissue paper and the upended plastic chair remained as a snapshot of the recent mayhem; that, and the thumping in Archer's chest and the pounding behind her eyes. Her legs were weak with failure. Her whole being deflated with defeat. She slid to the floor, surrendered her thoughts to Rory.

Rory as an infant, at the airport, love at first sight, love at first smell, her little butterball. Rory, catching frogs, learning to ice skate, riding the school bus, building with Legos, taking apart a bicycle, pushing a lawn mower, showing her how to work the DVD player. Rory, unable to sit through math class, fearful of airports and malls, obsessed with mechanics, fascinated with fans and knives. What was going to happen to her perfect butterball?

And then there was Roman. That was what they were going to name the baby in Texas. Wayne had picked the name, labeling his son the ideal citizen. But there is no Roman.

She pulled her knees to her chest and wrapped her arms around her calves and let herself go. The tears were soft and slow. All the guilt and anguish of her failures emitting in an orderly manner. Her mind raced back to her own childhood. Letting her parents down. Never being able to live up to her mother's opinion of her as the perfect daughter and mother. She missed her father. Missed being married. Wayne had replaced her with Marybeth. Would Rory replace her too? Did she matter to anyone?

The tears fell harder, bigger. Her body ached, her chest heaved, her throat constricted. She was going crazy, right in the corner of this sterile room reserved for crazy people, reserved for her. She was crazy. Crazy for thinking she could ever be good enough for Rory, crazy for thinking she could ever be of use to anybody, to herself, to anything. She pulled her legs tighter into her chest, moaning now, anguish perched on every nerve ending.

Spin, spin, spin.

She was a disappointment to Rory, to her mother, to her father, to Wayne, to herself, to Roman. Roman would be nineteen years old. Maybe she still would have adopted Rory and Roman would have been his older brother. So what if Roman was a Downs baby. So what? What was wrong with her? Why did she suck at everything she did? Why wouldn't she take Roman home and care for him?

She wiped her nose on the sleeve of her sweatshirt and slowly stood. Not a tissue in the whole sterile room. What kind of hospital was this? No mirror either, probably for the best so she couldn't see how awful she looked. She knew how awful she felt.

The vice around her head tightened. Her throat was dry. Her eyes and nose sore from rubbing and wiping. She had to get out of there. She wondered where Rory was. *Should she go see him?* She recalled the time several years ago when they had subdued him by placing a net over him. No, she didn't want to see that again, couldn't handle seeing her little butterball restrained, unconscious.

She went to the guard's vestibule. He hadn't returned yet. She wondered if there had been any problems getting Rory to a room. She picked up the phone. Without dialing, the operator came on the line.

"Darcy Cyr, please," Archer said.

She sat on the floor while she waited for Darcy to come to the phone.

Spin, spin, spin.

CHAPTER SIXTY-NINE

After speaking with Darcy, Archer felt strangely relieved. Rory was in a private room on the pediatric floor. He was asleep - or more appropriately passed out - for at least the next eight hours. The flood of tears had been cathartic for her. She wanted nothing more than to get home, go to sleep and dream that Rory was well; dream he was happy. It was only in that way that she felt she could be content. Archer knew, however, to reach this state of REM she would need help—the kind that warmed her belly and dimmed her thoughts.

It was after midnight. In the driver's seat, Archer squinted in an attempt to sharpen the edges around the blinking yellow traffic lights. The headlights of the few other cars on the roads were making her head throb harder. The only visible lights as she approached her neighborhood were at the Mobil To Go. Archer pulled into the parking lot, bumping the nose of the Subaru into a concrete pole intended to thwart lawbreakers. Inside the store, the fluorescent lighting felt like a million tiny knife blades in her spine.

"Archer," Connie looked up from a lottery scratch card. She pinched a tarnished nickel between her thumb and forefinger. "Do you know a man won five hundred dollars here the other day? It's costing me a fortune but the next winner is mine." She rubbed the card. "How's your mother doing?"

"My mother?" She had forgotten about her mother. Was she at the house?

"She was in here earlier this evening. Said she had really bad allergies. She was sniffling like the devil. Her eyes were all red. But she was dressed up like she was going out."

"Going out? Did she say where she was going?"

Why am I always asking the convenience store clerk where my family members are?

"To Martha's to return her van and play Canasta." Connie rung up the sale. "Seventeen dollars and thirty two cents."

Archer handed her a twenty, palmed the change. "I don't need a bag." She grabbed the bottle around the neck and hurried out of the store. To stay another second would be trouble. She wanted to blame Connie for everything. She wanted to blame everybody for everything. Yes, she needed to get out of there, fast.

Away from the lights of the convenience store, Archer reached for the bag in the seat next to her and took a long swig. Squinting at a set of head lights coming toward her, she savored the burn of the vodka as it traveled down her throat.

Driving into her garage, she caught a glimpse of the squatter squirrel who looked confused in the bright light.

"Not used to company this late, huh?"

She shut off the car, went into the house anticipating the clear elixir and her cuddle chair. In the kitchen, she poured vodka into a tall glass and added several ice cubes. She turned off the light in the kitchen, chastising herself for having left it on all day. She was about to sink into her cuddle chair when she realized it was already occupied. Trish was curled on her side, knees to her chest.

Archer rocked her hip. "Trish, wake up. You need to go home."

"Don't," Trish rolled over.

"Wake up honey," Archer patted her back then sat at the end of the chair. Trish stretched out her legs and put them on Archer's lap. Archer twirled the glass, listening to the ice tumble. "How did it go today?"

"I couldn't do it. I thought about how much you love Rory despite all the trouble he gets into and how you spend so much time taking care of him. I figured I could take care of the baby like you take care of Rory." Trish sat up. Her cheeks were rosy and her hair disheveled. She looked like a baby herself.

"Are you okay with your decision?"

Trish shrugged. "Why do you care what I do anyway? No one else does."

"I care about you. I just do. If you want the baby, you should have it. But it's very important you graduate from high school. You're a smart girl. You can go to college."

"This girl Taylor I know had a baby over the summer. She went to school while she was pregnant."

"Is she back at school since she had the baby?"

"I don't know."

Archer drained her glass, went into the kitchen and poured another. She returned to her chair, the glass in one hand, the bottle in the other.

"You have to do what's best for you," Archer said.

"You don't do what's best for you," Trish said. "Drinking that stuff is so lame."

Archer stared. What was it with teenagers? She never would have spoken to her friend's parent like that. In fact, she never even talked to adults when she was fifteen. Of course, she wasn't pregnant then either. And aside from Spin the Bottle, had no experience with the opposite sex.

Archer finished the drink. "I need to go to bed and you need to go home."

"Where's Rory?"

"Not now. Do you need me to take you home?"

Trish looked at the cup in Archer's hand. "No. But I can't go home anyway. They know I didn't have the abortion. My mom knows Raven is the father and she wants me to get rid of the baby. I'm not doing it."

"Is your mom still...?"

"What?" Trish asked.

"Is she still with Raven?"

Trish looked away then back at Archer. "It's complicated."

Archer emptied the bottle into her glass. She let the bottle tip over on the floor. She tried to think of something intelligent to say to Trish, something wise and motherly, but nothing came to her mind. The vodka was doing its job very well, thank you. "I'm going to bed."

She grabbed a quilt Grandma Rose had made and laid it over Trish's lap, kissed Trish on the top of her head and stumbled toward the stairs, positive she was hearing things when Trish said: "I hope I'll be as good of a mom as you."

CHAPTER SEVENTY

Archer carried the glass filled to the brim with clear elixir to her bedroom, wondering why Trish would ever want to emulate her as a mother. Was it Kara who had said Trish was nuts? Obviously, Kara was correct.

As she tackled the last step, a carpeted Everest, her body ached. Worse, her brain hurt. She put the glass on the bathroom sink and ran the water in the tub, adjusting the knobs to her favorite temperature—the hot all the way to the left, the cold in the middle. She tossed in chamomile lavender bath bubbles which were supposed to soothe but never worked. She found more comfort from the vodka. She raised the glass to her lips and drank, wishing she had bought a second bottle from that dumb ass Connie.

"Mrs. Falcon?"

She heard her name but couldn't figure out who was calling it or where the voice was coming from. Her legs were cramped. It was dark. Her head rested against something hard.

"Mrs. Falcon, where are you?" The voice was impatient, demanding.

Was that Trish?

Fabric draped around Archer's face and behind her back. It was rough like denim, coarse like flannel. Wires jabbed. Blades cut her. Underneath, was soft and fluffy. And then she figured out where she was. The comforter that cushioned her was Rory's long forgotten Lion King blanket. The fabric was the jeans and shirts he never wore. Dismantled motors and fans brushed her arms. She was in the depths of Rory's closet, unsure how she got there.

She moved her legs and kicked a fan. Her heel landed on a metal tool box buried beneath abandoned beanie babies. The closet door swung open. Archer shielded her eyes from the light.

"'What are you doing? I was going to call the cops. I couldn't find you." Trish stood over her, hands on her hips like a disappointed parent.

Archer crawled out of the closet, dragging wires and fan parts. Beanie crabs, dragons and poodles were tangled in her feet.

Trish sat next to her. "Why are you in Rory's closet?"

"Where is Rory? Is he okay?" Archer asked.

Trish put her arm awkwardly around Archer's shoulders. "I'm sure he's okay. He's always okay."

Archer trembled. With the unexpected shudder flowed a river of tears. "I miss him. I miss him so much."

"I know." Trish clumsily stroked her back.

Archer cried harder. "I miss the way he made coffee milk when he was nine years old. I miss Rory so much. And I miss my dad. He used to call liverwurst dinosaur meat and I'd laugh so hard when he made a mugwump face. Even if I was mad at him, he could make me laugh. And I miss Roman even though I never got to know him. And Wayne. Why didn't Wayne love me more than Marybeth? What's wrong with me? Why did they all leave me?"

"It's okay," Trish patted her back.

"No, it's not. Rory's in the hospital. In a straight jacket, for all I know. It's not his fault. He can't help the way he is."

"I know."

"If I wasn't his mother, he'd be okay, like other kids. It's my fault."

"No, it's not. Rory is the way he is."

"He blames me. I know he does."

"That's not true."

"Then why did he want to find his birth mother? How come I'm not good enough? What's wrong with me?" Tears salted Archer's tongue.

"He wants to find his birth family so he can be a better son," Trish said.

Archer stopped, studied Trish for a moment. "Did he tell you that?"

Trish shook her head. "C'mon, let's get you to bed." She pulled Archer up and walked her toward her bedroom.

"Did he really say that?"

"He thinks if he can meet a blood relative he can figure out why he is the way he is and be a better son to you."

Archer cried, leaned on Trish for support. "I thought he didn't love me. I thought I wasn't good enough for him."

Trish steered Archer toward her bed and under the covers. As Trish tucked the blanket under Archer and shut off the light, Archer spoke, her voice unsteady, her mouth dirty and dry.

"Don't be a mother like me," she said, "be a mother like you."

CHAPTER SEVENTY-ONE

Clanking woke the fire in Archer's brain. Pounding against the sides of her head, splitting her ears. Not even six in the morning. *Who would call this early?* Rory. He was in the hospital. She jumped out of bed, searched for her phone. She grabbed her clothes on the floor, rummaged through pockets, looked in drawers and on her dresser top. *Where was her cell phone?* She tripped over a pillow on the floor. No, not a pillow. Trish was asleep at the foot of her bed wrapped in Rory's old Lion King blanket as if she were a burrito. The one coping mechanism that even Archer thought worked—wrap yourself tight so only your nose and mouth stick out, ignore the rest of the world.

She finally found her ringing phone in the bathroom, breathlessly pressed a bunch of buttons and said: "Hello."

"Archer, it's me, Darcy."

"Is he okay?"

Archer gagged. The smell in the bathroom was awful. She saw vomit in the toilet. She flushed it. She hadn't heard Trish get sick during the night.

"He's fine," Darcy said. "He's still asleep. I checked on him a few times during the night. I get off in fifteen minutes and wanted to let you know."

"Thanks. I really appreciate it." She put her hand to her head to stop the dull ache. "Wayne is supposed to be there this morning. I'll be there later. I'm not feeling well right now."

The bathtub was filled with water. An empty mouthwash bottle floated in it. A drained glass was upended in the sink next to an empty bottle of cough syrup. She rinsed the cup and filled it with water, took a sip. The water tasted thick and nasty. She spit it out into the sink. Her stomach heaved. *Was she going to throw up? Was that her vomit in the toilet?*

"Wayne called the nurse's station a few minutes ago," Darcy said. "He can't get here until after lunch."

"You're kidding," Archer leaned over the sink. "Never mind, I know you're not kidding. Thanks for your help. Again."

She hung up, teetered on the side of the sink, waited for the nauseous feeling to pass. When it did, she called Kara.

"Hey," Archer pulled the drain to let the water out of the bathtub

"How's Rory?"

"Still asleep so I guess he's doing okay. I need a favor, as usual."

"Okay, as usual."

"Could you go to the hospital and sit with him for a bit? I would like someone he knows there when he wakes up and his father, of course, is too busy. I'm not feeling well right now and I need to run to the office."

"Sure, I'll be able to go there for a few hours. I'd like to spend some time with Rory. Have you seen Trish? She hasn't been to school in several days."

"She's with me."

"Really?"

"Long story," Archer said.

"I have a feeling when this is over, you're going to have a lot of stories to tell. Don't worry about Rory. I'll be there when he opens his eyes."

"Thanks. I may not tell you enough but I love you."

"I know."

Archer hung up before Kara could hear the quake in her voice. She crawled back into bed and wrapped herself into a burrito, only her nose and mouth sticking out.

CHAPTER SEVENTY-TWO

"Thank goodness you're back." Delores hugged Archer. "I almost e-mailed you my resignation thirty times."

"It's been a tough few days. I'm glad you didn't resign because then I'd have to fire you."

They smiled, knowing Archer had never fired an employee in her life; not even the secretary who spent hours picking and organizing paper clips so they were divided by color. The gold ones in one container; silver ones in the other. Fortunately, her husband had retired to Arizona and she had moved away.

Archer's office felt the same. Delores had made organized piles of reams of previously scattered paper but it was still her office. It was where she felt competent, where she could anticipate what would happen next. A world of four corners governed by statutes and laws. It wasn't real life. It wasn't a world with no boundaries, where pregnant fifteen year old girls rescued downhearted fools.

Delores' voice sang over the speaker phone. "Jim Strong, line two."

"Is he calling about the Kennedy case?" she yelled to Delores.

"He wants another extension of time."

Archer picked up the phone. "No."

"C'mon, Arch, what's the harm?" Jim asked. "It's a modification of child support. You know my guy is going to have to pay more. When we work it out, I'll get him to pay it retroactive. I promise."

"You have to drive another kid to college?"

"The younger one is still in high school, thank goodness. Hopefully this one won't be so smart so I won't have to pay for another Ivy League education. The things we do for our kids, huh?" he laughed. "Seriously, I'm preparing a lecture on the Salem Witch Trials for a convention next week."

"Why don't you give up law and write those books full time?"

"I wish I could but the books don't pay the bills. So can you give me another ten days?"

"No, Jim, we need to get going on this...wait, how about we make a deal?"

"I'm listening."

"I'll agree to another ten day extension if you give me a private lesson on the witch trials."

"Okay. What do you want to know?"

"Everything possible about the Warren family."

Archer wrapped her hands around a coffee mug, the warmth comforting. The temperature had fallen and she wished she had had brought a jacket with her. She thought of Rory, who took pride in not wearing a coat unless the temperature dipped below thirty degrees. She felt guilty not being at his bedside. But Kara was there and he was still sleeping.

Jim Strong shoveled a spoonful of oatmeal into his mouth. "Why the interest in the Warren family?"

They were seated at the counter of a local coffee shop, the same cafe Judge Murphy went to every morning. Archer was glad Murphy was in court.

"My son might be related to them," Archer said.

"To the Warren family from Salem?"

"Yes."

"Through your side or your husband's side of the family?"

Archer was stunned. She thought everyone had heard about their divorce. "Neither. Rory was adopted." She didn't correct the husband part.

"And you think he is genetically related to Mary Warren?"

"Who is Mary Warren?"

"One of the girls responsible for starting the hysteria that led to the hangings."

"Why are you so interested in this?" Archer asked.

"I read about the witch trials when I was in law school. It was a due process issue. They allowed spectral evidence. You know, ghosts. The girls would blame the ghosts of the accused. The judges led the girls mercilessly. They hanged the accused based on gossip and hearsay. Remember your favorite amendment? The Sixth. The right to confront your accuser. " Jim smiled.

Archer was taken aback. That interview seemed like ages ago. She half heartedly wondered if she got the appointment.

"It was a good answer. The committee was impressed by you. Too bad those accused of being witches back then had no rights. Okay," Jim shifted on the stool. "What do you want to know?"

"Start from the beginning."

"In 1692, a group of girls were in the forest in Salem dancing, playing, laughing and singing. They were caught."

"So?"

"This was a Puritan society. No dancing, no games, no fun. Work all day long. Go to church. Read the bible. Have sex only to procreate."

Archer blushed.

Jim paused. "Sorry. Anyway, Abigail Williams started the hysteria. Got the other girls to say they were dancing and singing because they were under a spell. Mary Warren worked for John Proctor. She told him the same thing. Proctor beat her then made her go back to work. The short of it is, the girls had to name the witches that had put them under the spells or else they'd get in trouble. "

"And the people they named were hanged."

"Only the ones who didn't admit they were witches. The interesting thing about Mary Warren was that she reneged on her statement that community members were witches. She told the judges that she and the other girls were lying, that there were no witches, no spells, no fits."

"What happened to Mary Warren?"

"She figured out if she continued to tell the truth she too would be hanged. So she changed her story again. She admitted to being a witch. She even named her master John Proctor. He was hanged."

"Were they actual witches?"

"Naw, I don't believe in that stuff. You know when we were kids and we used to play with Ouija Boards and do pretend séances? That's probably what the girls were doing. They were bored teenagers and found a way to draw attention to themselves. The people who were hanged were odd-balls like loners and widowers, maybe they were mentally challenged, or they were involved in land disputes with folks in power. Mary Warren's family died when she was young, that's why she was living with Proctor. In fact, most of the accusers had no parents. Mary Warren probably would have some mental diagnosis today – post traumatic stress disorder or something like that. I've tried to trace her history but I've come up empty. Her story is the most blatant example of how injudicious the Salem Witch Trials were. Why do you think Rory is related Mary Warren?"

"It's a long story," she sighed.

"I have all day."

"I thought you had a lecture to prepare. Isn't that why you're not working on an Answer on Kennedy?"

"You're not going to believe this."

"What?"

"The lecture I'm preparing is on Mary Warren."

Archer felt a hand on her shoulder, turned her head.

"Ms. Falcon, what a pleasure to see you."

"Your Honor," Archer said.

"Hi, Judge," Jim said.

"Mind if I join you both?" Judge Murphy sat at the stool next to Archer.

A waitress put a mug of steaming coffee in front of him. "The usual?" she asked.

"Please." He looked at Archer, "I hear there's been some trouble with Rory."

Archer was surprised. "What did you hear?"

"Suspended from school. The restraining order. The search for his birth parents."

"How…?"

"Connie is my mother in law's second cousin, or something like that. They tell each other everything. My mother in law tells my wife. Most of the time I don't listen to gossip. It's not very reliable evidence. But when I heard Rory's name, I was concerned."

"Connie tells her everything?" Archer asked.

"Everything."

Archer pictured bottles of vodka on the counter of the Mobil To Go. Hopefully Connie didn't tell everything.

"Did you know, Judge, that Rory may be a descendant of one of the major players of the Salem Witch Trials?" Jim leaned on the counter to involve himself in their conversation. "Archer and I were just about to get into some genealogy."

The waitress put a brown bag on the counter, its top folded over, sealed.

Judge Murphy laid down a five dollar bill. "I'll leave you alone then. I always take my breakfast to the office. Have to get that paperwork done." He placed a hand on Archer's shoulder. "How is he?"

Tears filled her eyes. "Not so good."

"I'm sorry. If I can help, let me know."

She nodded, the lump in her throat so thick she couldn't speak.

Judge Murphy stood, grabbed the paper bag, then leaned down and whispered in her ear. "Don't forget the Skittles."

CHAPTER SEVENTY-THREE

Thinking of the Skittles and Rory as a baby, tears streamed down Archer's face as she walked into her bank, hoping the sunglasses would hide her anguish; that no one would want to speak with her if they couldn't see her eyes.

She was in and out speedily, the documents from her safe deposit box tucked in her pocketbook. Back in the car, she looked at her phone, realized she had missed a call while in the vault.

The message from Kara was garbled due to poor reception in the hospital. Archer could barely make it out. Something about Rory. In trouble. Again.

Archer was once again matching her footsteps to Darcy's quick strides down the sterile, hospital hallway.

"When Rory woke up," Darcy said, "he was groggy. Even though my shift had ended, I didn't leave. He was calm but I think as the meds wore off, he got more and more agitated. That's when they restrained him again."

Kara was at the end of the hallway. Archer ran, turned into Rory's room, gasped. He lay in the bed, staring at the ceiling. His wrists and ankles were bound to the sides of the frame. A net was spread over him, clipped to the bed on the corners.

"Get that off of him." Archer screamed. She could no longer watch her son be fettered through no fault of his own. "Now. Before I sue everyone here. Get that off of him." Archer ran to the bed, tugged on the ropes and restraints.

Kara grabbed her arm. Archer shook her away.

"Release my son," she yelled.

Four nurses ran into the room.

"Now. Or else every one of you will lose your jobs," she shrieked.

They looked at each other, frozen. Another nurse walked in, authorized his release with wide eyes and a nod.

Free, Rory sat up. Kara and Darcy stood by the door.

"Can you leave us alone?" Archer asked.

The women hesitated then left. Archer took Rory's hand. He didn't pull away. She couldn't tell if it was his hands or hers that were shaking. Or both.

"Are you okay?" Archer asked.

"Yeah. I'm sorry, Mom. I really love you."

"I'm sorry, too. I really love you."

"I know my real dad's alive. Kitty told me."

"Why do you believe her? Can you trust her?"

Had Kitty relied on spectral evidence, Archer thought, like her ancestors? But in this circumstance, there were no ghosts. Jib Pero was long dead.

Rory leaned his head back then looked toward the door. Archer followed his gaze. Campbell was there. Her heart jumped.

"Give me a second, okay?"

"Yeah," Rory said.

Archer stepped outside the door, felt his big hands on her shoulders.

"You okay?" Campbell asked.

"As good as can be, I guess."

"How's Ror?"

"I can't tell. I'm so worried about him."

"I need to tell you something." He looked around the hallway. "Come here." He pulled her into a utility room, grabbed her, kissed her hard. Archer fell into his embrace.

"I'm sorry," he held her close.

"Me too."

"Maybe..."

"Yeah. Maybe." She looked up at him. "I don't want to leave Rory for too long."

They left the utility room. Kara and Darcy stood outside Rory's room, appearing dazed. Archer raced in. Campbell behind her.

Rory was gone.

CHAPTER SEVENTY-FOUR

Archer stared at the empty hospital bed, reminiscent of the time her car was stolen. She just stood on the street, staring at the parking spot in Forest Hills, New York. Her Mazda RX-7 replaced by a Ford something-or-other.

"Where is he?" Her question lingered in the antiseptic air.

Campbell was on her left. Kara to her right. Darcy at the door.

"I'll call security," Darcy left.

"Where is he?" Archer asked again, louder. "Somebody answer me."

Kara gently touched her arm. "We don't know."

"Where'd he go? I thought you were watching him." She stared at the bed.

"I was...I'm sorry," Kara stammered. "Darcy and I were talking and..."

"No," Archer took Kara's hand and squeezed it. "It's not your fault. He's probably at the soda machine or talking to another kid."

"I'll check the floor," Campbell trotted out.

Archer thought of all the times she did nothing after Rory had disappeared, all the times she took refuge in the cuddle chair, knowing he would come back. But this felt different. She recalled his episode the day before. His rising panic, the insistence his birth father was alive, his turns and spins on the floor, Wayne more interested in reconnecting with his buddy than helping his son. This time, the cuddle chair wasn't an option.

She looked at Kara. "We have to find him."

Archer turned to leave but stopped short. Wayne was at the door.

"Where's Rory?" he asked.

"Gone," Archer said.

"What do you mean gone?"

"Look it up in the fucking dictionary. Gone. No longer present. Not here."

Kara stood next to Archer, spoke calmly. "I believe gone is the past participle of go."

"Okay," Wayne said. "I got the message. I had something to do this morning but now I'm here. I can spend the whole day with him. Where is he? Have you checked the soda machine?"

"We don't know where he is," Archer said, softly.

"Have you called his cell?"

Archer grabbed her phone from her pocket, hiding any sign that Wayne had offered a good idea. She dialed, pressed send. Eminem's rap lyrics were muffled. Wayne picked up the pillow from Rory's bed, grabbed the phone and silenced it. Archer took the phone, sank to the ground, her back against the metal braces of the hospital bed.

Campbell ran into the room. "I've checked the entire pediatric wing. Darcy has security looking for him. The exits to the hospital have been sealed. Nothing yet. Did you try his cell phone?"

Archer looked up. "He's gone."

"What do you mean gone?" Campbell asked.

Archer sighed. "He left his phone. He never goes anywhere without his phone."

"He can't be far," Wayne said.

"I'll call it in." Campbell ran out of the room.

Archer held Rory's cell phone, recalling all that had occurred over the last several days. From Bangor to Gloucester to Salem back to Gloucester, now home in Bangor again. Rory in a rollover car accident with Trish. Trish pregnant. Rory meeting Kitty. Rory being accused of her murder. Rory taping their conversation. Rory in the car throwing pieces of his ghille suit. Rory spinning, spinning, spinning,...

It took Archer just a moment to figure out how Rory's cell phone acted as a recorder. Yes, she was correct. Rory had lied. He hadn't erased their conversation. She pressed play.

Rory sounded urgent. "Where are you going?"

Kitty's voice was soft and getting softer, like she was walking away from him. "I'm going to make things right."

"How?"

"My mother's gone. I have no one. I'd be better off if I end it."

"End it?" His voice began to panic.

"I have nothing."

"You have me."

Archer turned off the recorder. Blood rushed to her head, her throat closed and a weight sunk in her stomach. She couldn't stand to hear him so worried and so sad. She didn't want to hear Kitty reject him. But she had to know what happened. She looked at Kara, then at Wayne. She flipped the recorder back on.

"You can come with us to Bangor," Rory said. "You can open a Crow's Nest there. We don't have good restaurants like this. My mom can take care of you. She is really good at taking care of me. She loves babies and dogs. She would take care of you. I know she would." Rory spoke quickly, more to himself than to Kitty. "I don't know what to do. Maybe I'll call mom. But she'll be mad that I'm here. Maybe Detective Ellen. I don't know." Rory's voice grew louder, sharper. "You can't do that. That won't work anyway. You won't die. You'll only be unconscious from the gas. It's not like you're in a running car with the garage door closed. I always tell my mom not to do that."

Kitty chanted over Rory's rising panic. "Toads and frogs and whippoorwills, I cast you out. Toads and frogs and whippoorwills, I cast you out."

She continued in the background as Rory spoke. "My friend Trish cuts herself. She says she wants to die. I won't let her. I don't want you to die. Bad things always happen but there are people that need you. Like I need Trish so she can't die. My mom needs me so I can't die. I'm sure someone needs you."

"Toads and frogs and whippoorwills, I cast you out. Toads and frogs and whippoorwills, I cast you out."

Archer heard a thump.

"Oh no, oh no, oh no. 911. I have to call 911."

The recorder went dead.

Archer's phone rang. Archer, Kara and Wayne jumped.

"Rory?"

"No, Mrs. Falcon. This is Connie from the Mobil To Go."

"Is Rory with you?"

"He was. He loaded up with his usual supplies. Said he had a long trip."

"Was Trish with him?"

"No, he said he ran here from the hospital."

"Did he say where he was going?"

"No."

"Connie, this is very important. Rory is sick. I need to know where he is going."

"I swear, he didn't tell me."

"How long ago did he leave?"

"Just a couple of minutes ago. Wait…" Connie said.

"What?"

"What is it?" Wayne asked.

Archer held up her hand. "Connie, are you there? Connie?"

"Is Rory okay?" Wayne knelt next to Archer.

"Wayne, please, give me a minute. Connie, are you there?"

Connie's voice floated back over the satellites. "I'm watching Rory now."

"Can I speak to him?" Archer asked.

Campbell came back into the room. "Archer."

"Not, now," she said. "Connie, can I speak to him?"

"No, he's not here."

"Where is he?"

"He just left. He's driving Mr. Jenkins' riding lawn mower."

"I just got a report on Rory," Campbell said. "I know where he is."

"A riding lawn mower?" Archer asked.

"He just drove by on the street. I saw him through the window," Connie said.

"Where is he going?"

"He's getting on the interstate," Campbell said.

Archer dropped the phone. "What? On a lawn mower?"

"He's going to I-95."

"Don't tell me," Archer sighed, "he's heading toward Gloucester."

CHAPTER SEVENTY-FIVE

"There he is." Campbell had one hand on the steering wheel of the police car, the other held a microphone close to his mouth.

Archer recognized the lawn mower. Rory had pointed it out to her many times, called it the Monster Mowchine and talked about it frequently—the choke, the drive shaft, the horsepower. How Mr. Jenkins had let him drive it one day. How Rory's dream was to save enough money from mowing lawns and shoveling snow to buy one just like it, soup it up, maybe race it one day. Rory sat high on top of the yellow seat, his shoulders hunched forward, his hands grasping the handlebars.

Campbell spoke into the microphone. "I'm following a white male, fifteen years old, dressed in black and seated on top of a riding lawn mower. He's heading toward the interstate. He's going five to ten miles per hour." Campbell looked at the speedometer. "Closer to ten."

The blue lights of the police car slowly turned. Rory's black flannel pajama bottoms flapped in the wind. He wore a University of Maine hoody sweatshirt. In the opposite lane, traffic slowed. Archer twisted in the front passenger seat. A row of cars were stacked behind them.

"No need for back up," Campbell spoke into the microphone. "I don't want to scare him. We'll get him home."

Rory held out his arm, signaling a right turn. He pointed at the entrance onto the interstate heading south. Archer felt the tap on her left shoulder. She looked at Wayne in the back seat. She knew what he was thinking.

"I remember too," she said.

Wayne leaned forward. She felt his breath in her ear. "That was one of his first questions about riding a bicycle. How to let people know he was turning?"

"I think he's the only kid in the world who uses hand signals." Archer faced forward, watched Rory steer onto the ramp. "I wish he wasn't going onto the interstate. We should stop him. Cut him off or something. What do you think, Campbell?"

"No, don't." Wayne said. "He'll freak out and run away."

"We can't let him go on the highway," Archer kept her eyes on Rory who was halfway up the ramp, "The cars go too fast. He'll get hurt, or worse…." She looked toward Campbell. "Stop him."

"I think Wayne's right. Let's see what he does. This isn't a safe place to stop him anyway. If he runs off the road, he'll end up in that ditch. And if that lawn mower falls on him…"

"He's a good driver," Wayne said. "Always has been. Whether it's his bike or a lawn mower or a snow blower. He's good with machines. And I hear he's been collecting gas cans."

"On top of all the other junk in the house," Archer said," he now has a collection of different colored and shaped gas cans. I don't know what his infatuation with those things are."

"There's something about guys and gasoline," Campbell said.

"It would be a lot easier if he collected stamps," Wayne shifted his weight until he leaned into the front seat, equally between Archer and Campbell.

"You tried to get him into that, remember? He ended up decorating his room and Rutherford with them."

"Yeah," Wayne laughed. "We started with National Park stamps. Rutherford looked ridiculous covered in those stamps. There wasn't anything Rory couldn't do to that dog."

"He used to sit on top of him like he was a horse."

"Rory loved Rutherford," Archer said. "He was calmer when he was around."

"Yeah," Wayne said. "How come we never got him another dog?"

"Because you left us and I could barely handle Rory alone," Archer snapped.

Wayne sat back. The silence didn't last long.

"Hey, Campbell, you okay doing this while on duty?" Wayne asked. "You are on duty, right?"

"Yeah."

"I was wondering the same thing," Archer said.

"It's okay, as long as we're in Maine," Campbell said.

"Think he'll make it to Gloucester on that thing?" Archer asked. "It's over two hundred miles away."

"He'll run out of gas way before then," Campbell said. "A riding lawn mower like that only has about a five gallon tank. He won't be able to get more than twenty five miles tops."

"At ten miles per hour," Wayne said, "that'll take him over two hours. I don't know Rory to do anything for that long."

"Except mow lawns," Archer said as Rory steered into the right hand lane.

Campbell drove steadily behind him, blue lights reflecting off the back of the shiny yellow and green mower.

"Think there's anything we can do to stop Rory from this expedition? I mean, he's already met Kitty. His birth father is dead. Where do you think he's going?" Wayne leaned forward again.

"Back to Gloucester. He thinks his birth father is alive."

"What's wrong with us?" Wayne sat back. "When we decided on adoption, this wasn't part of the plan."

Archer sighed, watched Rory. "No, none of this was part of the plan."

"If I had known he'd be obsessed with finding out about his birth parents…"

Archer deliberately interrupted him. Wherever Wayne was going with this thought, wasn't going to make her happy. "I went to the safe deposit box and got the paperwork from his adoption. I thought I might get information to help Rory find out more about his birth parents, especially his father. We're not going to stop him from his search. We might as well help him."

"And. . ?" Wayne asked.

Archer reached into her bag and grabbed a packet of papers folded in half. "Let's see. We know about his birth mother." She read from the papers. "Kitty Warren, age thirty eight at the time of the adoption. His birth father was younger, thirty years old. His name was Jib Pero. Caucasian, five foot eleven inches, light brown hair, passed the physical exam." Archer looked up. "That could describe anyone – even Campbell." She playfully punched his arm.

"Hey, don't do that." He righted the steering wheel. "Keep your eyes on Rory."

"Why does he think the guy's alive?" Wayne asked.

"Kitty told him, but she was crazy. At least that's what Ellen said. And from meeting Kitty and hearing the tape of her conversation with Rory, I would say Ellen was right. Ellen and Kitty knew each other. Ellen was there when Rory was born, caught him even. She was the one who handed Rory to me at the airport. She had wanted to adopt him."

"Why such interest in Rory?" Wayne asked.

"Ellen is Jib's sister. She's Rory's aunt."

"Did she tell Rory?" Wayne asked.

"No. I told her not to."

Ahead, Rory slung his right arm out, bent down, palm out—the universal signal for stop. He pulled onto the shoulder. Campbell stopped behind him. Archer, Wayne and Campbell opened their doors at the same time.

"No. Just me." Archer ran around the front of the police car and stopped at the side of the mower. Atop the mower, Rory stretched his arms over his head like he had just woken from a long nap.

"Hi," she said, "Where are you going?"

"Gloucester. I know he's alive."

"We'll take you." She held out her hand.

He took it. Together, they walked toward the police car.

Rory stopped, looked back. "Think Mr. Jenkins will be mad if I leave the mowchine on the side of the road?"

Archer smiled. "I'm sure he'll understand."

CHAPTER SEVENTY-SIX

Rory slid into the back seat of the police car as Archer got in the front, turned her head, hoping Wayne and Rory would have a positive exchange.

"Hey, Big Guy," Wayne squeezed his shoulder.

"Hi," Rory cast his eyes down, leaned against the window. He dug into his pajama pockets and pulled out his I-pod and ear buds. A Vault energy drink and a bag of Funyons peeked out of the pocket of the front of his sweatshirt.

"How was the ride?" Wayne asked.

"Okay."

"Reminded me of when Teddy Roosevelt rode a cow catcher to Limoru in British East Africa. It was in 1909 so he wasn't President anymore but they still treated him like royalty. Do you know what a cow catcher is? It's mounted to the front of a train to prevent obstacles on the track from derailing it. Now, they call it a pilot. President Roosevelt took his son, Kermit, with him. It was slow going, that's for sure. Trains didn't move in those days as fast as they do now. Maybe we can go on a trip together one day."

Rory shrugged.

"There's a lawnmower museum in Lancashire, Great Britain," Wayne said. "We can go there. Just the two of us."

"Really?"

"Yeah, we'll have a blast."

Archer resisted asking Wayne how he planned to pay for the trip when he couldn't afford to pay his child support.

"How far do you think you made it on that thing?" Campbell pulled the police car back onto the interstate, heading south. No flashing lights, no siren.

"The tank wasn't full," Rory said. "I was stupid. Maybe made it ten miles. Did you clock it?"

"No, I should have but I'd think you're about right. We can check it another time. Put the odometer on zero, start at the Mobil To Go then end here. How fast did you get 'er?"

"I'm not sure if the speedometer is accurate and it doesn't have a seat belt so I didn't push it. Maybe nine miles per hour. Mr. Jenkins made that engine sweet. I was worried about blowing a tire. I wouldn't want to be on the interstate on the mowchine with a busted tire. Would you?"

"No way."

"Mr. Jenkins said he'd help me build a lawn mower to race. That'd be chill."

"Do all riding lawn mowers go that fast?" Wayne asked.

"They only go like five miles per hour unless you work on the engine," Rory said. "Everyone knows that."

"I was just asking, son. No need to jump down my back."

"Rory," Campbell eyed him in the rearview mirror. "I will not take you to Gloucester if you talk to your father like that."

"I don't need you to fight my battles, Officer. I can handle my son without your help."

Archer turned to Campbell. "You're going to Gloucester?"

"We're all going."

"I thought you couldn't take the police car out of Maine. I had assumed you'd turn around at the next exit and head home then Rory and I would go ourselves."

Wayne leaned forward. "I'm his father. I'm going too."

"Me too," Campbell said. "I'm his...friend."

"Why would you think you and Rory would go alone?" Wayne asked.

"Maybe because anything that involves Rory I end up doing myself."

The men didn't respond. Godsmack played from Rory's ear buds. If Archer hadn't heard the band hundreds of times, she wouldn't recognize the muffled sounds.

Campbell spoke into his microphone. "Have someone pick up a riding lawn mower on 95 South. About four miles from the Hammond Street exit. Might want to send a flatbed."

"A flatbed?" Rory asked. "Wicked. Sorry I'm going to miss that. Hey, Mom, can you call Detective Ellen?"

"Why?"

"Because."

"You want me to tell her anything specific?"

"Tell her I'm sorry I took her spray paint."

Ellen picked up on the first ring. "Is Rory okay?"

"As good as can be expected. We're heading your way."

"You are?"

Archer looked into the back seat. Rory's head was rocking up and down. He was consumed by the heavy metal of *Godsmack*.

Archer spoke softly. "He thinks his birth father is still alive. Kitty told him that. Do you know why she'd say that?"

"Because she's crazy."

"I don't know what to do."

"Where are you now?"

Archer looked out the window. "About forty five minutes from the Massachusetts border."

"Just you and Rory?"

"His father is here too. And Officer Campbell. He's with the Bangor P.D. and Rory's school resource officer."

"Let me speak to him."

Archer handed the phone to Campbell, who didn't move to take it. "What?"

"Detective Ellen O'Neill wants to speak to you."

"Tell her I'm driving." He put on his mirrored sunglasses.

"You talk on that microphone while you drive all the time," Archer said. "And on your cell."

"That's business. It's different."

"This is about Rory."

"Tell her I'm driving."

Archer put the phone back to her ear. "He's busy."

"Okay, fine. I'll meet you at the border. Give you a police escort into Gloucester. See you in forty five."

"Wait," Archer said, "I'm sorry for how I treated you at the hospital."

"I know this is hard for you."

"I just don't know the right thing to do. I wish Rory came with a manual. It would probably be the only one of its kind."

"Maybe you can write it."

"I'm too busy living it."

Ellen laughed. "Listen, I want to be part of Rory's life but the final decision is yours. If you say no, I'll meet you at the border, escort you into town and you'll never hear from me again."

"Really?"

"He's your son. I have to respect that."

Archer thought for a moment. "I think that's the right thing to do. I think this is too much for him. I need to get him stable."

Ellen was quiet.

"Are you there?" Archer asked.

"Yes," she said softly.

"I'm sorry if that hurts but it's what's best for Rory. And there's no reason for you to meet us. We can make it to Gloucester just fine."

"Please. I promise, let me do this one thing and I won't contact you or him again."

Archer looked into the back seat, considered getting Wayne's opinion. Wayne had one of Rory's buds in his ear, Rory had the other.

"Fine," Archer said.

"One more thing. Where is Rory going when he gets to Gloucester?"

"I don't know. He hasn't told me." Archer motioned toward the back seat to get Rory's attention.

Rory looked up, took the bud out of his ear.

"Detective O'Neill wants to know where we're going once we get to Gloucester. What should I tell her?"

"Tell her I'm going to see the man with the gas globes."

Archer repeated Rory's words.

"Clyde?" Ellen asked. "At the lawn mower shop?"

"I guess."

"He thinks Clyde is his father?"

Archer turned around, looked at Rory again. The bud was back in his ear.

"Clyde is not his father," Ellen said.

"Why would he think that?"

"I don't know."

"Wait. You told me at the hospital that Rory's birth father collected gas globes. He must have heard you. And Clyde has gas globes in his shop. He showed them to Rory."

"I know he has them," Ellen said. "I gave the globes to Clyde. He and my brother were best friends."

"Should I tell him?" Archer turned around again.

Rory leaned into Wayne. Wayne's hand was on Rory's knee.

"Awesome riff," Wayne said.

"I told you they were wicked good."

Archer wished she had that manual now. She looked at Campbell who seemed mesmerized by the road. As the cruiser rocketed toward Gloucester, Archer sighed.

CHAPTER SEVENTY-SEVEN

Lawn mowers surrounded the entrance to Clyde's shop as Campbell parked the cruiser in front. Ellen pulled in behind them. Rory jumped out of the car, ear buds swinging. Archer ran after him. The bells on the lawn mower shop door jingled as it swung open, then shut, open then shut again.

Inside, Rory stopped short in front of the counter. Clyde looked up from a gas globe he was polishing. The words Kendall DeLuxe sparkled in blue and red. For the first time Archer had ever witnessed, Rory was speechless.

"Everything okay, son?" Clyde looked over half rimmed spectacles.

"I knew it," Rory said.

"Knew what?"

"You called me son. You are my father."

Clyde carefully put the globe down. "Wouldn't that be nice. But I never had any children. At least any that I know of," he laughed, stopped when he saw Rory's expression unchanged. "You're serious."

"You collect gas globes. I collect gas cans."

Clyde looked at Archer who stood near the door of the store. Archer knew without hesitation the right thing for Rory. She nodded.

"Come back here, son." Clyde lifted a shelf that led behind the counter.

Rory shuffled through.

"Feel this," Clyde took Rory's hand and rubbed it over the globe. "Smooth, isn't it?"

"Yeah."

Clyde looked at Archer. "Women don't get it, do they? Men just love machines and anything to do with them. I have a John Deere behind the shop that I love like it came from my loins. Here," Clyde handed the globe to Rory, "I want you to have this."

Rory cradled the globe to his chest. "They told me you were dead."

"I'm not your father, but if I had a son, I would like him to be as handsome and polite as you are."

"You're not...?"

Clyde shook his head. "Your father was a wonderful man. Brave, strong, born a sailor, died a sailor. I don't know why you thought differently. I'm sorry if you're disappointed. If your father were alive, he would be with you. That was the kind of man he was."

Rory wiped his eyes. "I'm sorry. I thought..."

"That's okay," Clyde pulled Rory into him.

Rory buried his head in Clyde's chest. Clyde rubbed a big hand over Rory's back. The bells rang on the front door again. Archer turned, saw Campbell step in, his mirrored glasses reflecting the disarrayed shelves of the store. He brushed by Archer like she wasn't there, stepped to the counter and faced Clyde. Campbell removed his glasses. Archer took a step forward, thought better of it, stayed where she was. Rory's back heaved, his head still deep in Clyde's chest.

Clyde pulled Rory away from him, looked deep in his eyes. "If you want to see your father, turn around."

"What?" Slowly, Rory turned, faced Campbell.

The bells rang again.

Ellen sprinted into the store. "Jib?" She ran to Campbell, threw her arms around his neck. Campbell kept his arms at his side then grabbed her, pulled her into him.

The bells again. "What's going on?" Wayne asked from behind Archer.

"Rory's found his birth father," Archer said.

"What?" Wayne asked.

Archer turned her back on the reunion. "Campbell's a fraud," she said, "and I hope he rots in hell."

CHAPTER SEVENTY-EIGHT

Despite knowing they were mostly written by people living in pretend worlds, Archer had read too many self help books to keep count. Tomes from so-called experts who espoused on everything from perfect parenting to improving your self esteem to living in the Now. But she was far from the perfect parent, her self esteem sucked and she definitely hated the Now. She preferred the Never.

She watched Rory, excited and anxious like a kid at a circus, his head swiveling from the strong man to the bearded lady to the clowns, trying not to miss any of the strange acts. Campbell, Ellen and Clyde were huddled around him. Ellen's hands cupped her brother's face. Clyde patted the shoulder of his no-longer-dead best friend.

Where did she fit in? Wayne's fingers wrapped around her hand, covering her knuckles. Long ago, they had fit together well. Now, she felt uncomfortable with him standing so close; her fingers trapped.

"How are you here? What happened? Man, where you been?" Clyde's words spewed, quick and jumbled like the speech of an anxious auctioneer.

Campbell stepped back, leaned on the counter. He dropped his head into his hands. His broad back shook. Archer had never seen him cry before.

"It was my fault." The words struggled out of his mouth.

"What was?" Ellen asked.

"The Andrea Gail. It went down because of me. They died because of me. My friends. My brothers."

"What are you talking about? It wasn't your fault," Clyde said. "The storm was the worst ever. Nobody knew. How could you have known?"

"I knew, alright." He muscled his way past Clyde and stood near a rack of motor oil. He looked down at Ellen. "They all wanted to turn back. I said no."

"You weren't the captain," Ellen said, "it wasn't your decision to make."

"I talked him into it. I told him we could outrun her. I told him we would be the only ones left out there and all the kill would be ours. He didn't want to do it but I talked him into it."

"It's not your fault, man," Clyde shook his head.

"Those boys would still be alive if it weren't for me."

Rory grabbed his ear buds and shoved them into his ears. He plunged his hands into his sweatshirt pocket, tucked his chin into his chest. He paced his little dance. Archer knew he was listening though, heard every word. She tried to walk toward him but Wayne tightened his grip on her hand.

"How did you survive?" Ellen asked.

"I don't know. I was the last one. The rest...well, they were gone, drowned. I hung to a piece of the boat. I prayed for death. I don't remember anything else except waking up in the hospital."

"Where?"

"Nova Scotia. I told them I lost my I.D. The name Michael Campbell came to me. I created a new identity, a new history. I knew I couldn't go home."

"You could have always come home," Ellen said.

"Where'd you go?" Clyde asked.

"I bummed around for awhile, then I went to Bangor, joined the police department. I wanted to be close to Rory."

Rory picked his head up.

Campbell looked at him. "I knew you were living there with your adoptive family."

"How would you know that? He wasn't even born when you left, and, well," Ellen looked around the room, "we never told you."

"I found out from Kitty."

"You were in touch with Kitty?"

"Only once. Just to find out how you were. And to find out what happened to the baby."

Rory stepped toward Campbell. "You're my father."

Wayne moved forward this time. Archer tightened her grip on his arm, stopped him.

"It's complicated," Campbell said.

Ellen looked at Archer and Wayne. "Can we speak to you alone?"

"Not alone," Rory said. "I can handle it, Mom. I swear. This is about me. I'm not a kid anymore."

Wayne squeezed Archer's hand, puffed his chest. "Whatever you have to say, you can say in front of our son."

Archer felt the fear rise in her throat. "I don't know."

"Please," Rory took Archer's other hand. "I really really love you, Mom. I can handle it. I promise. No more secrets."

She looked at Rory, so handsome. Tall, lean, wisps of hair on his upper lip. Physically, he was almost a man. Emotionally, well...

Archer sighed. Maybe decisions weren't right or wrong, good or bad. Maybe they were just...decisions.

It was Now or Never. She chose Now.

She gripped Rory's and Wayne's hands firmly. "Whatever you have to say, you can say in front of our son."

CHAPTER SEVENTY-NINE

Archer ran out of the lawnmower store. She needed a drink. Now. And fast. Head down, she darted to the bar across the street and landed on a stool at the counter. The old bar smelled of the sea and stale beer. She and the bartender were the only ones there.

"Vodka on the rocks," she said. "Make it a double and keep 'em coming."

"We don't get many tourists in here," the bartender scooped ice into a glass. "Most of 'em go to The Crows Nest on account of The Perfect Storm." The bartender put the drink down, the clear liquid swishing over the sides of the short glass.

Archer took a quick sip and felt the heat of the elixir in her mouth, down her throat. The bartender stood in front of her. Probably in her mid-forties, she was wind burnt and tanned. The wrinkles around her eyes and mouth suggested a hard life.

The bartender wiped the bar top. "What brings you here?"

Archer had the same question for herself. What had brought her here? She recalled the letters Rory had written on the four fingers of his left hand. That was it, she thought, that was what had brought her here.

Archer swirled the ice in the glass, downed the remaining liquid in one gulp. "Fate. Do you have children?"

The bartender filled Archer's glass and placed the vodka bottle on the bar. "No kids. Never found anyone I wanted to have children with. Never figured I could take care of anyone beyond myself anyway."

"That's probably a good way to think about it. Some women shouldn't have kids. But you know, you don't have to find someone to have a kid with. Just have someone donate his sperm and bingo, instant baby." She knew she sounded bitter. Hell, she was bitter.

"That sounds wrong." The bartender wiped her hands on her apron. "It's not natural."

"Tell me about it." Archer sank the ice cubes in her glass and watched them float to the surface.

"It sounds like witchcraft or black magic." The woman continued.

Archer searched her eyes. Did she know?

"You're right," Archer gulps the second drink. "It's just like witchcraft. This pregnant woman freaks out. Reports hearing things and seeing things. She thinks she's a witch. She puts spells over the unborn baby, says he is the devil and has to die. When he's born, he can't stay around her. It's not safe."

"Freaky. Where does he go?" The bartender walked around the bar and sat on the stool next to Archer.

"He goes away to live with another family. And the sperm donor follows him. He pretends to like the boy's adoptive mother and the boy's adoptive mother is a dumb ass." *How could she have thought that Campbell, um, Jib, whatever his name, had really liked her? Had really loved her, for that matter.* "And now the boy is almost a man and he wants to find his real family."

Would he be happier with his real family? Isn't that what a good parent would do - make the sacrifice? Shit, hadn't she already sacrificed enough?

Dread filled Archer's stomach as she recalled the scene in Clyde's store. Rory and Ellen embracing; Wayne watching, dumbfounded; Campbell and Clyde reminiscing over the gas globe collection; and Rory, surrounded by his *real* family.

"Your son is Kitty's baby, isn't he?"

Archer pushed her glass toward the bartender who filled it. "How did you know?"

"Small town, big mouths. Kitty talked about him wanting to see her. Said something about it a day or two before she died. We've all been hoping it was true. That the boy had returned. He's a legend around here. We never knew what happened to Kitty's baby."

"He wanted to find his real family so he can figure out why he is the way he is. He got to meet Kitty before she died. He knows Ellen is his Aunt. And now, he's met his father."

The bartender stood, knocking the stool down behind her. "Impossible. Jib is dead."

Archer swallowed her drink. "True."

The bartender reached over the bar and grabbed a shot glass, poured a drink for herself. Archer considered the repercussions of Jib being alive after all these years; not only how it affected her and Rory, but how it affected the town of Gloucester.

Archer filled her own glass this time. "Campbell is Jib and he's very much alive."

The bartender righted the stool, sat on it. "I don't know anything about this Campbell guy but I can tell you your son is special. Not a lot of kids can say their mom's a witch and an entire town makes up stories about his fate. It's been a favorite pastime round here, like folk lore. To make up stories about what happened to Kitty's baby. To figure out his fate."

FATE. Of course.

"He's definitely special." Archer wiped her eyes.

"Why are you crying?"

"I don't want to lose him. I don't want to be a bonus." Tears flowed as Archer imagined life without Rory. "I'm sorry." She whispered and slid off the bar stool.

She wanted out of her skin, out of her life. She wanted someone else's life. Someone who was witty and charming and knew how to be a parent. She ran into the bathroom, leaned on the sink and dared to look in the mirror. She wanted a do-over.

Her cell phone rang. She looked at the caller ID, surprised that she felt relief.

"Hi, Mom." Archer tried to mask the quiver in her voice.

"Thank goodness you answered. I've been worried sick. What happened? Is Rory okay?"

Archer didn't know what to say. Was Rory okay? Would Rory ever be okay? Should she tell her about Kitty's suicide, Rory's break-down, Rory's new-found family? Should she say she was sorry for being a terrible daughter to her, a worse mother to Rory?

"Are you there? Are you okay?" Rose asked.

"Rory got to meet Kitty." Archer said.

"How did that go?"

"She said crazy things to him. Then she killed herself. Rory thought he made her do it."

"Kitty killed herself? Is Rory okay? I'm so sorry. I could have helped you . . . " Rose stopped. "I know. You don't need me."

"That's not true."

"Is he okay?"

"He's happy right now. He met his birth father and his biological aunt." Her voice broke.

"Are you crying?"

Archer couldn't respond. The tears mugged her voice.

"Where are you?" Rose asked.

"In the bathroom at a bar in Gloucester."

"Archer, Honey, listen to me. Blow your nose, drink water and sit down. I'll wait."

Archer grabbed a paper towel and blew her nose on the rough paper. She cupped her hands under the faucet and drank water. She sat on a toilet in a stall.

"Okay," she said.

"Better?" Rose asked.

"Yes."

"What are you afraid of?"

"That he won't need me." The words propelled from her mouth, without thought, without filters. "He'll know there are other people who can be his parent and who he can rely upon. It's always been just me. Even when Wayne and I were married. And now, it won't be just me anymore."

"He's always had other people he reaches out to," Grandma Rose said. "Officer Campbell. Wayne when Rory was younger. That lady at the Mobil to Go. Kara sometimes. And me. He has room to love all of us. We're his support system. Everyone needs a support system but we're not the same as a parent."

"What if he doesn't love me anymore?"

"Why wouldn't he love you? You're a wonderful mother."

"That's not true. You're the only one who thinks it and I wish you would stop saying it. Rory and I fight all the time. I yell at him. He curses at me. I let him keep his room like a pig sty. He disappears and I don't know where he goes. Sometimes I'm glad he's gone. I can't control him. He got into my vodka." Archer froze at her mention of vodka, hoping her mother hadn't heard.

"I know you're not perfect. Nobody is perfect. You're like a willow tree. You bend but you don't break. You have strong roots. And that's what Rory needs. I don't know how you do it. You give Rory all of those things in the best way you can.

"I don't know, Mom."

"Do you think Rory's perfect?"

"No."

"But you still love him?"

"Of course." Archer blew her nose.

"So why wouldn't that hold true for Rory, or for me? You're not perfect and I love you."

Archer sniffled, blew her nose again.

"So, is there anything I can do to help you?" Rose asked. "I would love for you to need me sometimes."

There was a lot her mother could do for her. There always had been but Archer had never felt she deserved her kindness, her assurances, her love.

Archer forced herself to say it. "Could you make some brisket? I'll be home for dinner. And, mom, could you shorten those pajama bottoms for me?"

Rose laughed. "I thought you'd never ask. And thank you for telling me about the vodka."

Archer walked out of the bathroom, paper towels in her hand. The bartender handed her a tall glass of ice water. Archer sat by the window, too exhausted to talk.

She lifted the glass to her lips as a horn sounded. It sounded over and over again like a persistent foghorn. Archer looked out the front window, put the glass down and stepped outside. It took a moment to register, but there he was, high on the top of Clyde's John Deere.

"Hop on, Real Mom," Rory said.

Archer smiled, ran to him and sat behind him. They drove off, blazing through the streets of Gloucester at five miles per hour.

CHAPTER EIGHTY

Archer and Rory stepped out of the City Forest into the backyard on Willow Street, completing the loop. Archer adjusted her glasses, finally able to see clearly. Rory grasped twigs, leaves and small branches in both hands. Trish came out to greet them.

"How'd you guys do?" Trish looked at Rory.

Rory turned, revealing the two month old baby in his pack. "Ryan slept the whole time. Didn't you, Big Guy?" Rory dropped the leaves and branches and reached an arm clumsily around his back to grab a chubby foot; then began slipping his arm and shoulder out of the pack. "I'm done. Take him. Is Campbell here yet? We need to get to work."

"Rory, wait." Archer leaped forward. "Let Trish get Ryan."

Trish unhooked the harness from Rory's bouncing back. "Stop moving." Trish slapped Rory's shoulder.

Free of the baby, Rory ran off.

"What's all that?" Trish waded through the forest debris Rory had dropped.

"He's making Ryan his first ghille suit."

"Wicked good." Trish positioned the baby and the Snuggli to her front.

Archer waded through a pile of leaves. Ryan let out a mew. Archer squeezed the baby's foot.

"He has such a little cry." Trish bent her head forward and nuzzled the baby.

When she picked her head up, Archer saw tears in her eyes.

"Do you think I'm doing the right thing, keeping him? I mean, Ellen would be a great mother. "

"You're a wonderful mother already. Trust yourself. You have good judgment and you're strong." Archer looked at the willow tree in the yard and smiled. "Everything will be fine." Archer pulled Trish close and kissed her head.

"Ellen looked so sad when I said I wouldn't let her adopt him."

"I know. But you told her she could be Ryan's aunt. And just like she's a wonderful aunt to Rory, she'll be a great aunt to RyRy."

A loud bang echoed into the backyard. Archer and Trish walked to the front of the house. Rory and Campbell were at the edge of the driveway, leaning over a smoking mower. Rory ran to them.

"You should have seen it. It was so funny. I told Campbell the spark plug was rusted but he wouldn't listen." Rory laughed and clapped his hands. "The spark plug back fired. Blew up like when that bullet exploded in my hand but without the fire. I told Campbell it would happen. The mowchine is sensitive. He didn't believe me."

Campbell slunk toward the house, wiping his hands on his jeans. Grandma Rose sat on the front porch in the presidential rocker from L.L. Bean.

"Are you hurt?" Archer asked Campbell.

He sat on the porch step. "Only my pride. The kid was right. I hate that." He winked.

Archer blushed. Rory beamed.

Archer sat next to her mom on the front porch, scanning the pile of mail on her lap. Trish and Ryan were in the house. Rory and Campbell were back tinkering with the mowchine.

"Is Kara meeting you at AA tomorrow?" Rose asked.

"Yes."

"I'm proud of you."

"I'm proud of me too." She handed an envelope to Rose. "This one's for you. It's from the bank."

Rose opened it, scanned the letter. "They're offering me a plan to buy-back my house. Part of some government program. What do you think?"

"I don't know. You've lived here for almost a year. Things are going well. Rory likes having you around. School's going to start soon for Rory and Trish."

Rose smiled. Tore the letter in half.

Archer opened an envelope addressed to herself, put it face down, looked up at Rory and Campbell. "They're hoping to race that thing in a month or so."

"Rory told me. Do you think it's safe?"

"No, but what I think doesn't matter. When those two get an idea, there's no stopping them."

"Two peas in a pod," Rose said.

Archer's cell phone rang.

"Wayne?" Rose asked.

"Yeah." She answered it.

"Can you give Rory a message?" Wayne asked. "I'm going to be in a play in Argentina for three months and I'm leaving next week."

"What about the trip to England to the lawn mower museum?"

"I refunded the tickets. I need the money to go to South America. I'll take him to England when I get back. He won't mind waiting."

Archer looked toward Campbell and Rory. Their heads were bent over the engine. Campbell pointed to some doohickey, laughed and patted Rory on the back. Archer pressed end on her cell phone.

"Everything okay?" her mom asked.

"Same old stuff. Let's play Scrabble."

"Right after I put the brisket in the oven."

Rose walked into the house. Archer turned the letter over, ran her fingers along the embossed governor's seal.

On behalf of the Governor's Judicial Appointment Committee of the State of Maine, we regret that you have withdrawn your application for Judgeship. if your family obligations change, we invite you to submit your name for consideration again. The State of Maine could benefit from your judicious temperament, intelligence and sensibility.

"Do you know where Ry's wipes are?" Trish sat on a rug near the fireplace. Ryan lay on his back on Rory's Lion King blanket.

"They're in your room," Archer said.

"Will you watch him for a minute? He's a mess."

Archer sat next to Ryan as Trish bounded up the stairs. She bent over him, smelled him, tickled his feet. He was her little munchkin.

Rory burst into the house. "We did it. We did it. The mowchine is running awesome. She's ready to race. Come see her!" He ran outside.

Archer picked up Ryan and went outside.

Rory stood over the mowchine, beaming. "Isn't she wicked good?"

"Yes." It was all wicked good.

END

ACKNOWLEDGEMENTS FROM THE AUTHORS

We have always had the support of our parents, Arlyne Lewis and Dean Lewis, in anything we have chosen to do. This book was no exception.

Our brother, Warren Lewis, was brave enough to take on the task of designing the front cover and we love what he did with it. Thank you to the photographer of the photo on the front cover, Sean Faircloth. It is a great photo taken one Thanksgiving in North Carolina. Beverly, Marianne and Ben – thank you for your support too.

Thank you to our "original fans" who supported Wicked Good since we began blogging it chapter-by-chapter. They are (in no particular order) Minda, Anne W., Ana, The Diz, Marilyn, Norman, Rhonda and Anne A.

We have countless friends to thank - friends who have specifically helped with the book and friends who have helped with life. Thank you Risa, Dawn, Karyn, Michele, Christina, Judy, Pam, Jill, Debi and Darla. You gals are the greatest friends anyone could ever have. And thank you to MA and Phil for your unconditional love and support.

Thank you to our mother's book group for its comments that helped make *Wicked Good* wicked better.

Thank you to all the people who have been touched by autism who have shared their stories with us. Thank you to the autism professionals who have supported *Wicked Good*.

And extra special thanks to Joyce Sweeney's Thursday night writing workshop group. Our fellow writers. Our friends.

Finally, thank you to all our Facebook friends who have helped make this adventure wicked fun.

And From Amy to Jo and Jo to Amy: There is no better friend than you.

PLEASE VISIT OUR WEBSITE
www.amyandjoanne.com

WE WOULD LOVE TO HEAR FROM YOU
amyandjoanne@gmail.com

FOR BOOK GROUPS

Please consider reading *Wicked Good* for your book group.

Invite Amy and/or Joanne to appear in person or via Skype.

Contact us at amyandjoanne@gmail.com

Suggested Questions for Book Group Discussion

1. Why do you feel Archer and Rory remain devoted to each other despite their conflicts?
2. There are three main mothers in Wicked Good. Archer, Grandma Rose and Kitty. How do they each deal with motherhood?
3. How does Archer gain strength from Rory?
4. How does Rory gain strength from Archer?
5. Besides the willow tree, what are other symbols in Wicked Good?
6. Discuss Campbell keeping his relationship with Rory a secret for years.
7. What if Rory didn't have Asperger's syndrome? How would you then view his actions and reactions?
8. Do you know anyone with Asperger's/autism? Whether your answer is yes or no, how has this affected how you related to Archer and to Rory in Wicked Good? How has reading Wicked Good affected how you relate to those you know with Asperger's/autism?
9. What role does Trish play in Wicked Good in relation to Rory? In relation to Archer?
10. Do you think you could write a book with your sibling?

COMING SOON

Wicked Wise